Thou Shalt Not Allow a Witch to Live

By

Laura Jo DeMordaunt

 **SDP Publishing**

Thou Shalt Not Allow a Witch to Live, Published October, 2013

Cover Illustrations: Randy Jennings
Cover Design and Interior Layout: Howard Communigrafix, Inc.
Editorial and Proofreading: Shannon Miller, Karen Grennan

Published by SDP Publishing an imprint of SDP Publishing Solutions, LLC.

For more information about this book contact Lisa Akoury-Ross by email at lross@SDPPublishing.com.

SDP Publishing
Permissions Department
36 Captain's Way, East Bridgewater, MA 02333
or email your request to info@SDPPublishing.com.

Library of Congress Control Number: 2012948887
ISBN-13: 978-0-9829256-6-9

Printed in the United States of America

*To the descendants of
Bridget Bishop, who have
adopted less-contentious
lifestyles.*

Preface

This is a true story of an American tragedy that occurred in the 1690s. The famous witch trials held in Salem, Massachusetts, escalated to over 200 persons being formally accused of witchcraft; 150 languishing in gaols and 19 hanged (14 women and five men). Another man, after having spent five months in darbies with his accused wife, refused to submit to a trial, hoping that by avoiding a conviction, his farm—which would otherwise go to the state—might go to his two sons-in-law. The refusal brought the penalty of pressing.

This witch hunt was fed by perjury at trials, no legal counsel for the accused, no formal avenues of appeal, no witnesses to testify under oath on their behalf, corruption of the legal system of the day, and a "kill witches" mentality that had originated in England. King James I would write a treatise, called *Demonology*, that further inflamed the Puritan mind to hunt for witches. Goodwife Bishop's narrative describes and defines from her viewpoint how these unjust conspiracies along with the turbulent conditions of her day combined and caused Bridget to become the first casualty of this villainy.

Glossary of Colloquial Terms

A

ade—insult directed at a woman

'afore—before

againe—again

all-a-mort—struck dumb

alsoe—also

amang—among

amen curlers—parish clerks

angrie—angry

anothar—another

arn't—aren't

arrivall—arrival

assemblie—assembly

autem mort—female beggar who uses her children to beg

'ave—have

B

bairn—child, children

barmy—crazy, insane

barn—born

bayle—bail

become—became

black magick—the appeal to the devil in order to accomplish evil

blat—wail, shout

blow the gab—to confess

blubber, blub—cry

bodkin—pin

'bout—about

brothar—brother

brung—brought

brush—to run away

bullies—sailors

bunkie—roommates

bushel bubby—full-breasted woman

C

cadge—being tied to apron strings

cap—to support another's assertion or tale

'cause—because

cild—linen

clapper—gossip

cloths—clothes

cock tease—flirt

cockish—uppish, forward

colly wobbles—stomachache

come—came

continuall—continual

cryed out upon—accused

D

darbies—irons, darbies, fetters

dimber—pretty

devill—devil

dismal ditty—a Psalm at the gallows

doe—do

dudds—clothes or goods

E

'em—them
eternity box—a coffin
evar—ever
everieone—everyone

F

forrin—foreign
furthar—further
fyne—fine

G

gaole—gaol or jail
goin'—going

H

hangman's wages—one
    shilling for the executioner
    and three halfpence for
    the rope
har—hear
hard—heard
harp—dwell upon a subject
hart—heart
hayr—hair
heaver—breast
hee—he
heeself—himself
hell cat—a furious, scolding
    woman
henpecked—a husband
    governed by his wife
herring pond—sea
hobbled—to walk lamely
hodgepodge—irregular

mixture of numerous
    things
hookee walker—expression
    signifying that the story is
    not true

J

jerry sneak—henpecked
husband
jurat in curia—document
    used in the trial

K

knob—head

L

laid by the heels—to be
    confined or put in prison
larn—learn
lawe—law
lett—let
lye—lie

M

magick—magic
mantua-maker—dressmaker
marke—mark
marrowbones—to make
    her beg pardon on her
    knees
maudlin—weepingly drunk
maul'd—drunk
mee—my, I, me
meeself—myself
messmates—companions who
    eat at the same mess

mish—petticoat

moabites—gaolers, bailiffs

mobility—the mob

moiety—signify a share or portion

morris—to hang dangling in the air

mothar—mother

muck—money, wealth

mum for that—I shall be silent as to that

N

nabbed—taken, arrested

noe—no

noodle—head

noozed—hanged

nubbing cheat—gallows

nubbing ken—courthouse

nutcrackers—stocks, pillory

O

o'—of

ond—and

ordinary—public place where people could purchase food and drink

othar—other

P

packed out—very crowded

pact—the witch is no longer merely invoking the devil's aid through her charms and spells, but actually believes she has made a contract to serve him.

pasting—beating

penance board—pillory

pike—run away

plump in the pocket—flush with money

prancer—horse

probablie—probably

pump—wheedle a secret out of

R

reliefe—relieve

S

s'd—said

sad trim—dirty

severall—several

shee will 'ave a hearty choke ond caper sauce for breakfast—she will be hanged

shee—she

sich—such

sitten on thorns—uneasy, impatient, anxious

sluice your gob—take a big swig of a drink

soe—so

stand the huff—to be answerable for reckoning in a public house

surgeon—doctor, physician

T

taradiddle—a fib or falsity
thar—their, there
tharby—thereby
tharfore—therefore
tharin—therein
tibs—young lass
tickrum—license
'til—until
togather—together
traipsing—walking about
trusty trojans—true friends
tryall—trial
trye—try
turk—cruel, hard-hearted man
'tween—between
twist down a pace—eat
   heartily
twisted—hanged

V

verie—very

W

w'th—with
w'thin—within
w'thout—without
waer—where
war—was, were
waren't—wasn't, weren't
wee—we
weel—well
wharin—wherein
what—that
whiffy—smelly, unpleasant
white magick—charms or
   spells used for benevolent
   purposes
wrighting—writing

Y

yar—year
ye—you
yer—your
yeth—youth

Some slang words adapted from Dictionary of the Vulgar Tongue, Francis Grose, 1811, which was adapted from 1736 Dictionary of Thieving Slang. Retrieved from www.fromoldbooks.org/Grose-VulgarTongue/

Notes from the Author

The modern Gregorian calendar didn't come into use until 1752. Prior to this date, the calendar used was the Julian calendar. All dates listed in this story use the Julian format.

In this story some women are called Goody, short for Goodwife, and others are Mrs. (short for mistress). These titles deal with the social status of married women. Goody is for lower-class folks, while Mrs. is reserved for gentry.

Bridget Bishop's Peas Porridge

1 pound dried peas	Veggies from mee garden
8 tablespoons lard	2 onions
1 tablespoon crushed dried mint or sage ond pepper	1/2 cup vinegar
	Slab o' bacon or hambone

Wash dried, peas, discarding any stones or forrin objects from ye garden. Place peas in a ceramic bowl o' fair water overnight. Drain. Chop onions ond veggies. Put onions, veggies, ond pepper in pipkin or pot. Cover w'th water ond bring to boil over coals. Add slab o' bacon or hambone ond cook 'til peas are squashy. Remove scum. Remove meat from pot ond slice into small pieces. Put back in pot. Stir in lard, vinegar, ond spices.

In mee ordinary, mee whip a batch ond it sits 'til it be gone. Each day mee warm mee pottage ond add a few veggies. Mee lykes it when it be two days ol'. Mee tweeted this old rhyme to mee bairns: "Peas porridge hot. Peas porridge cold. Peas porridge in the pot, nine days ol' Some lyke it hot, some lyke it cold, some lyke it in the pot nine days ol'."

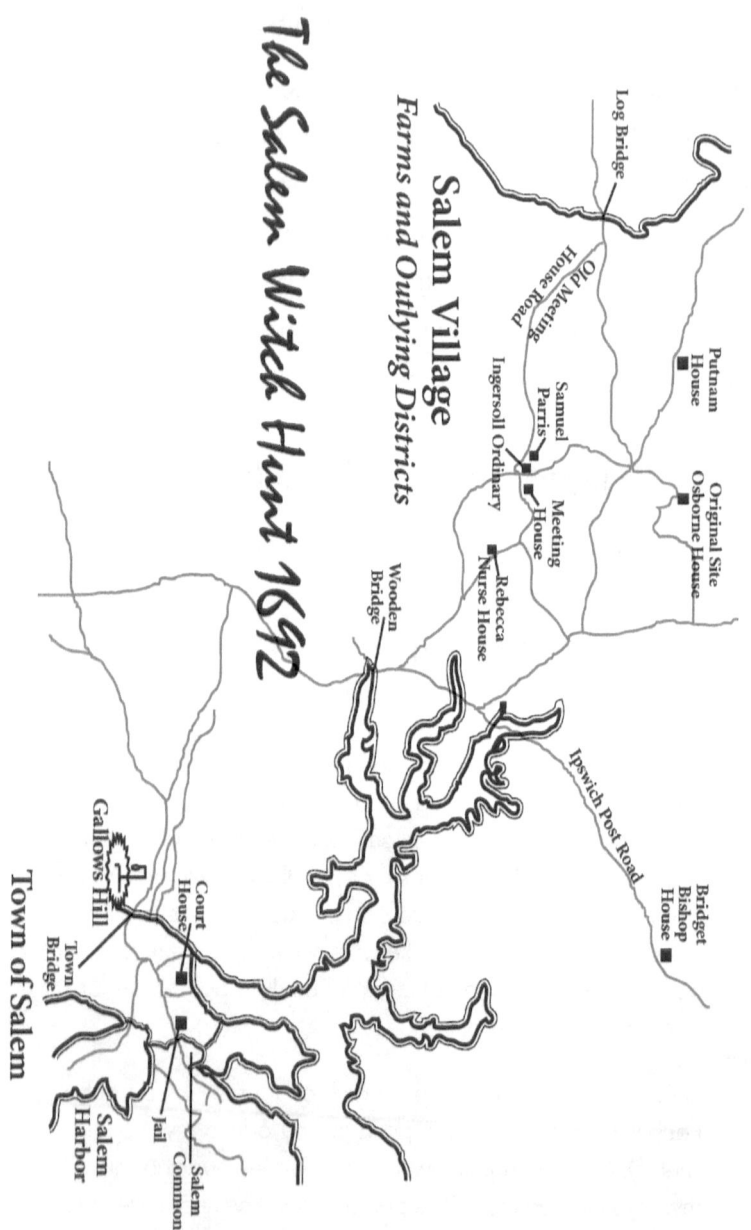

The Salem Witch Hunt 1692

Salem Village
Farms and Outlying Districts

Log Bridge

Old Meeting House Road

Putnam House

Samuel Parris

Ingersoll Ordinary

Original Site Osborne House

Meeting House

Wooden Bridge

Rebecca Nurse House

Ipswich Post Road

Bridget Bishop House

Gallows Hill

Court House

Town Bridge

Town of Salem

Jail

Salem Harbor

Salem Common

Salem Village and Salem Town, 1692

© Laura Jo DeMordaunt. Adapted from "Salem Witchcraft," by Charles W. Upham; Chpt 4, pg 25.

Mee don't give a fig what they say or don't say 'bout mee. Othars opinion o' mee don't matter. Mee goin' to continue to:

> *own mee taverns . . .*
>
> *express mee view on the treatment o' women . . .*
>
> *wear mee red paragon bodice ond othar lacy dudds o' mee choice . . .*
>
> *brew mee own hard syder . . .*
>
> *yell at mee husband if hee's grouty . . .*
>
> *invite all comers to play games o' chance . . .*
>
> *attend mee local congregation when mee wants to . . .*
>
> *attract patrons w'th jigs ond reels . . .*
>
> *use unmuzzled profanity when mee wants to . . .*
>
> *continue to drive hard financial bargains . . .*
>
> *hold penny-pitchin' contests . . .*
>
> *blat out mee arn't noe disciple o' the devill . . .*

In fact, mee goin' to continue to live mee life as mee sees it. Mee goin' to press ahead, regardless o' the outcome. Mee not goin' to be the red herrin' for all thar troubles ond woes.

Mee arn't responsible for thar bein' verie few yeng men for these yeng girls to marry . . .

> *The French ond King Philip's Indian War is.*

Mee arn't responsible for the bad feelin's 'tween the Salem Village ond Salem Town . . .

> *50-yar land feuds ond community tensions are.*

Mee arn't responsible for the poor crops ond disease . . .

> *Small pox epidemics ond*
>
> *Poor farmin' practices ond harsh winters are.*

Mee arn't responsible for neighbors who dislike mee . . .

> *Mee lifestyle ond defensive freethinkin' are.*

Mee arn't responsible for how ye suffer under these hypocritical pretenders o' religion . . .

The Puritan establishment's slippin' grip ond divine action to restore the flock are . . .

Mee arn't responsible for the restless political climate . . .

desires to be free o' England ond high levels o' taxes are.

Mee not responsible for yer convulsions, broken wagons, spectral delusions, ond bad dreams . . .

natural ond neurological causes are.

Mee arn't responsible for the jealousy what split our community . . .

geography ond social conflicts are.

Mee am mee own independent woman. Mee will not be forced to move. Mee am verie self-willed. Mee can be abrasive ond outspoken. Mee is a "rebellious innocent" livin' amang the pious watchdog eyes o' a Puritanical society. In othar times ond places, mee would be praised for these qualities. Along w'th these othar markers, mee dare say, ye might even label mee the first emancipated feminist in the New World.

As mee, Bridget, begin mee story to mee posterity, mee would like to thank mee descendant, Laura Jo, for not bein' shamefaced by mee stigma as a witch. Mee am 'preciative o' her courage to gather togather in a single record, the research on the hysteria, false accusations, ond conspiracy what surrounded mee tryall, teats ond all. Mee doe 'ave some verie famous, renowned posterity. From mee day up through the 1800s, mee descendants war too discomfited to claim mee. They would rather sweep mee under the rug. Mee am mostly remembered in history lessons ond at present-day tourist attractions. Mee is glad what one o' mee blood relatives took the time to compile mee story for distribution to those who want to keep mee memory alive. To the reader may mee say, mee story may seem a wee bit disconnected ond mee dates out o' kilter, but mee story flows as mee mind war pricked w'th facts ond recollections. It has been s'd, the darkest page o' New England history bore the record o' the Salem tryalls. Mee reader, mee hopes to relate mee part in this New World tragedy. Mee story embodies all the tentacles o' these tumultuous times. Mee war the first to fall victim to the travesty o' justice o' mee day.

Every yar, for more than a hundred yars, American children, to celebrate Halloween, bob for apples, eat lots o' candy, ond dress up like witches ond warlocks, not realizin' what to doe soe publicly in 1692 Salem, they would represent Satan's disciples. Mee thinks it hard for mee reader to understand, but it war verie plain in the 17th century what Satan ond his forces had broke forth ond the devill's desire war to break down the Puritans' "city on the hill." It war believed what the Prince o' Darkness, who is invisible, contracts w'th witches ond warlocks, who are visible, to serve him. Since witches ond warlocks are the consorts o' Satan, an act o' good citizenship in mee day would be to kill these disciples; to eradicate the devill from thar community. Secondly, mee devout neighbors strictly interpreted the Bible. The Bible is the word o' God. God commands what witches shall not be allowed to live.

> *Exodus 22:18 (King James Bible):* "Thou shalt not suffer a witch to live."
>
> *Deuteronomy 18:10:* "There shall not be found among ye any one what maketh his son or his daughter to pass through the fire, or what useth divination, or an observer of times, or an enchanter, or a witch."
>
> *1 Samuel 15:23:* "For rebellion is as the sin of witchcraft, and stubbornness is as iniquity an idolatry."
>
> *Galatians 5:19-20:* "Now the works of the flesh are manifest, which are these: adultery, fornication, uncleanness, lasciviousness, idolatry, witchcraft."[1]

To avoid God's wrath ond restore God's care for his covenant people, mee neighbors, believin' the Bible to be infallible, used these scriptures as the impetus for identifyin' witches, conductin' tryalls, ond condemnin' alleged witches to death.

One o' the myths mee gave a hearin' is what the first settlers in the New World war advocates o' religious freedom. In mee eye, this is a weel-intentioned untruth. The Puritans war not interested in freedom for all religions. They war verie intolerant, not only o' witches but alsoe o' any deviation from thar Puritan orthodoxy. Massachusetts Bay Colony had only recently expelled the Quakers ond Baptists. Likewise, mee hard tell, throughout the Dark Ages ond the supposed enlightened ages o' the 16th ond 17th centuries, whenever thar war challenges to the orthodoxy o' the time from reformers sich as Galileo, Martin Luther, Westley, Roger Bacon, ond Tyndale, the churches, in order to suppress these deviations, consolidated thar powers. When the establishment felt thar hold on thar flock slippin', the avenue o' choice to brung the waverin' faithless ond disloyal back into the fold war inquisition tryalls ond often the pronouncement o' death to eliminate defiance ond opposition. Europe hanged or burned 40 to 50 thousand people for witchcraft. Accused witches on the continent ond in Scotland war burned for heresy. Accused witches in England war hanged as it war a felony.

Thar is dispute to this day 'bout whether or not mee war a witch, or merely anothar innocent victim noozed at Gallows Hill in 1692. However, mee don't hold a grudge against Salem for mee fate. Mee can't pass judgement on those who war involved. Both the times in which mee lived ond the intrigue ond stress to which mee neighbors war subjected by religious leaders who used the fear o' witchcraft as a means o' bolsterin' thar slackin' power in the community, need to be sifted as causes. Mee thinks when people are fearful o' somethin', thar fears make it work.

As mee descendant, Laura Jo, discovered mee link to the witch tryalls, her laborious research has permitted mee true story to be told. Through these pages ond sources, mee hope ye will come to know 'bout the controversies what swirled around mee life, mee environment, arrest, tryall, conviction, ond execution. Alsoe, mee hope, ye as mee posterity will be vindicated by the attempts o' Salem ond by those involved in the tryalls to seek forgiveness. Mee am glad what ye will now read for the first time, mee real story. Mee am a human bein' who war unjustly accused, victimized, ond sacrificed in these ways:

a victim o' community feuds 'tween Salem ond Salem Village;

a victim o' zealot clergy who whipped the populace o' Salem Village into a state o' mass hysteria w'th thar sermons ond wrightin's on witchcraft;

a victim o' neighbors w'th whom thar war bad blood ond who disliked mee lifestyle;

a victim o' a conspiracy amang judicial ond church officials who through thar witch hunt, encouraged neighbors to be afraid o' neighbors;

a victim o' the political instability 'tween New England ond mothar England;

a victim o' a less-than-judicial court whar customary preliminary witch-marke examination procedures war held in public ond not in private. A course o' action condoned by the judges for the edification o' local residents;

a victim o' archaic legal proceedin's waer defendants war not permitted to retain counsel, nor could they appeal;

a victim o' spectral evidence what by its definition war invisible evidence, impossible to refute, war accepted;

a victim o' lax legal goin' on what allowed children under 14 to testify in capital felony cases;

a victim o' internal contentions what revolved around the church in Salem Village;

a victim o' unexplained losses o' livestock, strange illnesses o' thar loved ones, ond othar natural events;

a victim o' local natural ond political disasters ond community problems what caused mee ripe, explosive, stressed community to lash out against any local person who war not a mainstream chosen o' God; ond lastly,

a victim o' corruption in government waer the gaole fees levied on accused war an incentive to appropriate thar land ond possessions.

The theocrats o' mee day wanted to get rid o' mee. Mee superstitious neighbors who harbored animosities wanted retaliation against mee. How doe ye doe this? Ye accuse mee o' bein' a witch ond use a witch hunt as a tool to get rid o' mee in thar community. Soe what war the consequences o' this time ond season . . . consider the title o' this book.

Mee war fictionalized two hundred yars later, in an 1868 play/ poem on the Salem tryalls by Henry Wadsworth Longfellow:

ACT II Giles Corey of the Salem Farms

Scene I

Corey:

Poor soul! I've known her forty year or more.
She was the widow Warselby, and then
She married Oliver, and Bishop next.

She's had three husbands. I remember well
The games of shovel-board at Bishop's ordinary
In the old merry days, and she soe gay
With her red paragon bodice ond her ribbons!
Ah, Bridget Bishop always was a Witch!

Martha:

They'll little help her now, her caps ond ribbons,
And her red paragon bodice and her plumes,
With which shee flaunted in the Meeting-house!
When next she goes there, it will be for tryall.

 Who would believe such deeds could find a place,
 As these whose tragic history we retrace?[2]

Mee, Bridget Bishop, war barn in the yar ca. 1629-30 ond christened Bridget Playfer in St. Mary-in-the-Marsh Congregation . . . in a small village w'th 100 to 150 inhabitants. For yer interest, mee has cut down a wee bit a history 'bout Norwich, Norfolk County, England, by historian Tim Lambert:

> The village was part of the larger settlement of Norwich, Norfolk County, England. Norwich started as a small Saxon settlement north of the river Wensum. In time, it grew into a town, perhaps because of its situation on a river. In those days, it was much cheaper and easier to transport goods for sale by water than by land. It became known as North Wic (wic is an old word for port and Norwich was an inland port). The name Norwich first appeared on a coin minted in the early 10th century. In 1004, the Danes sacked and burned Norwich. Fire was a constant hazard since the buildings were of wood and thatched roofs. However, Norwich was soon rebuilt and flourished once again. By the time of the Domesday Book, in 1086, Norwich was one of the largest towns in England, with a population of about 6,000. By the 14th century, 1500s, the population of Norwich had

ably grown to about 10,000. In Norwich, as in most medieval towns, the main industry was the manufacture of wool. First it was woven then it was fulled . . . that means the wool was cleaned and thickened by being pounded in a mixture of water and clay known as fuller's earth. The wool was pounded by wooden hammers worked by watermills. Afterwards, it was dyed. Another important industry was leather working. In Norwich there were tanners, saddlers, and shoemakers. There were also many goldsmiths in Norwich. In 1505, Norwich suffered a severe fire. Two more followed in 1507.

In 1549, came Kett's rebellion. Enraged by their treatment by Landowners, some of the farmers of Norfolk rose in rebellion. They took control of Norwich and camped on Mousehold Heath. The first attempt to crush the rebellion failed. A small force led by the Marquis of Northampton entered Norwich and fought in the streets, but was then forced to withdraw. The government then sent a much larger force under the Earl of Warwick. This time, the rebels were driven out of Norwich. They withdrew to Mousehold Heath then to Dussindale. The earl's men attacked and routed them. Afterwards about 300 rebels were hanged, including Kett. In 1579, there was an outbreak of plague, which may have killed one-third of the population. However, Norwich soon recovered. There was always plenty of poor people in the countryside willing to come to the town to look for work. After 1565, many weavers came to Norwich fleeing religious persecution in what is now Holland and Belgium. The "strangers" may have boosted the population of the town to about 16,000 by the 1580s. In the early 16th century, Norwich seems to have suffered an economic decline but it began to prosper again in the late 16th century. The population of Norwich rose rapidly in the 17th century and reached about 25,000 in 1700. This was in spite of outbreaks of plague. It struck twice, in 1625 and again in 1665, but each time the town recovered. During the civil war from 1642-1646, most of the people of Norwich supported parliament. There was no actual fighting at Norwich during the civil war. However, there was a riot in 1648. The mayor was a royalist and parliament ordered his dismissal.

But the mayor was popular and his supporters rioted. They attacked the homes of well-known Puritans and then entered the committee house where gunpowder was stored. Somehow the gunpowder exploded, killing 40 people. Afterwards eight of the rioters were hanged.[3]

'Afore crossin' over to the colonies, mee married Captain Samuel George Warsselbe, 13 April 1660. By him, mee had two bairns, a son Benjamin, christened 6 October 1663, barn in England, ond a daughter Mary, barn 10 January 1665, in Boston, Massachusetts. On 26 July 1666, as a widow, mee married Lord Thomas Oliver, who war alsoe from Norwich. Hee had a considerable amount o' property . . . an estate called Bolloman outside o' Norfolk. Lord Thomas Oliver ond his first wife, Mary Leman, arrived in Boston on the ship "Mary Ann" in 1637. They brung w'th 'em two bairns ond two servants. One o' the bairn, a daughter, war married to a Constable Hilliard. Thar othar bairns remained in England. They moved to Salem, whar hee began to accumulate a great deal o' land. Over the yars what Mary Leman Oliver lived in Salem, shee war verie critical o' the Puritan treatment o' the Quakers ond Baptists, ond supported Roger William's preachin' o' separation o' church ond state. Shee war sentenced to whippin's for neglect o' church attendance ond callin' local ministers bloodthirsty. A cleft stick war placed on her tongue for slander. Shee war 'specially critical o' Major William Hathorne for whippin' Quakers in the streets o' Salem Town. Othar times, shee found herself in the nutcrackers for workin' on the Lord's day ond screamin' what the constables war thieves ond robbers. Shee war banished from Salem, but defied this order ond returned. Her husband's ability to pay her bonds kept her out o' the gaole. Thomas Oliver's hesitancy or failure to control his wife caused her to be exiled out o' Salem area in 1649, w'thin three weeks. W'th each banishment, Lord Thomas Oliver ond his wife Mary Leman returned to thar estate in Norwich. It warn't long 'afore Thomas laid his wife, Mary, in the grave. Thomas war residin' on his estate in Norwich in 1652. It war in Norwich what wee become acquainted. Thomas urged mee to immigrate to New England. Since mee first husband had previously passed on, mee acted upon Thomas's invitation to immigrate. Mee immigrated to New England in ca. 1664-1665 w'th mee one dependent child, Benjamin. It war a churned up crossin', as mee war in me late months with mee number-two bairn. Mee barely set foot on New World soil 'afore mee war delivered o' mee bairn Mary.

An interestin' twist to mee story is the Puritan persecution o' Thomas's first wife, Mary. As mee mentioned, Mary called the Puritan colony leaders white sepulchers who come to New England for religious freedom, but wouldn't allow othars freedom to worship. For her punishment, shee spent some time at the whippin' post ond nutcrackers. Mary war persecuted by Hathorne's father, Major William Hathorne, the most powerful magistrate in Salem. Shee responded to his oppressive treatment by blusterin' what shee hoped to live long enough to see his flesh torn in lots o' pieces. For 13 yars, her statement supposedly bedevilled William Hathorne ond shee war accused o' witchcraft in 1650 in Salem, in absentia. Shee war livin' thousands o' miles away in England. Mary died in England. 'Cause o' Mary, a bettin' man would wager what anyone who become Thomas's second wife would reap the venom o' Hathorne's son, the magistrate

John Hathorne. The "witch-hanging judge," as John Hathorne war called, become a judicious church official, ond saw to it what mee, Bridget Bishop, Thomas Oliver's second wife, war the first to be executed under the mask o' witchcraft. John Hathorne war the only one who never repented o' his actions.

Thomas ond mee war married in Salem on 26 July 1666. He war 30 yars mee senior. Mee war 36 yars old. Wee settled into Oliver's Salem home on the southerly corner o' Washington ond Church streets.

By mee second marriage, Thomas Oliver and mee had one child, a daughter, Christian, barn 8 May 1667 in Salem. Mee dearest daughter, Christian, died the yar after mee war executed, 1693, at the age o' 25. The hard times, ruinous scandal, ond humiliation o' mee accusation, arrest, ond execution war too much for her gentle constitution, resultin' in her early demise. Mee tragedy war extended to anothar generation. Mee daughter, Christian, married Thomas Mason 26 July 1666 in Salem ond died leavin' an only child, six yars old, Susannah, barn 23 August 1687. By mee third marriage to Edward Bishop Sr., probablie 'afore ca. 1667-1668, mee had noe issue. On 11 April 1694, the local magistrates pronounced what Edward Bishop Sr. war appointed guardian for his stepdaughter, Susannah. Mee don't know why Thomas Mason did not raise his own daughter, Susannah, heeself. What mee doe know is what Susannah, despite losin' meeself ond her mothar soe tragically at sich a yeng age, grew up to marry into the Beckett family, a prominent shipbuildin' family o' Salem. John Beckett's home war on three acres o' ground near the waterfront in Salem. His home war moved from Beckett Court to the Nathaniel

Hawthorne's House o' Seven Gables compound in Salem. In an interestin' twist, Jonathan Felt's first cousin, Joshua, married Anne Walcott, the yeng sister o' Mary Walcott, one o' mee accusers. Mee granddaughter, Susannah Mason, married John Beckett Sr. on 20 September 1711, ond by him had a son, John Beckett Jr., thar first child. Six daughters followed thar first son. John Beckett Jr., alsoe a shipwright, took Rebekah Beadle for his first wife on 30 May 1738. John Beckett Jr. ond Rebekah Beadle's second daughter, Hannah (or Susannah, after her grandmothar) Beckett married David Felt on 8 Nov 1758. Hannah died ca. 12-13 October 1778. David Felt war a fisherman, shore man, ond merchant. He war drowned at sea 26 April 1807. David Felt's son, Nathaniel, married Hannah Reeves ca. 8 Apr 1791-1792. Nathaniel's son, Nathaniel Henry, moved west ond married Mary Louise Pile on 7 Dec 1856. Firmly established in the state o' Deseret, Nathaniel Henry's son, Nathaniel Henry Jr., barn 2 December 1861, married Mary Elvira Clark, 30 November 1887. Nathaniel Henry Jr.'s daughter, Luzon Elvira Felt, married Seymour LaVar Christensen on 28 November 1917—these are the author o' mee history, Laura Jo's grandfather ond grandmothar. David Felt, barn 1729 at Salem, is the progenitor through which Laura Jo descended. Mee ancestor, Laura Jo, can alsoe trace her genealogy to George Felt Sr., who come to Massachusetts w'th John Endecott ond 50 or soe planters ond servants aboard the Abigail in ca. 1628-1629. The settlement they established war founded at the mouth o' the Naumbeag River on the site o' an ancient Indian village. It war first called Naumkeag, after the local Indian tribe. Endecott's responsibility war to establish the colony ond to prepare it for the arrivall o' additional settlers.

For the notin', on 8 October 1673, Edward Bishop Sr., husbandman o' Beverly, bequested to his son, Edward Bishop Jr. o' Salem, 57 acres or thar'bouts in Essex County, New England. At this time, 40 acres o' s'd land war situated in Salem ond war in the possession o' Edward Bishop Jr. Part o' this 57 acres war five acres lyin' in Topsfield. Twelve acres lyin' in Beverly, six acres lyin' near a beaver pond, ond six acres lyin' in the rail field, commonly soe-called for bein' bounded on the west w'th the common road or highway, war in the possession o' Edward Bishop Sr. ond s'd 12 acres would be his property rightfully durin' his natural life ond then to fall unto Edward Bishop Jr. ond his heirs forever, after his death. Mee relates this registry o' deed to still the confusion as to waer Edward Bishop Sr. ond meeself resided after our marriage. Wee lived on Edward Bishop Sr.'s 12 acres on Ipswich Post Road, Beverly, Essex County, Massachusetts, for five yars 'afore mee war cryed out.

Mee probablie don't 'ave as many descendants as the othar 19 people who war executed durin' the witch tryalls o' 1692. But mee descendants embrace some o' the oldest ond most respectable families o' Salem ond branch widely from 'em. Mee 'ave hard thar could be up to 20 million descendants o' some o' the accused witches in the United States.

The 17th century, especially 1692, war a sad, degradin' time in colonial history ond left its marke on American history. Those o' us freethinkers, who immigrated to the New World, left a life expectancy in England o' 30 yars. In London, may mee say, what disease war soe rampant, deaths outnumbered births. Wee suffered from lack o' food 'cause thar war noe food to be had. Thar war many o' us competin' for the same job. Plus, mee society in mothar England war a verie compound social society waer citizens like mee couldn't rise above our birth conditions. Thar war noe room for aspirations. Mee hope ye will give a hearin' to the wide-held belief what Satan war behind these diseases, deaths, ond unseasoned happenin's. This frame o' mind war commonplace, even amang the educated o' Europe.

'Afore mee time, the persecution o' accused witches did not become widespread 'til King James I (formerly King James VI o' Scotland). James I had spent most o' hee life in the wings, but in 1603, the 37-yar-ol' become King o' England, Scotland, ond Ireland, in the newly united Great Britain. James I believed heeself to be king by divine right. Mee hard it s'd what King James I felt kings should rightly be called gods. What a bunch o' bunkum— mum for that. Thus bein' God on earth, hee could alter the word o' God. The Scottish people, amang whom James war raised, war verie superstitious. Thar state church war the unrelentin' enemy o' witchcraft. When James become king o' all Great Britain, hee inherited a theologically divided kingdom. To settle matters, hee convened a conference o' 47 scholars, mostly Church o' England clerics who had thar fingers in the pie, to reconcile his beliefs w'th the "Great Bible." Odd to mee what in the old Hebrew, 'afore the King James version (authorized ond instigated by King James I, same king), thar war few references to malefic witchcraft as sich. Mee feelin's seem to tell mee what those good ol' translators, knowin' King James I's concern ond interest on the subject o' witchcraft, went 'bout puttin' in a slightly different choice o' words what deleted, then altered, then added ruinous prose what war baneful ond carried great theological consequence. All o' these flip-flops war brung 'bout by the crusade of scholars to make what grand ol' kind happy. The new King James version o' the Bible reads in Leviticus 20:27: "A man also or a woman that hath a familiar spirit, or that is a wizard, shall surely be to death . . ." The scripture war one o' many what war modified. Thus accordin' to the new King James's version o' word o' God, anyone who has an familiar evil spirit or who consorts w'th conjurers are guilty o' felony w'thout benefit o' clergy. The charter what the early colonist brung w'th 'em adopted King James I's lawe against witchcraft. Durin' King James I's short tenure, women, especially aged women, war the prey o' persecution. Mee gave this some thought ond concluded what our wrinkles, our greyin', ond our stooped frame labeled wee older women as nonproductive ond flawed. Wee women who war noe longer able to produce ond suckle a child war not useful. These negatives made wee older matrons more likely to be social outcasts who 'ave detoured from the norm ond who are liable to critical Puritan censure. Mee understand what women who war accused o' witchcraft in mee day war commonly 'tween the ages o' 50 and 60. Mee hard tell almost 20 women for everie one man war executed for witchcraft in King James I's 22 yars as king. Since King James I knew soe much 'bout witchcraft, hee wrote a book entitled Daemonologie. It had a profound influence in startin' the wave o' witchcraft persecutions what flooded over England ond Scotland. As a consequence o' readin' this publication, a Puritan, named Matthew Hopkins, war inspired to lead a campaign, beginnin' in 1645, to exterminate everie witch in the eastern counties o' England. Hopkins witch-findin' lasted 'til 1647. Mee hard tell Hopkins war called the "witch-finding general." Reformation leaders Calvin ond Knox believed ye war denyin' the word o' God if ye denied witchcraft. Mee dedicated Puritan saints brung these witchcraft lawes ond beliefs w'th 'em over the pond. When the charter war revoked in 1684, these witchcraft lawes war rescinded.

Pope Innocent VIII (Giovanni Battista Cybo) (1432-1492), Pope from 1484-1492

Public domain image reproduced from Wikipedia Commons

Speakin' 'bout history, lett mee share w'th ye some ancient, as weel as local, history concernin' witchcraft what set the stage for this Salem witch hunt. Mee friends ond neighbors o' Massachusetts Bay war by noe means the first to believe in witchcraft. Belief in Satan, soothsayers, ond evil spirits go way back to the ancient Hebrews o' the Old Testament as mee 'afore made known. It war told to mee what the attitudes towards witchcraft in Europe took a decidedly violent turn from 1231 on. In 1484, Pope Innocent VIII declared in his papal bull what those who had given up thar Catholic beliefs war the devillish bein's who brung 'bout natural disasters ond the resultin' scourges. He war the first to use accused magicians ond witches as scapegoats ond to use severe punishment for those convicted o' witchcraft. The ol' lecher, King Henry VIII, proclaimed witchcraft war a treasonous capital crime against the king ond church w'thout benefit o' clergy. Punishment war death by twistin'.

To the reader, may mee relate just a side note 'bout King Henry VIII. It war way 'afore mee time, when King Henry VIII made over the Catholic Church in England into his own state church. The Puritan purists felt this change war in name only, for King Henry retained much o' the ceremonies ond rites o' the church o' Rome. 'Cause the Puritans felt the new Church o' England war a double o' the church in Rome, they separated 'emselves from the state church ond a new religion war barn. This new religion espoused a simple theology based on scripture ond nothin' else. Since Biblical scriptures like "And I will cut off witchcrafts out of thine hand; and thou shalt have no more soothsayers," (Micah 5: 12-13) regarded witches as evil to be cut off ond destroyed, to mee it war day-follow-night natural, when the settlement o' new colonies began in the early yars o' the 17th century, what the Puritan British citizens should bring articles wrighten by clergymen who prosecuted, common lawes by jurists who condemned, ond pamphlets which justified the persecution ond execution o' witches. This war especially true o' mee Puritan neighbors who settled Massachusetts Bay.

Mee hard thar war a few cases o' witchcraft in the colonies even 'afore 1692. Each o' these cases war handled in a normal judicious New England way ond thar war noe public executions relatin' from these charges o' witchcraft. For the tellin', is the tryall o' Mary Glover, a part-time housekeeper o' Boston. Shee worked as a domestic in the Goodwin home. In 1688, four o' the Goodwin children: Martha, 13, John, 11, Mercy, seven, ond

Benjamin, five, took on convulsions. When questioned at her tryall, Goodwife Glover admitted what shee believed shee had made a pact w'th the devill. Thar war five ministers who fasted ond prayed for the children. One o' the four children war cured by this wonder-work, but poor ol' Goodwife Mary Glover war noozed for bewitchin' 'em. On her way to the gallows, Goodwife Mary Glover give cry what shee warn't the only who had a hand in the witchcraft ond shouted out thar names. Cotton Mather wrote down thar names, but kept 'em to heeself. The children's afflictions continued in a violent manner. By-ond-by, Cotton Mather brung the oldest Goodwin daughter, Martha, to live at his house soe hee might pray, fast, ond exorcise this daughter vexed w'th Satan, ond alsoe to observe w'th his own eyes someone who believed herself to be possessed o' the devill ond his witches. Mee hard hee kept her under constant watch durin' her stay w'th him, ond hee later wrote hee larned more 'bout witchcraft from this observance than any book hee evar read on the subject o' witches.

Mather later wrote a pamphlet, which hee made public in ca. 1688-1689, called *Memorable Provinces Relating to Witchcraft ond Possessions*, wharin hee included his account o' Goodwife Glover ond the Goodwin family ond described witchcraft ond the invisible world in detail. Mee am persuaded this pamphlet had a profound effect on the New England area ond provided the magistrates o' 1692 w'th relevant valuable models in the Goodwin children ond Goodwife Glover, upon which to base standards for the 1692 tryalls. Mee think the larned wrightin's o' church men from mothar England ond early colonial clergymen war anothar bias what carried weight w'th the justices in mee Court o' Oyer ond Terminer.

The central concerns o' mee neighbors ond thar clergy war thar religion. Mee could say what thar religion war the only purpose the Puritans had for comin' to the New World. Most o' Massachusetts colony felt they war a chosen people ond if they lived saintly lives, God would never permit the devill to afflict the saints.

Massachusetts Colony Puritan ministers wanted to be separated not from the Church o' England, but from the corruption w'thin the church. This circle o' Puritans disapproved o' wee nonconformists who did not emigrate for religious purposes. King Charles I war verie glad to rid England o' mee overly pious neighbors. Thar rigid religious practices war a constant burden to the king ond to those who lived around 'em. Mee thinks it war almost 11 yars what King Charles I purged the Church o' England o' its Puritan members. After disbandin' his parliament, autocrat King Charles I commissioned Archbishop Laud to punish those who wouldn't conform to the Church o' England. Mee war just a small bairn when these Puritan ministers, reactin' to the repressive religious policies o' this king o' England, made the sea voyages w'th thar parishioners. They arrived in New England havin' a different vision o' how best to strictly live the Bible ond reform ond convert society around 'em. Historian Nathaniel Philbrick states:

> At issue at the turn of the 17th century—and long before—was the proper way for a Christian to gain access to the will of God. Catholics and more conservative Protestants believed that the

traditions of the church contained valid, time-honored additions to what was found in the Bible. Given man's fallen condition, no individual could presume to question the ancient, ceremonial truths of the established church. But for the Puritans, man's fallen nature was precisely the point. All one had to do was to sit and witness a typical Sunday service in England in which parishioners stared dumbly at a minister mumbling incomprehensible phrases from the Book of Common Prayer—to recognize how far most people were from a true engagement with the word of God. Appalled by these Sunday services, Puritans believed it was necessary to venture back to the absolute beginning of Christianity, before the church had been corrupted by centuries of laxity and abuse, to locate divine truth. In lieu of time travel, there was the Bible, with the New Testament providing the only reliable account of Christ's time on Earth, while the Old Testament contained a rich storehouse of still vital truths. If something was not in the scriptures, it was a man-made distortion of what God intended. At once radical and deeply conservative, the Puritans had chosen to spurn thousands of years of accumulated tradition in favor of a test that gave them a direct and personal connection to God. A Puritan had no use for the Church of England's Book of Common Prayer, since it tampered with the original meaning of the Bible and inhibited the spontaneity that they felt was essential to attaining a true and honest glimpse of the divine. Hymns were also judged to be a corruption of God's word—instead a Puritan read directly from the Bible and sang scrupulously translated psalms where meaning took precedence over the demands of rhyme and meter. As staunch "primitivists," Puritans refused to kneel while taking communion, since there was no evidence that the apostles had done so during the Last Supper. There was also no biblical precedent for making the sign of the cross when uttering Christ's name. Even more important, there was no precedent for the system of bishops that ran the Church of England. The only biblically sanctioned organizational unit was the individual congregation. The Puritans believed that a congregation began with a covenant (a term they took from the Bible) between a group of believers and God. As a self-created and independent entity, the congregation elected a university-trained minister and, if the occasion should arise, voted him out. The Puritans also used the concept of a covenant to describe the individual's relationship with God. Ever since the Fall, when Adam had broken his covenant with God, man had been deserving of perpetual damnation. God had since made a covenant with Christ upon the fulfillment of that covenant, God had offered a covenant of grace to just a small minority of people know as the saints. The Puritans believed that the identity of the Saints had long since been determined by God. This meant that there was nothing a person could do to win salvation. But instead of being a reason to forsake all hope, what was known as predestination became a powerful goad to action. No one could be entirely sure as to who was one of the elect and yet, if a person was saved, he or she naturally lived a godly life. As a result, the Puritans were constantly comparing their own actions to those of others, since their conduct might indicate whether or not they were saved. They were constantly searching themselves for signs of damnation. It was a religion of endless striving and uncertain rewards. Underlying this compulsive quest for reassurance was a person's conscience, which one divine described as "the voice of God in man." A Puritan was taught to recognize the stages by which he or she might experience a sureness of redemption. It began with a powerful response to the "preaching of the Bible," in which God revealed the heights to which a person must aspire if he or she were to achieve grace. This was followed by a profound sense of inadequacy and despair that eventually served a prelude to, if a person was destined to be redeemed, indwelling grace. From this rigorous program of divine discipline a Puritan developed the confidence that he or she was, in fact, "one of the chosen elect."[4]

Mee just can't embrace the Puritan doctrine what' God had already decided through noe acts o' thar own who can be saved or damned. These self-assured preachers seemed to think this doctrine war found in the Bible. It warn't in mee Bible ond baffles mee sense ond reason. Doesn't seem to mee to pass muster what thar warn't anything a person can doe to escape heaven or hell. Mee could see how it happened what mee Puritan friends war always comparin' 'emselves to those around 'em to see if they war masterin' thar evil actions faster than somebody else. Bein' able to 'ave mee free will to choose eternal bliss in heaven or hot hell war mee religion.

Over generations, cracks began to appear in the pious coverin' o' thar saintly lives. Cotton Mather war o' the opinion what the New England churches "were in danger of complacent stagnation. The Lord's chosen needed a reformation." In mee opinion, Cotton Mather used his inflamed wrightin's ond preachin's to stimulate Puritan parishioners to look inside 'emselves for the devill's influence. Our local clergy's speeches emboldened mee neighbors to look outside, as weel, at thar neighbors ond to be afraid o' each othar, denounce each othar, ond to purge by accusations thar village o' Satan. These Sunday sermons whipped up mee local neighbors into a witch-accusin' frenzy. Mee hard Mather bears the title o' the New World's most committed witch-hunter. A witch hunt didn't mean what mee neighbors went door to door askin' if thar war a witch tharin. But they did join in a campaign to punish individuals who fit a criteria o' witchcraft, on the pretext o' safeguardin' our little community against those who worshipped the devill.

One o' the first ministers to arrive early on in our Bay Colony war the Reverend Francis Higginson. He talked the town fathers into bestowin' the name Shalom, a Hebrew word for "place of peace," on thar newly established town. 'Cause o' many people pronouncin' it wrong, the name become Salem. Mee hard the Bible city o' Jerusalem had once been called Salem. Hard tell, the word Salem has many special meanin's like eternal peace, prosperity, friendship, ond security. However, mee neighbors the Puritans did not offer friendship, prosperity, or security to those outside thar fold. The fact o' the matter, they come to practice thar religion as they pleased ond they did not allow wee nonconformists the same religious freedom. Historian Tom Juergens added, "Anything too much fun registered somewhere on the Puritan wickedness scale, even if it did rank low . . . leaping and dancing merited a fine of 20 shilling." Thar war noe exceptions to attendance at Sunday services. Noe exceptions! The penalty for non-attendance war fynes or expulsion—not just from the church, but alsoe from the whole community. Thar war some o' us who went in the front door, out the back door, ond paid the fyne to avoid expulsion. In mee view, those ol' blue lawes war laced w'th too many does ond don'ts. The Lord's Day war spent listenin' to four hours o' sermon warnin' o' sin ond punishment w'th an intermission. Durin' intermission, mee neighbors had time 'tween to walk home, eat a meal what they had cooked the day 'afore, ond walk back to the meetin'house for four hours o' the same. Those o' us who war highest in social standin' sat in pews below the preacher pulpit. Poor farmers, servants, ond children sat in the back. Noe talkin', sleepin', nor music war allowed. It seems like plainness

New England Puritans debating an issue, 1600s
Reproduced with permission by North Wind Picture Archives

to mee, what it waren't hard to enforce noe labor o' any kind on
Sunday 'cause ye didn't 'ave time to doe anythin' else but be in
church. Mee felt trapped in thar rigid, repressive meetin's. Mee
always seemed to find chores to be done in mee ordinary on thar
Thursday lecture day.

Fifty-seven yars ago, in 1636, the colonial court o' this
community o' peace cast out Roger Williams, whose opinions
war deemed seditious ond heretical. Nonconformist leaders who
disagreed w'th Puritan orthodoxy ond who wanted to establish
congregations independent o' the Puritan congregations war sent
across the herring pond. Othars, sich as Baptists ond Jesuits,
who war denied thar religious freedom war, in many cases,
driven out by force. The Puritan theocracy felt they war the open

door through which thar parishioners approached ond received acceptance o' God. Quakers believed what everieone had direct admittance to God w'th noe intermediaries. If this point o' view war true doctrine, Puritan ministers warn't needed.

This Quaker philosophy war just one doctrine the Puritan clergy considered heresy. In an effort to purify, protect, ond police thar parishes, the Puritan clergy o' the Massachusetts Bay Colony war the most active persecutors o' the Quakers. Those Quakers who landed in Boston war banished, under fear o' death, if they returned. William Leddra war hanged at Boston for practicin' the Quaker religion. Endecott had four Quakers put to death by twistin' for returnin' to the colony after thar banishment. For holdin' true to her faith, a Quaker women war ordered to strip to the waist ond half-naked, shee war tied to a cart's tail, dragged, ond whipped not to exceed 30 lashes at each town, 'tween the streets o' Salem ond on towards Boston. Puritan punishment war harsh ond severe. The Puritan theocracy felt it necessary to make punishment visible to thar neighbors, soe in many cases, an "H" war branded on thar cheek for heretic. Ears lopped off ond holes bored through a tongue war outward signs o' punishment for a heretic belief. Our Native Indian neighbors war considered agents o' the devill ond less than human.

May mee marke an Indian banishment what occurred in 1638. In this yar, native Indians war forcibly deported to Barbados ond Jamaica on one o' many ships. 'Cause, in the words o' our illustrious Governor o' Plymouth Colony, Josiah Winslow, "They had joined in an uprising against the colony and were guilty of many notorious and execrable murders, killings, and outrages."

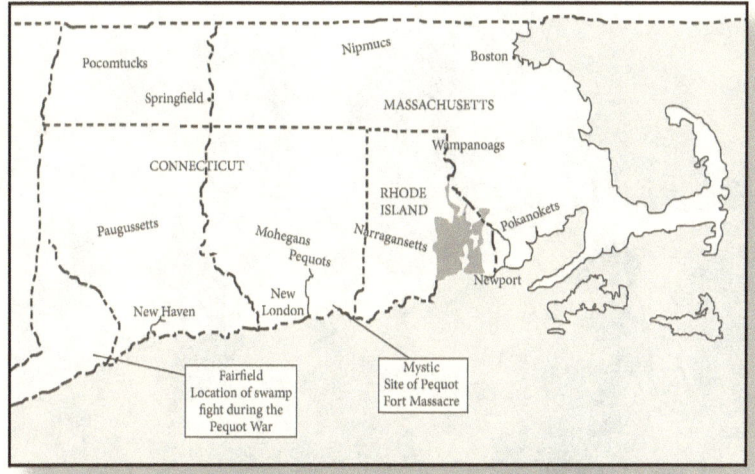

Map of Indians in Southern New England, 1600s

Reproduced with permission by North Wind Picture Archives

This removal war the offshoot o' the Pequot War, which ran a course o' 1634 through 1638. Mee war not in the New World at the time, but it war referred to as the first armed conflict for the Puritan colony against a powerful Indian tribe. As the story war retold to mee, it looked like the Indians desired to control the trade on the Missituk ond Pequot Rivers. The waves o' new Puritans arrivin' needed good farmland ond they felt they had a God-given right to extend thar settlements into the Connecticut River Valley. Mee Puritan neighbors had noe royal charter for this land, but they wanted the rich soil ond the furs. A Puritan business venture built a fort ond John Winthrop Jr. war appointed governor. All o' this war done on land occupied by the Pequot. It warn't long 'afore John Stone, a noted smuggler ond slaver, killed one o' thar chiefs. In retaliation, the Indians killed Mr. Stone ond his seven-man crew. The Bay Colony officials made two

Endicott Block Island

Public domain image reproduced from Wikipedia Commons

demands for retribution: the Indian responsible be turned over to the colony ond the Pequot war to pay a tribute in wampum. The Pequot chief Sassacus refused.

Then in 1636, John Oldham, a trader, ond his crew war murdered in a boat off Block Island. News o' his death become the subject o' sermons in the Bay Colony. Many o' the colonists insisted what the Pequot be punished for these deaths. The Bay Colony sent John Endecott to exact payment for the deaths.

In an attempt to avenge, Endecott's party o' 90 men sailed to Block Island ond attacked two recently abandoned villages. They carried away crops ond destroyed what they couldn't carry. The Pequot retaliated by raidin' unsuspectin' settlements. A yar later, Endecott sailed along the coast to a Pequot village, waer they repeated the demands. The Pequot stalled ond escaped into the woods. Endecott burned down the village ond took the crops.

Durin' the fall ond winter o' 1636, the Pequot laid siege to Fort Saybrook. Furthermore, a Pequot force attacked a small settlement in April 1637, killin' nine ond kidnappin' two young girls.

Eventually the Pequot tribes war defeated at the village o' Mystic. Captain John Mason ordered what the Pequot be burned. It war recounted to mee, as many as seven hundred people, women ond children included, war burned alive in thar homes. The Puritan leader, Captain Mason, praised the Lord for "burning them up in the fire of his wrath, and dunging the ground with their flesh. It is the Lord's doings, and it is marvelous in our eyes!" The remainin' Pequot war hunted down by the Mohegan ond the Narragansett, who decapitated some ond sent thar severed heads to the Puritan leaders in Boston.

Those Pequot who remained, 200 old men, women, ond children, offered 'emselves as slaves in exchange for life. Sadly, these war the castoffs what war banished to Barbados ond Jamaica. Mee colonist ancestors appropriated Pequot lands ond declared the Pequot dissolved. The colonists attributed the defeat o' the aggressive Pequot tribe to an act o' God. "Let the whole Earth be filled with his Glory! Thus the Lord was pleased to smite our enemies in the hinder Parts, and to give us their land for an inheritance." The Bay Colony proclaimed a day o' thanksgivin' 15 June 1637.

The war ended in September o' 1637 ond the Puritans officially declared the nation o' the Pequot extinct. The thoroughness o' the elimination o' the Pequot tribe made a deep impression upon the othar tribes. Othar Indians war fearful to rise up against the colonists ond for a long period, peace w'th the Indians come to the Bay Colony. In mee mind, mee can't seem to understand the Puritan's reasonin' o' the sixth commandment, "Thou shalt not kill." It seemed to mee it war a bendin' commandment w'th 'em. W'th each battle, militiamen in thar prime war lost from our Massachusetts Bay Colony. Mee am heartbroken to make public what the Pequot Battle war the beginnin's o' slavery in the colonies.

Salem, Salem Village, ond Beverly/Danvers war portions o' the Massachusetts Bay Colony settled in 1630 by this religiously devout group. In 1632, the capital war moved from Salem to 15 miles south in Boston. But the sheltered harbors o' Salem, anothar attraction for the great migration o' Puritans, continued to allow people to make thar livin' from the sea, ond eventually from the timber, enablin' Salem to become a skilled shipbuildin' center.

The territory administered by the Bay Colony Puritans included portions o' Massachusetts, New Hampshire, Maine, Connecticut, ond Rhode Island. These British Christian soldiers considered nonconformist settlers o' different faiths or nationality, like meself, to be forms o' the devill heeself ond felt it thar duty as God's chosen people to wage a battle against wee agents o' the devill. Since the colony believed thar should be noe separation o' church ond state, any sinful behavior war treasonous conduct against the entire community, ond appropriately dealt w'th by the theocratic hierarchy who controlled both church ond state. The Bible scripture in Matthew—wee shall be as a "city upon a hill" ond to be "a light to the world," oft-quoted by John Winthrop to his Puritan shipmates 'afore thar arrivall in Massachusetts, expressed his desire what they would 'ave a new, perfect society what would be an example for all othar people to show 'em how to live in God's way. Puritans war to live in the world, but not become part o' the world. Winthrop added, "So what if we shall deal falsely with our God in this work we have undertaken, and so cause Him to withdraw His present help from us, we shall be made a story and a byword through the world." This Zion city would be founded upon strict clergy interpretation o' the Bible ond clergy enforcement o' God's lawes. Any wrongdoers disobeyin' the Puritan interpretation o' the Bible would be weeded out ond find 'emselves in the nutcrackers, whipped, or havin' to find anothar place to live. Mee can bear a truth what public whippin's war common. Mee slanderous speech earned mee a few at the whippin' post in front o' the public meetin'house on Sabbath Day. Mee war humiliated, but not deterred.

The Puritan treatment o' women had not changed from earlier days to mee current livin'. It war mee point o' view what Apostle Peter callin' women a "weaker vessel" by virtue o' Eve's bein' deceived by Satan war demeanin'. Dwellin' on how people war weak ond vulnerable ond in need o' help war disturbin', in mee opinion. It war felt anciently ond in mee own day what women war daughters o' Eve. 'Cause Eve deserted divine devotion, ate the fruit ond tempted Adam who had been valiant to eat the fruit, ond brung death into the world, wee as women carried the weight o' the beginnin' o' the original sin upon our persons. Puritan clergy held women war naturally lustful, not to be trusted, ond war more inclined to error. In times long past, Christian theologians considered women to be the doors to sin. The *Malleus Maleficarum* states: "Because the female sex is more concerned with things of the flesh than men; because being formed from a man's rib, they are 'only imperfect animals' and 'crooked' whereas man belongs to a privileged sex from whose midst Christ emerged."[5]

Since Puritans believed what women war inferior to men, it war a man's world mee lived in. Mee felt mee war equal to mee menfolk. In the Puritan religion, women war expected to be silent, submissive, ond docile helpmates to thar husbands ond mothars to thar children. Mee war an independent thinker in conversation ond doin's. Mee war reminded more times than mee can remember what ideal Puritan woman had these characteristics: him outside, shee w'thin; him in public, shee at home; him preachin', shee harin'; ond him speakin', shee listenin'. Lawes for the punishment o' swearin' war passed, as many like mee had a sharp tongue ond war addicted to swearin'. Women war to be subservient to thar fathers 'til they war married ond then subservient to thar husbands. Mee often had clashin's ond fistfights w'th mee husbands. A Puritan woman desired to be a perfect housewife ond to please God. A woman's salvation depended upon the goodness o' her children. A good wife taught her children 'bout the Bible ond God. Durin' the meetin's on the Sabbath, women sat togather on hard, cold benches ond war not allowed to speak. "Let your women keep silence in the churches: for it is not permitted unto them to speak; but they are commanded to be under obedience, as also saith the law. And if they will learn any thing, let them ask their husbands at home; for it is a shame for women to speak in the church," as s'd in Corinthians 14:34-35. To be a covenant member o' the church, a person had to 'ave a conversion story. Only when sharin' thar conversion stories war women allowed to speak in church. Mee war strong-willed ond rebellious. Rebellion war a Puritan punishable fault. Mee had a reputation as a troublemaker 'cause mee went against the grain o' the community. Mee refused to regularly attend church. Not bein' one o' the chosen people, mee deportment war watched carefully. Women didn't participate in town meetin's ond war excluded from any church decisions. Mee war upper class ond had mee say at Salem town meetin's. Mee drove difficult financial bargains, war reluctant to pay mee bills, ond war prominent in business activities. If a woman didn't read the Bible, it war thought shee war worshippin' the devill. Women war taught to read, but few larned to wright, as thar war noe reason for women to wright. Women had few legal rights on thar own ond rare economic independence. They didn't often own property. Women war to repress thar feelin's o' anger ond frustration. Mee war verie independent, could both read ond wright, spoke mee mind, ond inherited a house ond property from Thomas Oliver, mee second husband. Thomas died grantin' our Salem Town house ond land for mee use. Mee turned this house into a ordinary ond ran it by meeself 'til mee remarriage. Mee stepdaughter Mary, Thomas Oliver's daughter, war jealous what mee received this property. May the reader give a hearin' to what's what. Mary war married to Constable Job Hilliard, who mee thinks had causes for bringin' charges against mee. May mee say, mee don't feel shame what mee are a woman. Mee admits what many o' mee gowns war cut low to sport blubber. Puritan women war to wear a simple, noe frills, modestly cut cloth from head to toe ond avoid bright colors ond ornamentation. They war to cover thar hayr w'th a cild cap. Mee never covered mee hayr. It war the most beautiful part o' mee. They war to sew thar own smocks, mish, ond jackets. Mee either imported mee cloths or had 'em tailor-made.

Since mee deviated from the Puritan standards for women, mee war ostracized. Mee war constantly under suspicion. In mee ordinary, thar war drinkin', shove ha'penny, shovel board, wagerin', ond dancin'. The pious clergy ond parishioners felt all o' these activities opened the doors to sin ond Satan. Mee means o' support war a direct challenge to the will o' God. Many o' the ordinaries in our colonies war small ones operated by women out o' thar homes, especially widows like mee. The local magistrates who awarded "liberty to keep a house of common entertainment" preferred widows. They felt wee had good business sense, war hard workers, ond might otharwise be down ond out ond become a drain on the colonies. In mee opinion, the church controlled our little village too tightly. Mee felt the rigid religious practices war a constant burden to mee townspeople. Any signs o' differences war interpreted as the presence o' evil. Puritans even thought crippled, aged, poor, deformed, ond sickly people war possibly the offspring o' Satan. Puritan lawes left noe room for the weak ond old.

Mee think for people o' yer day, the 21st century, the Puritan religion would be an incredibly difficult religion to follow. Mee live in hope what ye don't impose ye moral standards on mee people o' 1692. From thar verie yeth, everie Puritan larned to fear death, destruction, ond the devill. Mee 'ave seen more corruption ond more vice hidden beneath a somber, sad-colored frock in this colony than mee evar saw in the motharland. These rural Puritan farmers lived in fear o' the forest dangers what ringed thar fields. The forest war the realm o' Satan ond against him ond his forces, guns offered noe protection. In like manner, the forests could conceal an Indian attack. Each small village in our colonies had a blockhouse waer wee could flee from an Indian attack. Mee farmer neighbors always attended thar mornin' ond afternoon Sabbath meetin' carryin' thar muskets. From thar pulpits, Cotton Mather, John Hale, Nicholas Noyes Jr., ond othar local ministers warned thar parishioners what the Massachusetts forests had once belonged to the devill ond what the devill would conquer the Puritans ond take his kingdom back if they war not steadfast in all the lawes ond ordinances o' the church. These backwoods farmers war warned what Satan war all around 'em ond it war his desire to break down the godly community ond tempt people to sign his book ond to become witches. The ministers o' the day preached what witches war human manifestation o' the unseen world. To add to superstition, thar sermons warned what the devill's favorite way o' testin' Puritans war to place witches in thar communities. Reverend Cotton Mather, co-minister w'th his father o' Second Church, Boston, wrote what witchcraft war a horrible plot against the country, which if not seasonably discovered, would probablie blow up ond pull down all the churches in the country. The parishioners trusted in what thar ministers preached. The more thar clergy preached witchcraft, the more the parishioners believed in witchcraft. Mee know it as a truth, thar war verie few who didn't believe in the unseen world o' the devill ond witches. Those who had doubts kept 'em to 'emselves ond war careful not to say thar views, leastwise they 'emselves might be suspected, become the enemy, ond thar verie lives would be in danger.

Thar war 'bout 500 people o' lower class livin' in the wilderness community o' Salem Village. The village war an outlyin' farmin' community o' Salem Town. When mee immigrated to the colonies, mee lived in Salem Town as the wife o' Lord Thomas Oliver. Since mee war a member o' the merchant class, mee usually referred to the village as the farms ond those livin' thar as the farmers. Most o' the farm people had little or noe formal education, ond shared the insecurity soe often found in those whose livelihoods depended on natural factors beyond thar control. Most o' the farmers war barely hangin' on. Many o' thar sons, ten percent, had lost thar lives in the King Philip Indian War or othar conflicts. Many war now off fightin' in Maine against Indians, Dutch, ond French, ond did not return. 'Cause o' the decline o' marriageable men, Salem Village war overflowin' w'th unmarried girls w'th noe prospects.

In mee view, history wouldn't 'ave a reason to remember the names o' Abigail Williams ond Elizabeth Parris, if these two girls would 'ave kept Tituba's tricks, spells, ond games to 'emselves—mum for that. As the experimentin' in spells ond fortune-tellin' tricks grew more intense, Betty ond Abigail, who war both God-fearin' Puritans, began to worry what they war committin' evil. Mee suppose on the one hand, they war ashamed ond frightened 'bout bein' disobedient, but on the othar, war excited o' doin' somethin' what war strictly forbidden in Salem Village. Even though the two girls, Betty ond Abigail, war enchanted by Tituba's stories o' her childhood in Barbados,

Tituba telling tales to Salem children
Reproduced with permission by North Wind Picture Archives

these tales o' voodoo ond white magick war soe real they gave 'em a sense o' doom. Mee am sure they war terrified o' what Reverend Parris might doe to 'em if hee found out how they had been practicin' white magick in his home. They would be severely punished ond maybe even publicly disciplined in thar church. Mee thinks these girls war feelin' the heavy weight o' thar disobedience ond livin' a lye. In Cotton Mather's wrightin's, *The Good Education Of Children,* he states: "They which lie must go to their father the devil, into an everlasting burning . . . God will pour out his wrath upon them; and when they beg and pray in hellfire, God will not forgive them, but that they must lie forever. Are you willing to go to Hell to be burnt with the devil and his angels? Oh Hell is a terrible place, that's worse a thousand times than whipping."[6]

It warn't long 'afore Betty Parris, plagued w'th shame over the Puritan lawes shee war breakin', would lapse into distraught guilt-ridden stares. When called to reality by her loved ones, shee would scream, ond upon bein' pressed to explain, shee would make senseless babblin' sounds. Mee hard tell what these sounds war followed by chokin' noises what come close to a dog barkin'. Abigail Williams not only copied the starin' ond noises o' Betty, but shee went beyond Betty's antics, to include crawlin' on all fours over ond under the furniture ond lyin' on the floor in a screamin' fit. Reverend Parris ond his wife at first sought noe help w'th the sickness o' these two girls. Words war rumored around in mee ordinary, by those who attended the Salem Village meetin'house, what they war surprised to see Mrs. Parris come down the aisle at church w'th her two bairns in tow . . . since the girls war racked w'th some malady.

Mee guess it war hard to keep thar dark secret to 'emselves. Soe Betty ond Abigail invited othar yeng girl friends ond the mothar o' one o' the girls to join thar forbidden gatherin's in thar parsonage home. Bein' churchgoers, it war easy for all o' 'em to find an excuse for visitin' Reverend Parris's parsonage. Mee soon discovered what they all lived close to the parsonage ond they watched for times when the coast war clear ond they could slip unnoticed into the warm kitchen w'th its roarin' fire. This handful o' bored girls war switched on by Tituba's tales, spells, ond white magick. Mee suppose thar answer would be, if detected ond questioned, the reverend war out ond they war waitin' for him to return.

As mee explained previous, most yeng girls war concerned 'bout thar future status. To be manless ond w'thout a possible future marriage war to be w'thout a direction in thar lives. Noe greater misfortune could be one's fate than to be unmarried. Ye war an old maid if ye reached the age o' 25 unwedded. These girls war noe exception. Mee guess thar curiosity 'bout thar future love, thar own marriages, ond thar sweetheart's callin' drew 'em to these small informal meetin's. A soldier, a sailor, a tinker, ond a tailor—all yeng girls knew what thar future depended upon thar husband's trade. It war January 1692, a time close to St. Egnes Eve, a date 'tween winter ond spring; a traditional time for fortune-tellin'. The tellin' o' future events war Tituba's specialty. Tituba war an import from Barbados. Shee war one o' the two slaves what Mr. ond Mrs. Samuel Parris brung to Massachusetts. Shee knew a good deal 'bout witchcraft. All the black people in the West Indies believed in it. West Indies witch doctors war feared ond had great power over the slaves. W'th Tituba's help, mee hard tell what one o' the girls devised a primitive crystal ball. The girls pricked a hole in the eggshell ond then held it over the water in a glass. As the egg whites began to drip into the water, they diffused ond created shapes. The girls asked to see the faces o' thar future husbands or thar callin'. When ye held the water glass up to a candle, ye could see the shapes the egg whites take ond it would tell ye 'bout yer future husband or his callin'. Mee hard Ann Putnam Jr. received a chillin' answer. In the glass thar floated a spectre o' a coffin. Mee could imagine the hysteria these girls felt when the image o' a coffin appeared in the glass. Mee dare say what her curious attempts in fortune-tellin' war

Tituba and Mary Walcott-Longfellow

Public domain image reproduced from Wikipedia Commons

justly rewarded by this sordid prediction. Ann Putnam Jr. war terrified. This apparition proclaimed her a "bride of death." The Reverend John Hale later wrote shee war afterwards bothared by satanic visions to her death ond soe died a single person. Mee dare say, in spite o' the fact what curious girls 'ave been doin' this sort o' thing forever, the othar girls who met at Reverend Parris's home w'th inquisitive attempts in white magick, even though a game for sport, war likewise justly rewarded. It is mee view, what thar forbidden attempts to foretell the future war dealin' w'th the devill.

As the winter passed, it continued to be easy for all o' 'em girls to find excuses for visitin' Reverend Parris's parsonage. Tituba continued to unfold her stories ond white magick to Betty ond Abigail Williams, along w'th othar neighbor girls: Mary Walcott,

20; Elizabeth Hubbard, 17; Mercy Lewis, 19; Susanna Sheldon, 18; Ann Putnam Jr., 12; ond off ond on, Goodwife Ann Putnam Sr. All the partakers managed to keep these meetin's secretive for a while. It warn't long 'afore it war noised 'bout the village ond even in mee ordinary what thar war parishioners in our midst who war practicin' fortune-tellin'. As the girls grasped the seriousness o' thar scandal, they knew a truthful disclosure war not an option. Instead o' ownin' up ond to avoid chastisement ond penalties, mee guess the girls devised a plan to display bein' possessed by evil spirits. Soon the girls began to display a hodgepodge o' actions—odd postures, contorted gestures, loud cries, ond unintelligible words ond sounds. Mee thinks if these antics, at this time, war regarded as childish pranks, it would 'ave prevented the hysteria—mum to that. But not to be, they war taken note o' ond received serious attention. Eventually, this foolish magick transformed these girls into hysterical, evil public accusers ond testifiers, who hooked the devill ond his unseen world to Salem Village in order to hide thar participation in the forbidden art o' the fortune-tellin' glass ond othar games o' white magick. This circle o' girls, hitherto unnoticed as bairns usually are, now received daily attention. As these girls played at thar evil games, a circle o' watchers war either fascinated in what they observed or war panicked what these foolish girls war carryin' thar sport too far. Mee should touch on two more girls who war considered on the outer circle o' accusers . . . Sarah Churchill, 25, a maidservant ond relative o' the Ingersolls ond Mary Walcot; Elizabeth Booth, 18; ond Mary Warren, 20, a servant in the household o' John Proctor. In addition, thar war othar older matrons who cryed out ond testified . . . Sarah Bibber ond Gertrude Pope. Wee can't forget John Indian ond Tituba. Mee want mee reader to know, mee lived on Ipswich Post Road for 'bout five yars ond hadn't evar been in the Salem Village meetin'house 'afore ond mee didn't know the yeng girls who war experimentin' in fortune-tellin'.

As mee mentioned, thar war contentions 'tween Salem Town—the tradesmen, merchants, upper class, ond Salem Village—the farmers. Wee residents o' Salem Town wanted tax revenues for the upkeep o' the Salem Town meetin'house to be contributed by residents o' the farms. For thar part, the farmers, though usually outvoted by the more numerous town-dwellers, sought to avoid civic obligations owin' to thar bein' a distance from town. By the early 1670s, the farmers fightin' for an independent town status ond greater rights o' self-government, focused on thar desire to build thar own meetin'house ond to support thar own minister. Like othar residents who lived in outlyin' settlements in New England, they complained o' the long weekly journey to Salem Town center to attend church services, arguin' what they should be able to establish thar own congregation. In October 1672, the Massachusetts General Court agreed to thar request. Salem Village become independent. For yars tharafter, however, wee merchants in Salem Town still claimed the right to assess farmers for the maintenance o' our meetin'house ond the civic expenses o' buildin' bridges ond roads.

Ironically, the long-sought meetin'house ond minister, who war the subject o' soe much contention 'tween Salem Village ond Salem Town, proved to be the major source o' discord w'thin Salem Village itself. The first three ministers who served

Salem Village in the 17th century
Reproduced with permission by the Corbis Corporation

the village war caught 'tween the two factions what wanted to control the congregation. Reverend James Bayley war not weel-liked ond failed to earn consistent support from the parishioners. He war spied on, hounded, ond when the villages refused to pay his salary, hee finally left. Likewise, Reverend Burroughs war put in the uncomfortable position o' a mediator in the disagreements 'tween the two feudin' factions in the village. Since Reverend Burroughs war unable to subsist on what the parishioners paid him, hee left the village. Reverend Deodat Lawson answered the call to come to the Salem Village congregation. Once againe, tempers flared quite often amang the parishioners. Reverend Lawson feared for his stability. He war denied the position o' full ordained minister, soe hee

resigned ond returned to Boston. It war whispered to mee in
mee taproom what this lack o' conciliation amang the village
parishioners war the beginnin's o' an evil work. Parris had been
refused by a number o' larger churches 'afore hee submitted his
name to Salem Village. Reverend Samuel Parris war the last to
be hired. Mee hard what Parris arrived in the village w'th an
attitude o' takin' charge. He named severall conditions what
hee felt needed to be met 'afore hee would accept thar position
o' thar minister. He kept the congregation danglin' for almost
a yar hopin' to achieve his demands. He demanded title clear
ond free o' all encumbrances to thar parsonage ond 30 cords
o' wood cut ond stacked outside his parsonage. Mee tee-heed
a wee bit when mee hard the parishioners clipped the wings o'
what ol' minister. Parris would 'ave to find his own wood spell.
The humiliated Parris at last accepted the clergy position on the
parishioners' terms ond signed his agreement in the fall, 1689.
Thus, the congregation at Salem Village war againe established
w'th a charter, 19 November 1689, w'th 27 parishioners.
Reverend Parris commenced to minister in the Salem Village
congregation w'th a high hand. Mee needs to interject what from
this time on, Reverend Parris had a long, bitter struggle w'th
his parishioners. It war noised 'bout what Parris dismissed some
nonmembers from his meetin'house after his sermon 'afore the
members took communion togethar. Parris objected to ordainin'
deacons 'til they war proven by a test period. In mee ordinary,
mee hard the grumblin's by many o' the farmers against Parris.
They war organizin' for his removal. The villagers felt hee had
created a division in thar ranks by his exclusion from his church

o' the non-baptized. Thar bein' two generations removed from our Puritan roots o' 1629, many farmers war more worldly ond warn't in lockstep w'th severe doctrine. Hard-liner farmers felt the rite o' baptism should be performed for children o' full church membership. Then in 1690, Parris instituted the soe-called Halfway Covenant, which permitted the baptism o' infants barn to parents who had 'emselves been baptized, but who hadn't stepped forward ond recounted a conversion experience ond become full members o' the covenant. These partial unconverted members couldn't receive communion ond vote. Thar children wouldn't be admitted to full membership 'til they war at least 14 yars old ond could profess thar own conversion experience. This halfway covenant become a matter o' controversy ond contention in the Salem Village Congregation. By ond by, the discontented Salem Village farmers vowed to drive Reverend Parris out o' Salem. Othar discontented farmers considered quittin' Sunday services, but war afraid what the Putnam ond Parris camp would accuse 'em o' witchcraft. Just a bit o' titillatin' dirty linen. It warn't but two yars later, in 1691, when five Parris committee supporters war voted out ond replaced w'th five anti-Putnam/ Parris supporters. W'th the balance o' votes tipped against Parris, the committee voted not to pay Parris's salary ond declared null ond void the temporary ownership o' the parsonage. Mee oh my, what a blow to Parris, who war now facin' a future o' makin' a livin' off handouts from the powerful Putnam family. Mee hard it s'd Salem Village had been targeted for destruction by the devil by reason o' the people bein' divided ond thar differin' w'th thar minister.

Over the yars, our settlements in New England endured disappointin' harvests, harassment by the hostile Indians, disease, ond theological battles 'tween Puritans in high government positions who refused requests by England's current king ond the king's agents to allow the Church o' England to become established. As life in the Massachusetts Bay Colony become increasingly difficult for all o' us, the Puritan ministers preached w'th greater zeal what the Book o' Revelations war 'bout to be fulfilled. All signs—lack o' piety in the parishes around the colony—pointed to doomsday, conflicts, rumors o' future battles, ond God's anger. God's chosen people must repent ond repair.

One o' 'em battles mee lived through. It war the bloodiest ond costliest forgotten Armageddon in the history o' Massachusetts Bay Colony—King Philip's War. Metacomet, Metacom, or Pometacom, in his language, war the yenger son o' Massasoit. Most o' us in the colony called him King Philip. Philip become sachem o' the Wampanoag in 1662. He had noe trust in the colonists ond began immediately to negotiate w'th othar Indian tribes to gather allies for harassment ond attacks on the dispersed, lonely farmhouses ond unprotected settlements. The Narragansett ond Nipmuck Indian tribes joined him. Thar weapons o' choice war knives, tomahawks, ond flintlock muskets. Those ol' French Canadians ond Dutch dandies supplied the Indians thar muskets, musket powder, ond lead. Wee had a shaky peace w'th the Indian tribes, but it quickly escalated to war 'cause the colonists' livestock kept tramplin' on Indian cornfields, colonists went out ond shot thar game, ond colonists shared thar diseases. Compoundin' the above problems, the colonists war profitin' by unfairly tradin' English-manufactured goods, sich as pots, beads, guns, ond dry goods, for Indian lands. English-manufactured goods war creatin' a dependency for the Indian tribes. To the colonists, the purchase or tradin' o' the Indian lands meant ownership. To the native tribes, it meant only access to the land by colonists. The concept o' ownership by one person war strange to the Indians. They had noe settled places ond changed thar habitation from place to place. They expected to continue thar livelihood o' huntin' ond fishin' on the land as they had for hundreds o' yars. King Philip felt his people should return to thar traditional Indian ways, thus eliminatin' this reliance. Hostilities eventually war brung to a climax over these steady land sales ond the colonists' heavy-handed treatment o' King Philip. Suspicious o' Philip, the Plymouth administrators, in 1671, brung King Philip in for questionin'. He war fined ond released only after surrenderin' a cache o' guns ond promisin' to submit to English lawe. He vowed to heeself what it would be his last humiliation.

W'thin three days, the Wampanoag war on the warpath. W'th the request o' the Plymouth Colony, the Massachusetts Colony come to thar aide, expandin' the King Philip's War to include much o' the militia manpower o' New England. Signboards nailed to mee ordinary admonished mee local militia farmers what each soldier shall 'ave arms complete ond knapsack ready to march. 'Em Indians sure ravaged the countryside when they attacked. In the space o' a few yars, 1675-1678, more than half o' our towns in New England war laid to ashes ond many more damaged ond abandoned. Thar war 1,200 buildings destroyed. Our colony's economy war all but ruined as our debt amounted to 15,000 pounds. Much o' our cattle war killed—8,000 mee hard tell. Sadly, mee report much o' our population war killed, includin' one-tenth o' all men available 'tween the ages o' 16 ond 60. Two thousand women ond children war killed. Historian Charles Hudson stated: "During this short period, six hundred of our brave men, the flower and strength of the colony, had fallen, and six hundred dwelling houses were consumed. Every 11th family was houseless and every 11th soldier-at-arms had sunk to his grave."[7]

It seems to mee, loss o' property seemed to be counted first 'afore the loss o' human life. But even soe, one-third o' our white population war wiped out. King Philip's War resulted in the virtual extermination o' tribal Native American life from the Bay Colony. For each colonist killed, three or more Indians died—if not from bullets, then from starvation, disease, ond exposure. The combined deaths totaled 5,000, w'th more than three-quarters o' those losses suffered by the Native Americans. Thar war scarcely a fireside what war not a home o' mournin'. Thar war othar losses. France's Indian allies seized cod ketches right from thar ports ond the French corsairs captured our fishin' ketches at sea, reducin' our fleet from 60 to 15. In addition, our rapid expansion westward war halted. This conflict lasted only 'bout 14 months, yet it had taken those o' us who lived in the colonies two decades 'afore all o' the devastated frontier could be reoccupied, 'afore loss o' life to recover, ond 'afore our debt to be retrieved. Even w'th the conclusion o' King Philip's War, thar had been continuall Indian raids by othar Indian tribes, settin' our New England nerves on edge. King Philip's battle war a warnin' to all o' us livin' in the colonies what the father o' lyes war at work amang us. God war punishin' us.

Thar war severe epidemics o' sickness w'th high death rates. The smallpox epidemics o' 1677 ond 1689-90 reached a mortality rate o' 30 percent. Inoculations war opposed by mee Puritan neighbors. Thar ministers s'd inoculations caused many deaths ond spread the infection ond violated the natural lawes o' medicine. Thar clergy sermonized what inoculation war fightin' w'th the most high. Puritan ministers preached what smallpox epidemics war given to us by God as punishment for not adherin' to covenants. Attemptin' to shield ourselves from God's fury via inoculation would only serve to provoke him. Mee am hard-pressed to understand why these Puritans war always findin' God's disregard in thar afflictions. As mee sat in meetin'house on the Lord's Day, it seemed to mee thar sermon subjects harped on "personal suffering were required to earn redemption from the original sin." Can ye believe what they sit men ond women on opposite sides o' the church lest lustful thoughts might distract those who war worshippin'? Anothar stumblin' block for mee war listenin' to a reverend teach what God uses Satan to test faith ond punish w'th smallpox. 'Cause the subject o' inoculation warn't found in the Bible, it warn't the will o' God ond tharfore unlaweful. The pious clergy believed uncontrollable epidemics o' sickness war an evidence o' Satan's temporary success.

A blight epidemic spread through New England, destroyin' an entire season o' wheat ond corn. Thar war caterpillars ond othar crop-eatin' insects what wiped out whole orchards ond entire fields o' barley, oats, ond corn. Cotton Mather described the situation:

I believe there never was a poor plantation more pursued than our New England. First, the Indian Powwow, then seducing spirits, after this a continual blast upon some of our principal grains, here withal, wasting sickness. Next, so many adversaries of our own language, desolating fires also and losses by sea. Besides all which, the devils war come upon us with such wrath as is justly the astonishment of the world.[8]

These natural disasters war anothar sign o' God showin' his disfavor. Our commitment to our covenants w'th God war slumpin', soe God war allowin' the devill to spread his wrath upon us.

The dramatic statement by Puritan minister Jonathan Edwards seems to square w'th this drama: "The bow of God's wrath is bent, and the arrows made ready."

To continue mee story . . . in 1688, the contentious parsonage in Salem Village what bordered our crowded seaport o' Salem Town, agreed to consider Reverend Samuel Parris as minister. In the early 1670s, upon the death o' his father, hee cut short his studies at Harvard to return to Barbados to settle his father's estate. Mee hereby get on to cap the facts what war told around mee taproom o' mee ordinary 'bout Mr. Parris. Hee didn't doe weel at the import/export trade in the West Indies. Since his income war verie uncertain ond his plantation in Barbados war not prosperin', hee decided to give up his West Indies business ond become a minister. Hee put forth his name to some o' the big churches in Boston, but none wanted a minister who had not completed theological studies at Harvard. In the spring o' 1689, after a number o' larger churches refused his services, hee submitted his name, along w'th some demands, to the little church

o' Salem Village what needed
a minister. Parris tryed to use
his ability as a merchant to
drive a hard bargain w'th
the farmers. Mee hard tell,
Samuel Parris alienated
many o' the parishioners
by his sharpness in tryein'
to negotiate an agreement
in his favor. At this time,
Captain John Putnam war
one o' the most influential
elders in the Salem Village
church. Hee war a mover
w'th decided opinions. The
Putnam family ond extended

Samuel Parris (1653-1720),
Puritan minister in Salem Village
Public domain image reproduced from Wikipedia Commons

family owned large tracts o' land. May mee put 'afore ye this fact,
when ye own a lot o' land, ye can wield considerable political
power over yer neighbors. It war the Putnam family who war
the motivators to keep the farms o' Salem Village separate ond
independent from the tradesmen in Salem Town. To accomplish
this, Thomas Putnam's main strategy war to establish a church
what war independent from the Salem Town congregation. Thar
war many in the village congregation who war supporters o' the
Putnams. By 1688, after three ministers had been forced to leave
thar posts, it war the Putnams who put pressure on thar farm
neighbors to hire Samuel Parris as thar new minister. It war told
to mee what the farmers warn't happy w'th this arm-twistin'.

Mee farm neighbors war poor ond couldn't afford to pay the high taxes demanded to support a high-salaried minister who only had a limited amount o' trainin' at Harvard ond who had allegiance to the Putnams. After a yar o' negotiations over his salary, Reverend Parris accepted the job as the minister o' the Salem Village. Once hee war hired, Parris began to press for ownership o' the parsonage. The parsonage as a rule remained the property o' Salem Village. Irate farmers come steamin' into mee ordinary complainin' what Reverend Parris didn't know when to stop. Thar war many up-in-arms villagers who war fumin' w'th Thomas Putnam's desperate measures ond his attempts, to give in to Parris's request. In October 1689, a vote war taken by the parishioners. Salem Village parsonage, barn, ond two acres adjoinin' war given to Samuel Parris on a temporary basis along w'th 66 pounds a yar. May mee account for the sentiment o' the farmer protestors . . . since noe legal document war drafted, this ol' agreement warn't legally bindin'. Mee could see this sore spot warn't goin' to go away. Parris got to enjoy a comfortable house rent free, pastureland for cows ond othar livestock, but only while hee war livin' in it. Hee war to keep the parsonage in good repair. Over ond above, Mr. Parris would 'ave to take part o' his salary in corn ond othar things produced on the farms o' his congregation ond hee would 'ave to find his own wood spell. Putnam saw to it what Parris war quickly ordained by neighborin' clergy. This war a major mistake . . . an important step war skipped. It warn't the normal protocol to 'ave a minister ordained 'afore hee war approved. The normal custom for establishin' a minister in a Puritan congregation war to 'ave the covenanted body o' the saints approve the minister by vote. Putnam bypassed this order. In the eyes o' some o' mee flouted farmer friends, Putnam ond Parris, in designed haste, had leaped over proper order ond thus Parris didn't 'ave proper authority to administer communion or baptize babies. It is mee judgement this passover added fuel to the already bickerin' blaze in the village.

Heedless o' this fallout, Samuel Parris, w'th his family ond two slaves, journeyed to Salem Village. Mee sees what Reverend Samuel Parris's arrivall w'th his slaves, who war barn ond had lived in Barbados, wharin the atmosphere war saturated w'th faith in voodoo, witches, ond demonic magick, opened the curtain to our community scene o' witchin' hysteria. Mee hard tell what one o' his first sermons war directed to his farmer foes, wharin hee s'd the main drift o' the devill war to pull the church down ond the devill asserted what hee war assisted by wicked ond reprobate men.

Mee hard when Reverend Parris moved into the parsonage in November, hee ond his wife entered into his congregation duties w'th much energy. John Indian ond his wife Tituba war the names o' his two slaves. W'th two slaves to perform the household duties ond to watch over thar daughter, Betty, ond thar niece, Abigail William, the reverend ond his wife spent most o' thar time makin' congregation calls. It war an uneasy time for Reverend ond Mrs. Parris, as mee thinks Parris's position as Reverend war up for grabs. W'th the Parrises soe much away from thar parsonage, the two girls spent a lot o' idle time w'th Tituba. These girls hadn't evar held a doll or othar toys, it bein' forbidden. W'th nothin' to busy 'emselves w'th, thar idle time become the devill's playroom. Tituba war a believer in the existence o' evil spirits ond had become adept in white ond black magick ond othar voodoo sorceries. Mee hard it mentioned what shee war a great storyteller.

It war late January when Mr. Parris's nine-yar-old daughter, Betty, ond his 11-yar-old niece, Abigail Williams, become torn w'th fright ond guilt ond suddenly fell sick. The children's illnesses took the form o' complainin' o' pain, blattin' strange animal sounds, bizarre contortions o' thar arms ond legs, ond screams what burst on mee ears. 'Cause they war gettin' soe much attention, they commenced to doe more extraordinary things. Reverend Parris took Betty ond Abigail to various herbists to identify thar ailment. Parsnip seed, spirits o' caster oil, ond all the usual remedies war used. None war effective. Mee think they should 'ave tryed ignorin' 'em ond thar antics would go away—mum for that.

The distraught Reverend Parris war familiar w'th the Goodwin children bein' possessed by evil spirits, as the Parris family war livin' in Boston at the time o' Goody Glover's hangin'. Mee fancy what poor ol' Goody Glover had a hard life ond war a wee bit demented 'cause o' her age. Back-fence talk tittled what Reverend Parris realized this war noe ordinary illness what had taken root in his household. Hee suspected demons war causin' the strangeness o' his children.

Early on in February, durin' the cold idle winter afternoons while Reverend Samuel Parris, minister o' the Salem Village Church, ond his wife war out visitin' thar parishioners, Betty ond Abigail war joined by a group o' girls, none o' whom mee knew.

They gathered around the kitchen fire to entertain 'emselves w'th scary stories o' ghosts, spirits, ond the forbidden practice o' fortune-tellin'. The practice o' foretellin' information 'bout a person's life war known in the Bay Colony ond war strictly forbidden by the Puritans.

It war severall weeks 'afore Parris summoned to his parsonage a local physician, one Dr. William Griggs. Dr. William Griggs had just moved into the village. Even though hee war self-taught, Dr. Griggs war the only physician in Salem Village. Most likely, it war probablie his first house visit. Mee put forth what if mee war a doctor lookin' to start a practice, it would be useful to 'ave the congregation minister's good opinion in mee pocket. But Dr. Griggs war at a loss to understand the behavior o' the girls, as hee found noe physical symptoms to explain thar behavior. Thar behavior warn't the behavior o' good Christian girls. Dr. Griggs believed in witchcraft ond considered it the cause o' some diseases. Mee feel what Dr. Griggs acquiesced to the opinion o' Reverend Parris. Since the girls lacked any physical evidence o' an illness, mee feel what Dr. Grigg's conclusive compliance to Reverend Parris's suspicions resulted in Dr. Grigg's declarin' the cause for the strange, grotesque gestures to be supernatural in nature. Betty's fits war soe extreme what ripples o' fear spread quickly throughout Salem Village. On 14 February, Reverend Parris preached on Psalm 110:1 and spoke o' "God sending forth destroyers as a consequence of men's slighting of Christ." Reverend Parris ond his wife thought it best to send Betty away from the village. Shee war sent to live w'th stuffy Stephen Sewell. A bit o' side tittle, Stephen Sewell war the one-sided partial clerk o' the court at mee Oyer ond Terminer jury tryall. Even though Dr. Griggs didn't join the village congregation, hee war verie sympathetic o' Reverend Parris.

By the end o' February, othar girls in the village, includin' 12-yar-old Ann Putnam, daughter o' Thomas ond Ann Putnam Sr.; 19-yar-old Mercy Lewis; ond 17-yar-old Elizabeth Hubbard, niece o' Dr. Griggs, war taken sick ond began actin' in the same terrifyin' manner. Sich symptoms as loss o' hearin', speech, ond sight, loss o' memory, ond chokin' sensations in the throat war exhibited. It war sure strange to mee what all these girls war members o' the circle o' sin what visited the parsonage what past winter. Nobody knows what mysteries the girls had tampered w'th or how thar spirits had been disturbed. Did guilt weigh heavy on all thar minds? War they tryein' to break out from under the suffocatin' Puritan rules they lived under? They never told. Perhaps they didn't know 'emselves. It war the grownups who began to trye to put into words what war happenin' to thar children: odd postures; foolish, ridiculous speeches; ond fits. As mee marke, mee feel what if the community had paid noe mind to the exhibitions o' the girls, Salem witchcraft would 'ave never existed—mum for that.

When Thomas ond Ann Putnam Sr. noticed what somethin' war wrong w'th thar daughter, Ann, they thought thar daughter war dyin'. Thomas quickly saddled his horse ond rode to fetch Dr. Griggs. By the time Dr. Griggs got to the Putnam's home, Mercy Lewis war on the floor, along w'th Ann, writhin' ond screamin'. Dr. Griggs examined these two girls as hee did Betty ond Abigail. Hee dosed 'em w'th herbal medicines none o'

Ann Putnam Jr. makes an accusation of witchcraft.

Reproduced with permission by the Corbis Corporation

which had any effect. Hee sought answers in his medical books. But in the end, his belief in witchcraft caused him to yield his assent to the inference o' Reverend Parris ond the othar Puritan ministers—devillish bein's war tormentin' 'em. Usin' plain words, Dr. Griggs s'd the evil hand is upon 'em. But to put it in more technical terms, the cause war malefic witchcraft. If this war indeed the case, then the problem w'th these girls warn't a disease they had caught, but an authorized one. If these girls suffered from witchcraft, they war victims o' a crime committed by someone else.

Crowds followed Dr. Griggs from house to house to watch him make a diagnosis on girls afflicted unto death. Some o' the crowd would find thar way to mee ordinary. They war eager to spell out Dr. Griggs's sizin' up. 'Em girls warn't heated w'th fever. Thar

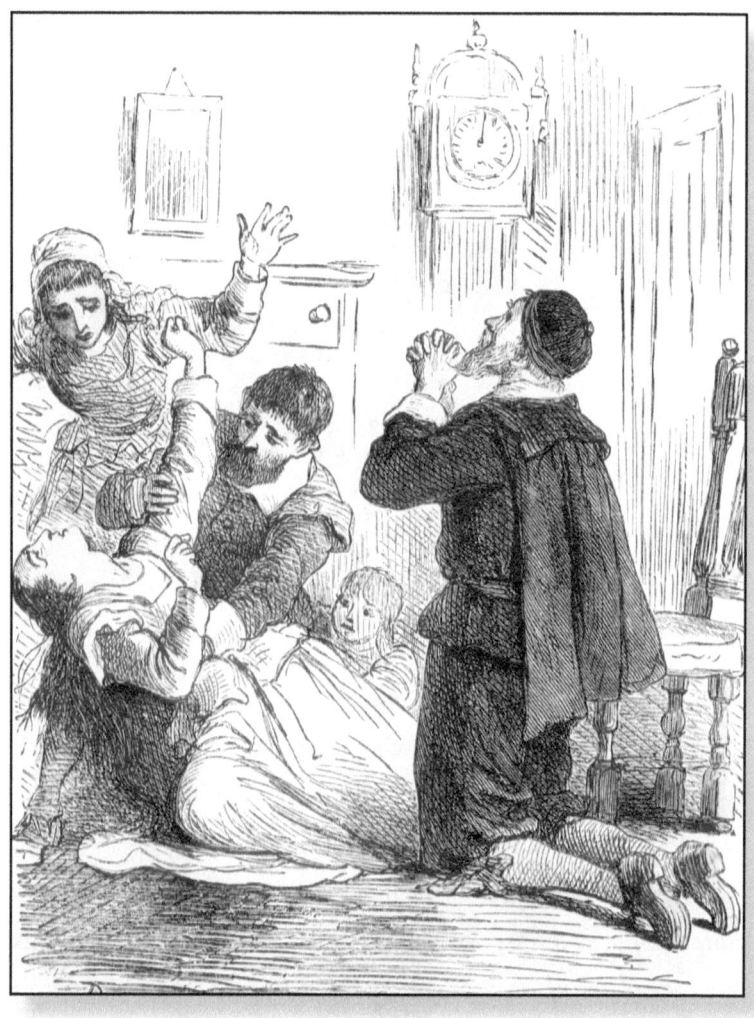

Reverend Samuel Parris attempts to save a woman from witchcraft by praying for her soul.

twitchin' limbs ond rigid jaw would indicate epilepsy, but thar whole body warn't rigid ond thar war noe loss o' consciousness. Epilepsy it warn't. They warn't madwomen 'cause they still seemed to be touch w'th the world around 'em. Plus, those blimey girls come out o' thar fits lookin' none the worse ond had noe recollection o' what they had undergone. What the evil hand war upon 'em didn't surprise the crowds. Now if this warn't a taradiddle. The results o' Dr. Griggs's diagnosis brung puzzled townspeople to mee ordinary askin' 'emselves who would be afflicted next. News o' the doctor's interpretation spread rapidly to othar parts o' the colonies. In this superstitious age, the mere rumor o' witches frightened most people. Suddenly, all the locals in mee neighborhood buzzed w'th talk o' witchcraft. From the pamphlet, *Memorable Provinces Relating to Witchcraft and Possessions,* wharin Cotton Mather attempted to demonstrate the reality o' evil spirits, mee know what people believed what witches gladly did the devill's bidin'. Superstitious neighbors began to nail horseshoes over thar doors to keep these disciples o' the devill away. Someone needed to speak out. Thar war noe witches tormentin' these children—mum for that.

In order to exorcize these evil spirits through an informal quiet means, Reverend Samuel Parris invited a number o' nearby ministers to join him in a day o' fastin', faith, ond prayer. Since all in the Bay Colony certainly knew what Cotton Mather had used faith, fastin', ond prayer to cure the Goodwin children a few yars 'afore in Boston, Reverend ond Mrs. Parris ond othars applied these methods as a more certain cure for witchcraft rather than turn over the problem to the magistrates ond the lawe. At the end o' the day, the girls' condition remained the same, forcin' the ministers to retire to thar homes in defeat. Reverend Parris war advised by some o' the Puritan ministers in Boston to abide in patience ond wait upon the providence o' God. Prayers ond sermons continued to be offered up by the local ministers for relief from these dramatic events. Even as Parris ond the othar local ministers fasted ond prayed, the legal process o' conveyin' witches to pre-tryall had already begun w'th the first warrants issued on 29 February 1692 ond the first pre-tryall examinations on 1 March 1692. Reverend John Hale, a minister in Beverly, visited the Parris home ond, after observin' the girls' sufferin', concluded "the hand of Satan was in them."

Mee know what a few yars afterwards in 1694, the sorrowin' Reverend Parris, tryein' to receive some consolation, stated what hee felt rebuked o' the Lord for the late horrid calamity to break out first in his family. Mee just can't imagine what Reverend Parris didn't know wharin to turn to brung his daughter ond niece under control. After the tryalls, Reverend Parris war forced to leave Salem Village. The new minister, Joseph Green, tryed to reach out to those families o' the accused ond brung 'bout resolutions what reversed the judgements against all the witches.

On 25 February, Mary Sibley, Mary Walcott's aunt, decided to trye some counter-magick to break the spell rather than the prayin' ond fastin' attempted by the clergy. Mee thinks Goodwife Sibley sought some how to does from Tituba. Shee ordered Tituba ond John Indian to prepare a witch's cake consistin' o' a batter mixed w'th Betty ond Abigail's water ond rye meal to be baked in ashes. When the cake war finished, it war fed to the Parris's dog. Accordin' to Tituba, who knew 'bout how witches afflict, "the witch herself would be hurt because invisible particles she had sent to afflict the girls remained in the girls' water, and her cries of pain when the dog ate the cake would identify her as the witch." Mee never hard what happened to the dog, but it war spilled in mee ordinary what Tituba ond John Indian war now able to see spectre 'cause they had put togather ond baked the ol' witch cake.

It war reported to mee what Reverend Parris found out 'bout the witch's cake ond become infuriated by attempts to use witchcraft in his own home. Parris s'd, "Until the making of the witch cake, there were no suspicion of witchcraft." The chatter round 'bout mee ordinary war Mary Sibley confessed her crime o' usin' witchcraft to Reverend Parris, ond hee helped her to script a notice to thar parishioners askin' thar forgiveness. On 27 March 1692, 'afore communion, hee publicly denounced Goodwife Sibley for summonin' the devill amongst us—it went down somethin' like goin' to the devill for help against the devill.

W'th noe reservations, mee feel what Parris from this moment on began to play on the fear what evil war breakin' loose in the village. Reverend Parris began to focus his sermons on witchcraft amang his parishioners. Parris knew his duty ond his duty war to single out ond brung witches to tryall—mum for that.

Mee local neighbors war anxious 'bout Reverend Deodat Lawson, former Salem Village reverend, bein' invited to speak at the Salem Village Congregation by Thomas Putnam. Mee village customers who attended his April 1692 sermon s'd visitin' pastor Reverend Lawson offered a more evenhanded approach. Lawson counseled:

We find no means instituted of God to make trials of witches. Nor could one rightly defend oneself against witchcraft with white magick, such as boiling one's urine or nailing a horseshoe over the door, because such charms were in themselves a kind of witchcraft and might well give a more secure foothold to the devil. Careless accusations of suspected person might also backfire.

Rash censuring of others, without sufficient grounds, or false accusing any willingly . . . is indeed to be like the devil, who . . . is a calumniator, or false accuser . . . The only "Shield Against Satan's Malignity" was faith in Christ, and the application of that faith in prayer. And such prayer would be answered, particularly if it came from a people bound to the worship of God, like those of New England, by their church covenants: whensoever God hath declared a person or people to be in covenants with Him, as the objects of His special mercy and favor, he will assuredly and shortly suppress the malice of Satan, however violently engaged against them.[9]

Thar war a few o' the afflicted girls at Lawson's village sermon. These tibs had some fits what interrupted Reverend Lawson's first prayer ond parts o' his sermon. Lawson warned what those who warn't in sympathy w'th the painfulness bein' suffered by the girls war in sympathy w'th the devill. Who could be responsible for reapin' God's punishment upon the village? Mee brain tells mee what Satan war puttin' ideas in the girls heads ond didn't need to call on the devises o' witches.

Reverend Parris ond othars demanded to know who tormented the girls. At first they war mute ond offered noe names. Tharupon, it become apparent to the girls what those around 'em, specifically the ministers, expected 'em to reveal a clear-cut culprit. The townsfolk war seekin' for someone to blame. It is mee judgement, what at this point in time, the girls realized they could deflect some self-guilt ond put the blame onto othars—mum for that. Terrified what thar crimes would be discovered, sich as usin' the fortune-tellin' glass ond othar white magick spells, the tibs opened the door to Satan. The yeng girls began pointin' fingers ond namin' names, even though they knew they warn't possessed ond thar accusations war lyes. It war told at a later time, what the girls worked togather to concoct thar stories. These tibs made a vow 'tween 'em to be consistent in thar accounts ond stick to 'em.

Enraged, Reverence Parris returned to his home to pump his girls w'th renewed vigor hopin' to jar thar memories. Time ond time againe, hee demanded Betty ond Abigail name the women who tormented 'em. Hee named severall people who might be responsible for thar sufferin' . . . mainly local women who had failed to attend church regularly ond then watched to see the girls' reaction to the names. When hee mentioned Tituba's name, Betty repeated her name over ond over againe. Parris accepted this as an accusation. It seems natural to mee what Betty would name someone w'th whom shee war intimately acquainted. Hee continued to badger the two girls 'til Abigail repeated the names o' Sarah Good ond Sarah Osborne, two o' the most unpopular women in the community. Reverend Parris tied up Tituba ond pasted her, then at his own dictation, shee confessed herself a witch ond what shee had seen Sarah Osborne, Sarah Good, ond two othar women, neither o' whom shee could identify, tormentin' 'em. Months later, after the tryalls ond imprisonment, Tituba would say what Reverend Parris pasted her to make her confess ond name her sister witches, ond what all her confession stories war due to this physical intimidation. To stop the pastin', Tituba told Reverence Parris what hee wanted to hear.

The singlin' out sickness spread fast through the village. Eager for the attention what the othar girls in thar circle war receivin', Mary Walcott ond Susanna Sheldon war next to take sick.

Upon returnin' to his home, Dr. Griggs found what hee had the same trouble w'th his niece Elizabeth Hubbard ond alsoe a house servant. As these new girls become subjects o' notice, they varied ond expanded thar modes o' sufferin'. Now as mee count 'em, everieone o' the girls who come down w'th this mysterious ailment war one o' the girls who had met w'th Tituba at Reverend Parris's home—mum for that.

As mentioned heretofore, news o' the doctor's malefic interpretation had spread rapidly throughout the colony. The mere rumor o' witches in our region alarmed mee easily deceived fellow colonists. Village townspeople would gather at the homes o' the afflicted girls ond watch thar strange antics, fits, ond outcries. Leadin' questions war put forward ond always the girls war asked, "Who torments you?" Thar war a few, like meself, who war hard-hearted souls who declared the whole thing war a lot o' fiddle-faddle. Mee ordinary cronies suggested what a good hidin' would put a stop to it sooner than Dr. Griggs's remedies. But instead o' bein' severely punished, the townsfolk looked upon the girls w'th terror ond awe—mum for that.

Prayers, fastin', ond sermons failed to stop the agitated girls. Mee even hard tell what some parishioners felt what previous

Puritan ministers, who had left unhappily over the course o' yars, war responsible. Had James Bayley, George Burroughs, ond Deodat Lawson spitefully drawn down God's punishment upon the village ond its girls?

Mee thinks Reverend Parris must 'ave had somethin' wrong w'th him, for noe minister worth his salt would come to Salem Village congregation after knowin' o' the quarrelin' ond smitin' amang the parishioners what drove away thar first three ministers. As mee 'aforementioned, mee know o' those who would 'ave Parris gone by now—hee warn't a popular preacher. Late fall, 1691, anti-Parris farmers from Salem Village war in mee ordinary ond reported on a meetin' held by some o' the parishioners who vowed to stop payin' Reverend Parris's wage ond to discontinue comin' to the meetin'house for worship services. Farmers who stopped 'round mee ordinary s'd a month had gone by ond they 'adn't paid his salary. Mee had visited w'th some o' his parishioners ond they war angrie w'th his inability to resolve thar disputes. Thar anger war furthar kindled when Parris took it upon heeself to use thar congregation funds to purchase gold candlesticks ond new vessels for the sacrament in thar meetin'house. It appeared to mee what Reverend Parris clearly had quarrels in his own congregation.

A part o' the congregation desired what George Burroughs, the former minister, should be reinstated, to the exclusion o' Parris. Burroughs had moved to Maine ond had been servin' as a minister in the backcountry for nine yars. Thar war great animosity 'tween the parishioners who backed the former Burroughs ond the present pastor. Burroughs disbelieved in witchcraft, ond openly expressed his contempt o' the system. Both Cotton ond Increase Mather felt hee war a troublemaker ond remarked hee war closer to a Baptist than a Puritan. Here, then, war an opportunity for Parris to use the confessions o' a foolish girl, Ann Putnam Jr., to overthrow his rival, Burroughs, ond perhaps silence those who opposed his ministry. Gamblin' on the superstitions o' some patrons in his congregation what thought Burroughs war evil ond a willin' servant o' Satan, Parris skittered ond proceeded hurriedly to brung 'bout the possibility o' 'avin' Burroughs arrested, tryed, ond put to death. It war told mee what George Burroughs war nabbed while eatin' his evenin' meal at his home in Maine ond immediately transported. Three days later, 7 May 1692, hee found heeself in a gaole in Salem. One o' his accusers testified hee war the leader witch. Durin' his pre-tryall, the sufferin' o' the girls war soe extreme, the magistrates ordered 'em removed from the courtroom for thar own safety. After his examination, hee war moved to Boston gaole. Thar war many respected citizens what signed a petition declarin' Burroughs' innocence. Mee believe this whole scheme originated in the murderous, malice mind o' Reverend Samuel Parris. Events war unfoldin' to give him new ond fearful power. Mee believe Parris war the chief author o' the terrible scenes what ensued. Thar war othars ready to aide him. First amang these war Cotton Mather, minister o' Boston. Mather, acclaimed for his knowledge ond wisdom, had recently preached much on the subject o' witchcraft, teachin' the people what witches war dangerous ond ought to be put to death. In one o' his sermons, Cotton declared witchcraft war high treason against the king ond queen ond witches warn't to be endured on earth or in heaven. Cotton Mather thus become a natural confederate o' Parris. They war thick as thieves. Second cohort, Sir William Phips, war a member o' Cotton Mather's church. Cotton Mather had baptized William Phips. Increase Mather, the father o' Cotton, had nominated Phips to his present office, Royal Governor. Third conspirator, Stoughton, the deputy governor who war appointed judge ond presided at the tryalls o' the witches, war the tool o' Parris ond the two Mathers. These 'aforementioned men, in mee judgement, must be charged w'th the full infamy o' what followed. Those who favored Reverend Parris war those who controlled the witch tryalls. Those who opposed him war those who either spoke out against the tryalls or othars in Salem Village who found 'emselves accused.

As the end o' February dawned, the girls' conditions worsened, provokin' Ann Putnam's father, Thomas Putnam, along w'th his brothar Edward, Joseph Hutchinson, ond Thomas Preston, to travel the wet dangerous road to Salem Town, whar they swore out official accusations 'afore magistrates John Hathorne ond Jonathan Corwin, chargin' the three accused women—Tituba, Sarah Good, ond Sarah Osborne w'th suspicion o' witchcraft, waerby "there had been much mischief done to Elizabeth Parris, Abigail Williams, Ann Putnam, and Elizabeth Hubbard sundry times within the past months and lately." Even though devillishness had taken place in the individual homes o' the four male accusers, mee thinks thar accusation war more a neighborhood accusation against the supposed evil spirits o' these three women. What's more, it war obvious to Ann Putnam's parents ond othars what witches had tempted thar children. The girls' wrenchin' bodies, loss o' sight ond speech, contraction o' the throat, ond screamin' war thar reactions against this malefic temptation. Mee townsmen assumed, w'thout proof, what this circle o' girls war strugglin' not to subscribe or yield to be witches 'emselves. When these complaints war received, Hathorne ond Corwin, who war alsoe Justices o' the Peace, personally issued warrants to the accused. The warrants required constables to brung the three women to a pre-tryall at Nathaniel Ingersoll's ordinary on 1 March 1692. Hathorne ond Corwin would conduct the examinations at the pre-tryalls. Weel ye can image what happened when news o' thar examination got out. Farmers, townspeople, sightseers from othar counties, ond meeself, come to witness thar pre-tryalls. Thar war soe many spectators what the place o' the examination had to be moved to a larger building. It war moved to the Salem Village Meeting House located just down the roadway from the Ingersoll ordinary. W'th regards to the legality o' the accusations, complaints, apprehensions, tryalls, ond convictions, may mee throw in somethin' o' interest at this point in mee story. Thomas Hutchinson s'd: "At the first trial, there was no colonial or provincial law against witchcraft enforce at this time; no charter with which to try witchcraft; and that the proceedings were under an act of James the First, passed in 1603. By that act, persons convicted were to be sentenced to the pains and penalties of death as felons."[10]

Thus under what lawe did Jonathan Corwin ond John Hathorne, the nearest members o' the upper house o' the provincial legislature, travel the five miles out from Salem Town to Salem Village w'th warrants in thar hands for Sarah Good,

Sarah Osborne, ond Tituba herself? Mee needs to work in here what w'th our charter repealed, thar war noe lawes against witchcraft under the Puritan legal cannon. Thus the ol' theocracy what appointed Corwin ond Hathorne, dug deep ond chose to reactivate a historical lawe o' mothar England . . . a statute under an act o' King James I, passed in 1603, to be in force. Two days 'afore mee execution, 8 June, the General Court o' Massachusett met to revive and rewright a provincial lawe found in our 1629 royal charter makin' witchcraft a capital offence—a felony. Thus the theocracy arrested, tryed, ond convicted mee outside the realm o' what war currently legal. Ye 20th-century lawyers call it ex post facto (from after the action or after the fact); lawe what retroactively changes the legal consequence (or statutes) o' actions committed what existed prior to the enactment o' the lawe. Ye could convict a person o' acts committed prior to lawes bein' passed. W'th Puritan clergy determinin' lawe for 'emselves, mee war guilty 'til proven innocent. How lucky are mee ancestors who live in a time when thar are checks ond balances to protect the civil rights o' people.

Mee war just barn when Charles I granted a group o' merchants ond landed gentry o' the New England Company a royal charter in ca. March 1628-1629. The New England Company war reorganized as the Massachusetts Bay Company. A group o' Puritans w'thin the Bay Company adopted a pledge known as the Cambridge Agreement. They agreed to carry the charter w'th 'em, tharby to control the company management. Since what day, the charters w'th our English monarchs war a political pain in the head for mee neighbors to be sure. This colonial charter incorporated the colonies into one body under a perpetual succession governin' council w'th supreme power to manage matters o' the soul, as weel as to correct, pardon, ond punish the people o' the colony. Mee learned from listenin' what from the moment the Puritans war granted self-governin' o' thar lands in the Massachusetts Bay Company Charter, compliance to the charters w'th English kings war a bothersome boil.

In our Massachusetts Bay, colonists could obtain ownership o' land from local officials appointed by the governin' council. Industriously they cleared the forest, bush, ond brush off thar land ond built homes. Each generation improved on thar land. Governance o' our own land war verie important to all o' us in the colony. Everie time the guard changed in England, the colonists feared what the new majesty would diminish or completely void our land ownership. The majesties looked on our charter as an obstacle to thar control o' the colonies. Mee needs to speak mee piece on control. Mee saw the governin' council as a small group o' pious clergy makin' decisions for all o' us in the colony. Powers what bear on mee war thar ability to enforce public morality. Mee town ministers spent a whole lot o' time preachin' on the evils o' wealth ond extravagance in cloths. Thank goodness for mee, thar war fines mee could pay to go around these decisions. Some o' thar powers bear upon mee ordinary, sich as mothar England's right to tax mee sixpence per gallon o' molasses arrivin' on forrin ships. Our Puritan governors felt verie independent o' the mothar England. As mee already touched upon, they war given power to distribute ond assign portions o' land w'thout interference from the king. This independence helped the Puritan theocracy to maintain thar religious fervor w'th verie little supervision by the king. Mee know they thought what the colony war beyond the reach o' the lawes o' England. The governin' body, the General Court o' Massachusetts, wished to be left to 'emselves to determine thar destiny. The freeman, w'th votin' rights ond the right to hold office, war limited to the Puritan church, ond the new governors war regarded as agents o' God's will on earth w'th the charter as the constitution o' the colony.

Off w'th King Charles I's head in 1649. Durin' the yars 1649-1660, thar war noe kings or queens in England. Massachusetts Bay Colony, w'th its Puritan settlements ond theocratic leaders, had supported the commonwealth ond the protectorate o' the republic. Under the leadership o' Oliver Cromwell, the first o' the Navigation Acts war passed, which lasted continuously long after mee death, up 'til 1849. As mee understand it, the navigation lawe reinforced the ol' 1650 ordinance waer noe forrin ships war allowed in New World ports. In the yar 1663, w'th the commonwealth on the rocks, stiffer ond more strict restrictions required all o' our imported goods bound for the New World to be shipped through mothar England first. What a tonnage o' twaddle! Once in England, mee goods war unloaded by bullies, inspected, taxed, ond reloaded. Our cargo war then to be portaged by English vessels or our own colonial ships 'afore goin' to othar forrin lands. Meeself ond mee fellow merchants war verie angrie w'th these acts o' trade restrictions. These ol' laws increased mee shippin' time ond mee shippin' costs. Like othars o' the king's obstructive lawes, wee merchants found ways to bypass 'em ond to go 'bout tradin' w'th all othar countries ond thar colonies. The Frenchies ond Dutch dandy suppliers' shippin' rates allowed mee to brung in mee sugar ond molasses from the West Indies much cheaper. Can ye believe mee war a smuggler? Mee warn't. Smugglin' war respectable 'cause thar war no way o' enforcin' the navigation lawes. Mee hard what a few merchants even purchased thar goods from pirates. Mee feels what wee merchants warn't represented in that ol' English parliament so why should wee be stopped in our trade by 'em.

W'th the collapse o' Cromwell's commonwealth ond the protectorate, English, Scottish, ond Irish monarchies war all restored under Charles II. The Puritans war reluctant to accept the English restoration, w'th its strict Anglican orthodoxy. The Puritans war unwillin' to accept what kings, noe matter thar name, had any sort o' right or power to govern thar colony. In 1661, Charles II issued a mandamus forbiddin' furthar persecution o' the Quakers. Hee alsoe requested specific changes be made to Massachusetts lawes to increase suffrage ond tolerance for othar Protestant religious practices. The governin' council continued to violate the terms o' the mandamus ond continued to practice intolerance. Moreover, our ol' Puritan governin' council unearthed ond passed an ol' commonwealth lawe what imposed death on anyone who might attempt to alter or subvert thar theocratic form o' government. The colony either evaded or ignored othar royal orders. Wee set up our own naval office. 'Cause o' a shortage o' hard currency in the colony, the colony war prompted to establish its own mint ond print our own currency. This war illegal in the eyes o' the king. Our governin' body continued to disregard the navigation acts. Our colony felt

these acts war an invasion o' our liberties ond wee couldn't obey
'em. King Charles II ordered the colonial governor to return
to England to answer for our colony's behavior. The governor
refused this direct order from the king. Edward Randolph, the
king's enforcer o' the Navigation Acts, wrote the king sayin':
"The colony was acting as high as ever and it was in everyone's
mouth that they are not subject to the laws of England nor were
such laws in force until confirmed by their authority."[11]

This outright non-compliance, 1660s through 1670s, brung
Massachusetts Bay colony under the inflamed inspection o'
Charles II. W'th the royal patience exhausted, his Majesty,
along w'th the lords o' trade, began steps to nullify our colonial
charter. The Chancery Court in England, on 23 October 1684,
voided the charter ond changed us to a royal corporation w'th
a corporation charter. W'th the charter repealed, the power o'
the Puritan ministers war limited. This come as a blow to the
Puritan clergy, who had previously enjoyed both political ond
ecclesiastical powers. W'th the loss o' the charter, the Puritan
leaders felt the colonies war under an evil spell. Mee arrived in
the colony shortly after Charles II war restored, to marry Thomas
Oliver, mee second husband.

King James II succeeded King Charles II in 1686. Againe James
II revoked the corporation charter ond unified all o' New England
in order to connect them ond to unite the colonies in a common
defense against France. King James II, in an effort to expand the
crowns' control o' the uncooperative trade ond intolerant religious
practices o' the unruly, insubordinate colonies, sent a tyrannical
governor, Sir Edmund Andros, to Boston, 3 June 1686, to rule

over all o' the dominion ond enforce the laws w'thout any local representation or assembly. Mee theocratic Puritan leaders hadn't ever had a royal governor 'afore. The Puritan General Court o' Massachusetts war noe longer in charge. Mee gave a silent huzzah when they war kicked out o' power—mum for that. Captain General ond Governor Chief o' our Territory ond Dominion o' New England didn't make heeself popular w'th the Puritans. Bein' a member o' the Anglican church war a capper. Hee tryed to conform our lawes to more closely resemble mothar England's. To take firmer control for the crown o' England, hee did away w'th town meetin's. Mee noticed governor appointees, who war members o' the Church o' England, replaced local officials. Hee instituted taxin' w'thout our representative's givin' agreement. Our right to a tryall by jury war hampered. Our press war censored ond our freedom to leave the bounds o' the Dominion war hedged. Hee tryed but failed to abolish elected assemblies. Being a soldier, hee took command o'er all o' our local militias. Hee revoked the Puritan ban to celebrate Christmas ond festivities on Saturday nights. Mee ordinary business benefited by this recant. Easter ond Christmas had been banned for 64 yars. Mee customers toasted 'round ond 'round to celebrate bein' sprung from fears o' spies smellin' Christmas in thar homes. Wee war let go o' cruel punishments like pillories, ears chopped off, and removal from the colonies for celebratin'. Andros's appointment brung shifting o' former land titles. Governor Andros claimed title for the crown to all uncultivated land in all o' our villages ond towns. W'th our land governance taken away, we war plunged into community distress ond dread. Anothar goal o' Andros war to brung 'bout

Increase Mather (1639-1723)

Public domain image reproduced from Wikipedia Commons

religious freedom. Andros asked "each of the Puritan churches in Boston if its meetinghouse could be used for services of the Church of England. When he was rebuffed, he demanded and was given keys to Samuel Willard's Third Church in 1687. Services were held there under the auspices of Reverend Robert Ratcliff until 1688, when King's Chapel was built."[12]

The great abhorrence amangst the Puritan ministers, o' the fickle power o' Anglican ond papist kings in mothar England, war as real as thar fear ond terror o' satanism ond witchcraft. The Dominion o' New England lasted three yars from 1686 to 1689. Governor Andros served as governor in our colony for three yars.

It war durin' the reign o' King Charles II what Puritan hierarchy sent Increase Mather, pastor o' the Boston North Church, to England to see if hee could persuade King Charles II to grant the colony a new charter. Mather arrived in London on 25 May 1687, ond war granted an audience w'th the king five days later. Although King Charles II flattered this Puritan envoy, leadin' him to believe what hee would act favorably on his request, hee did nothin' more 'bout it ond looked w'th disfavor on the project o' renewin' it. King Charles II died in 1681 ond hee brother, James, became king. While Increase war still in England, the English people rebelled ond ousted King James II. W'th the deposition o' the hated Roman Catholic James II in the Glorious Revolution o' 1688, the dominion dissolved. William o' Orange come from Holland in 1689 to rule England. Increase Mather pleaded w'th the new king to grant the New England colonists the same liberties they had enjoyed under the old charter, but hee war unsuccessful in his efforts to convince King William III.

Back to mee story. In 1689, soon aftar the news reached Boston o' the topplin' o' King James II, the colony suffered a major constitutional setback. By all accounts, the overthrow brung Andros's governorship to an end. King William III, sent a declaration to inform the Massachusetts Bay Colony o' his coup via messenger John Winslow. Hopin' to repress the news o' King William III's victorious overturn, Andros demanded the declaration copy o' Winslow. The flutter at mee ordinary war what Winslow refused ond Andros had him arrested. Mee hard the charge against Winslow war carryin' false ond treasonous papers into the country. Edward Randolph, a royalist who visited mee ordinary often, lett mee in on a secret. It seems Cotton Mather had a meetin' o' armed men at his home ond they entered upon thar strange work o' an uprisin'. Under the leadership o' Cotton Mather, the Bay Colony overthrew the ad hoc government o' the autocratic English governor, Sir Edmund Andros, in a glorious revolution. Mather ond his political conspirators secretly organized ond bought to pass the "Happy Revolution," as Cotton called it. This conspiracy forced Andros to surrender his government ond his title. Andros war nabbed runnin' down the street in a women's dress. Mee 'ave to laugh at this 'cause his boots war showin'. Hee war arrested in April 1689. Hee war held in confinement for ten months ond then war sent to England to be tryed. The colonies what war joined in the dominion reverted back to thar previous governin' bodies . . . most w'thout charters.

By overthrowin' the governor, the Puritan theocracy gained control once againe o' the government ond enjoyed thar ancient privileges—noe separation o' church ond state. They could continue thar pious Bible-based community o' saints as an example to the rest o' the world to be safeguarded 'til Christ's second comin'. Everythin' seemed right 'tween 'em ond God.

This Happy Revolution soe angered King William III o' Orange, what hee dissolved the Dominion o' New England under the British Crown. Newly arrived bullies from England visitin' mee ordinary lett slip what King William III war secretly opposed to the liberal provision o' our original Massachusetts Bay Company 1629 charter. Once againe, the loss o' the charter what had allowed the clergy to hold legal proceedin's ond to rule both church ond state under the lawes o' God produced deep local tensions. Puritan leaders thought God had turned from his chosen people ond war punishin' 'em. Devoted Puritans war to search thar own harts, thar actions, ond repent, for the devill war on the loose in Salem Village.

Meanwhile, goin' on five yars, Increase Mather war still in England continuin' to plead for an audience w'th King William III to negotiate the old charter. Despite efforts by Increase Mather, who pled w'th the new king to grant the New England colonists the same liberties they had enjoyed under the old charter, King William III o' Orange felt the rebellin' colonies needed a change. King William III invited the Reverend Increase Mather, as the colony's ambassador, to take part in the negotiations o' the new charter. King William III ond Queen Mary issued a new charter May 1692. The charter granted by King William III ond Queen Mary gave the colonists far less than they had hoped to receive. Mee gabbin' neighbors rumored what thar war widespread anxiety in our colony over loss o' liberties granted in the new charter. Our loss o' unlimited sovereignty had a hand in the witchcraft panic what reached its climax in Salem in the summer o' 1692. Under the William and Mary charter, Massachusetts Bay, Plymouth, Maine, New Brunswick, ond Nova Scotia become a single royal colony, called Province o' Massachusetts Bay. Legal claims to some land war taken away. Under the new charter, the royal governor ond deputy governor war now appointed by the king instead o' bein' elected by the people. All freeholders o' estates valued in excess o' 40 pounds war eligible to vote in all elections in the colony, regardless o' which church they chose to attend. Previously, only Puritan freemen in good standin' war allowed to vote. Our militia warn't outlawed. Eventhough legal claims to some land war taken away most land titles war reconfirmed. The royal governor ond deputy governor would 'ave to be men who war recommended by three agents from the Province o' Massachusetts Bay. Increase Mather war verie affectin' in the crown's appointment o' the new royal governor ond deputy governor o' the new Province o' Massachusetts Bay. Since Increase Mather war the most influential ond distinguished minister in Boston, King William III accepted Mathers's recommendation to 'ave his friend, Sir William Phips, appointed the new royal governor. Sir William Phips hadn't much education or experience in public service. Hee war a simple farm boy from the wilds o' Maine. It war rumored 'bout what hee raised a Spanish buried treasure in the West Indies what gave him the funds to invest in businesses in England. These businesses war a success ond earned him a knighthood granted by King James II in 1687. His military exploits are legendary, havin' snatched in 1690, w'th his fleet ond troops, the whole o' Nova Scotia from those ol' Frenchys. Massachusetts Bay Colony rewarded Phips for his limited conquest in Nova Scotia by bein' appointed ambassador to England. May mee be a tattler ond dish some dirt w'th mee reader. In August 1690, due to dilatory delay, Phips, in command o' his fleet, approached a garrisoned ond provisioned Quebec. Havin' sufficient time to prepare for a battle, Quebec sent Sir William Phips home in humiliation w'th a defeat ... losing 200 men ond a cannon. The expedition cost the Bay Colony 50,000 pounds.

The Mathers strongly swayed the new Royal Governor Phips to ask King William III to appoint the politically unpopular William Stoughton as his Deputy Governor. The Mathers war in like manner, instrumental in groupin' influential Puritan men in the Court o' Oyer ond Terminer to sit in judgement o' the accused witches. The Puritan justices war all from Boston ond war personal friends o' the Mathers. The 19th-century historian George Bancroft states: "Intercession had been made by Cotton Mather for the advancement of William Stoughton, a man cold of affection, proud, self-willed, and covetous of distinction. Apparently the Mathers saw in Stoughton an ally for church-related matters and a hard line hysteria promoting judge. Cotton Mather is quoted as sayin', 'the time for a favor is come, yea the set time is come.'"[13]

Both William Phips ond William Stoughton war ardent Puritans. Along w'th soe many othars in our town, mee war disappointed in Stoughton's appointment. Wee felt hee war a true turk.

At long last William Phips, along w'th Increase Mather, arrived on 14 May 1692, w'th a new provincial charter for the Province o' Massachusetts Bay. Phips ond Stoughton war sworn in as Royal Governor ond Deputy Governor. Some o' the hardline Puritans wanted our old charter restored ond nothin' else.

Sir William Phips war eager to assume his duties ond Massachusetts war eagerly awaitin' the arrivall o' a new governor bearin' a new charter. 'Til Phips ond the new charter establishin' the future form o' government war physically present in Massachusetts, it would be illegal to proceed w'th formal prosecution o' the accused witches owin' to this legislative obstruction. Noe courts could be held 'til a new charter had been granted. Simply put, noe charter, noe authority to conduct tryalls.

Sir William Phips (1651-1695)

Public domain image reproduced from Wikipedia Commons

Mee needs to return to mee story. The Salem Meeting House war the first scene o' judgement. At 10:00 a.m. Sarah Good, a weathered 39-yar-old war standin' w'thin one o' the front elongated pews. Sarah war leanin' on the railin' around the pew. Thank God mee say, this railin' war thar, as it allowed meeself ond othars to stand up when mee legs felt like cavin' in. It war suppose to be an informal pre-tryall court, to establish whether the accusations war true ond whether thar war enough evidence to conduct a tryall. Salem magistrates Jonathan Corwin ond John Hathorne conducted the public examination. They war joined at the meetin'house by a verie large assemblie, includin' all the girls who war afflicted. Each o' the accused war interrogated separately. Both Sarahs war asked many questions.

New England colonists arresting a witch, 1600s

Reproduced with permission by North Wind Picture Archives

The girls war asked if these war the witches who tormented 'em. Every one o' 'em s'd they war. Day after day, Osborne ond Good denied they war witches. Finally, due to Hathorne's daily heckle, Sarah Good broke down ond accused Sarah Osborne o' bein' a witch. To wee spectators ond the magistrates, a witch validatin' anothar witch proved sorcery war amang us. Only when Tituba war brung forward did the crowd har thar first confession o' witchcraft. The tribunal war 'bout to har from a woman who considered herself to be witch. Shee confessed ond even volunteered what shee had spoken w'th the devill for three days right here in Salem Village ond gave a description o' the devill as bein' hairy all over w'th a long nose. Shee talked 'bout the devill comin' to her in the forms o' black dogs, hogs, black cats, ond a wolf. Shee spoke 'bout ridin' sticks through the air to different places in the village. Shee raved 'bout a yellow bird what flew w'th her on missions for the devill. Shee told the farmers o' Salem Village what they wanted to hear. Tituba insisted what sickly Sarah Good ond the old bag o' bones, Sarah Osborne, war witches. Sarah Good had been survivin' w'th her four-yar-old daughter, Dorcas, by beggin' on the streets. Beggin' war an occupation the Puritans detested. Tituba confessed shee had seen Sarah Osborne associatin' w'th a creature w'th a head o' a woman, two legs, ond wings. Tituba s'd shee saw the Sarahs tormentin' the girls. The more shee talked the more shee implicated the two Sarahs. It war apparent to mee ond those spectators in the court what the more this ol' hen babbled the more wee all become convinced what the Prince o' Darkness war unbarred ond w'thin strikin' distance o' all our homes. As one day turned into four, thar war more interrogations ond the Sarahs continued to deny any evil. Tituba's vivid, detailed confessions set Salem Village into a frenzy as Tituba revealed sordid details 'bout Satan ond his disciples performin' evil acts amang the saints ond doin' harm. Tituba's statement covered the whole spectrum o' witch fantasy. Each tale gave trueness to witchcraft claims. Shee lett slip the secret what shee saw nine othar names what had signed the devill's book. Since mee war accused o' signin' the devill's book, mee inquired 'bout this little ol' book. It seems what a person made a covenant w'th the devill by signin' or makin' thar marke in the book w'th pen ond ink. Only w'th sich signin', did a person actually become a witch ond war given demonic powers, sich as appearin' in spectral form to doe harm to anothar. Who war these nine othars in thar community? It war but a few days 'afore nine ond many more war accused by the hysterical girls. Mee hard tell what accusations lengthened as far as London town. Tituba's disclosure set neighbor pointin' finger at neighbor. Mee thinks Tituba sure did blow the gab. Mee gut told mee what the hysteria w'th this witch hunt would increase 'fore wee saw it end. It war hogwash in mee opinion. Seein' spectre could be turned off ond on. The moment Tituba made her confession, her spectre noe longer tormented the girls.

After thar examination, the three women war finally transferred to the Boston gaole, 1 March 1692. Sarah Osborne died o' natural causes on 10 May 1692, insistin' to the end what shee war not a witch. Sarah Good war pregnant ond had her bairn while shee war in prison. The little boy died shortly after hee war barn. It seems a bit unjust to mee what even though Tituba dabbled in sorcery, witchcraft, ond satanism, shee war never tryed or executed for her role in the witchcraft tryalls. Shee war sent to ond later released from the gaole. Shee war later sold by Reverend Parris to pay off her gaole fees. I think mee reader will be o' mee same mind what the legal reasonin' o' the Court o' Oyer ond Terminer jury war a bit daft. All o' the persons who

Signing the devil's book

Public domain image reproduced from Wikipedia Commons

confessed to witchcraft in Salem lived, ond all o' the persons who denied the witchcraft charges war hanged. Thus the nub o' the matter war, those who war stuck in gaoles by the afflicted girls' damnin' testimonies saw confession as an exemption ond a way to avoid the gallows. Mee would guess what circle o' sin squirmed ond agonized as they hard Tituba recount her dealin's w'th witches, warlocks, the devill, ond his demons. War shee goin' to incriminate 'em? These hitherto unnoticed girls war now givin' Tituba thar rapt attention hopin' shee wouldn't reveal thar secrets.

Puttin' Tituba, Sarah Good, ond Sarah Osborne in the gaole didn't stop the afflicted girls' torments.

During the first few weeks of the hysteria, the afflicted girls constantly complained that they were still being tormented by the specters of the accused witches who were in the gaol, inferring that this was because these prisoners were allowed complete freedom of movement. When Sir William Phips arrived in Boston on May 14, to assume his duties, one of his first official acts was to order the prisoners shackled. The girls stopped complaining after this, unaware that several of the more humane gaolers kept most of their prisoners in irons only when they feared a visit from the ministers of one of the higher-ranking authorities, allowing them the same freedom they had enjoyed before Phip's edict.[14]

Now mee asks, how can shacklin' a witch lessen her power o' afflictin'?

When our newly appointed Royal Governor, Sir William Phips, ond Stoughton finally made thar way from Boston to Salem, more than 69 accused witches war already in the various Massachusetts gaoles waitin' to be tryed. Most o' those accused war women ond the warrants had been issued by men. Thar war a few men who war accused o' witchcraft, ond in most cases, these men war related to the women who war accused o' witchcraft. In mee opinion, our colony wouldn't 'ave had the witch hunt if our men had tempered thar tolerance ond hadn't been soe eager to brung these accusations to the attention o' the legal system. But be what as it may, Governor Phips war unprepared legally, politically, and theologically for the problems regardin' the witches what needed immediate attention. Even as the tryalls began, the finger-pointin' continued to flood ond showed noe signs o' the flow stoppin'. The gaoles war overflowin' w'th the accused who war demandin' tryalls ond release. The magistrates, sheriffs, gaolers, ond constables war under strain 'cause o' the crowded gaoles ond the demands placed on 'em to house, interrogate, ond torture the suspected witches. As mee stated earlier, the basic problem war what not one tryall had yet been held. Indeed, thar could be none durin' these early spring months. Thar war noe legally established government. 'Til the new charter war physically present in Massachusetts, it would be illegal ond extremely foolhardy to proceed w'th formal prosecution o' the accused witches knowin' what legitimacy might be called into question. Ironically, then, the most severe challenge to confront the judicial system o' Massachusetts durin' the entire colonial period come at a moment when what system war nearly immobilized.

Massachusetts war beset by calamitous adversities durin' the five yars what Increase Mather war in England. The yars o' 1689 to 1692 war difficult ones. Military units o' French ond Abenakis Indians, armed by the French, ravaged frontier communities. York war attacked ond burned. The French burned grain fields soe tons o' food war lost. A great fire broke out in Boston ond most o' the town war destroyed. Shortly 'afore noon, on 7 June 1692, an earthquake destroyed almost 90 percent o' Port Royal in Jamaica. Port Royal war a mercantile center o' the Caribbean. Thar large storehouses supplied all o' our sugar ond molasses. Only our own Boston rivaled Port Royal in size ond importance. It war a pirate city ond mee ordered ond received mee rhum for mee taverns from Jamaica. Many o' the Port Royal's 2,000 buildings, densely packed into 51 acres, war made o' brick (a sign o' wealth), ond some war four stories tall. Thirty-three acres, 66 percent o' Jamaica, sank into Kingston Harbor. An estimated

2,000 persons war killed in an instant. An additional 3,000 citizens died o' injuries ond disease in the followin' days. Many o' those who war killed or who died afterward war Puritans who had friends ond relatives in Massachusetts. The easily deceived Puritan populace war convinced by thar clerical leaders what these disasters war caused by the devill ond his evil spirits, who wished to drive the Puritans from New England. From the Puritan pulpits resounded the alarm what some dark powerful influence war over the colonies.

Phips had verie little trainin' soe hee yielded heeself to a council what recommended a special Court o' Oyer ond Terminer. Phips acted as quickly as hee could. In mee view, hee acted w'th unjustifiable haste. It war debated in mee taverns what this special Court o' Oyer ond Terminer had a shade o' illegality to it. Mee ain't noe legal mind, but some o' mee patrons seemed to know what this new charter didn't give the royal governor ond his Harvard cronies power to create this special court w'thout the concurrence o' the voice o' our representatives. Our legislators war to establish a general court. But thar war noe time to hold an election for this purpose. Thar war a backlog o' witches to be tryed ond disposed o' soe Royal Governor Phips, as the personal representative o' King George, ond royal governor o' the province, issued a commission for sich a court. Alsoe, the Court o' Oyer ond Terminer normally had power to handle civil cases. Thus hee exceeded his legal authority when hee set up a special commission o' Court o' Oyer ond Terminer, as the voice o' the people hadn't been hard ond noe general court had been elected.

This here trickum legis affected all o' us who war on tryall for our lives. It seems to mee what in a free government, the head man ought never to make a decision on a difficult matter w'thout checkin' w'th the representatives o' the people. Time to convene our representatives might 'ave carried our community beyond the insane moment ond saved us from one o' the greatest blemishes on our American history. Unfortunately, mothar England had a custom, in cases o' emergencies like this one, waer the king appointed a Court o' Oyer ond Terminer to har ond decide certain actions. The Court war to act "according to the Law & Custom of England and of this their Majesties Province." The frenzied public demanded action from Phips. Relyin' on recommendation o' Increase Mather ond othar uppity persons, Phips appointed a committee o' 12 o' the leadin' ministers to set up guidelines to govern ond aide the Court o' Oyer ond Terminer in the comin' witch tryalls. The 12 ministers went to work almost immediately. The ministers recommended, amang othar things, what spectral evidence—instances in which the spectre o' a person war seen performin' acts o' witchcraft while what same person war actually elsewaer ond unaware o' what war supposedly takin' place—be disallowed in the comin' court cases. They s'd spectral evidence, though it might serve as evidence to begin investigation, shouldn't be hard in court as evidence to decide a case.

What war spectral evidence? Mee hopes mee can explain it to thee. It war believed what witches gained thar powers through the devill, who would only work w'th those who signed a pact or contract w'th him. The devill would allow witches to take a form o' man or woman spectre or beast any time they desired. Cotton Mather reasserted this point o' view in *The Return of Several Ministers Consulted,* wharin hee stated what demons by God's permission can appear in the shape o' an innocent, virtuous man or women ond doe evil. Thar now, don't ye agree w'th mee, by his statement, Cotton Mather gave credibility ond validity to spectral evidence? Tharfore, when a person's spectre, ghost, or the person in an animal form appears to the victim bein' tormented doin' somethin' evil, or molestin' 'em in some way, the crimes war perpetuated by the spectre. Furthermore, the spectre war evident only to the victim accusin' not evident to the judges or othars in the courtroom. It wouldn't be the actual man or woman pinchin', hittin', bitin', or committin' othar mischievous wickedness. But in most cases, the justices didn't choose to distinguish 'tween the accused ond thar spectre. Even though it war thar spectre, the evildoer, supported by the invisible world, had to be a witch, ond couldn't be an innocent person.

Once the 12 ministers completed thar task, they assigned Cotton Mather the responsibility o' wrightin' the final draft. This set the stage for the manipulation o' the guidelines by Cotton Mather. It war in this festerin' atmosphere what Cotton Mather perceived what the iron war hot to create a letter entitled *The Return o' Several Ministers Consulted.* The final draft o' this letter war published 15 June 1692, ond sent to the justices o' the Court o' Oyer ond Terminer in Salem. His duplicitous design war to create a document worded in a double sense ond meanin'.

It affirmed the reality of the afflicted state of our poor neighbors, that are now suffering the molestations of the invisible world. It acknowledged the success of our honorable rulers to detect the abominable witchcrafts that have been committed, humbly praying that the discovery of these mysterious and mischievous wickednesses may be perfected. To please those questioning the validity of spectral evidence, the document states, convictions ought certainly be more considerable than barely the accused person being represented by a spectre unto the afflicted, inasmuch as it is an undoubted and notorious thing, that a demon may, by God's permission, appear even in ill purposes, in the shape of an innocent, yea, and a virtuous man. This final paragraph appears to undercut caution, and recommended the detection of witches. The document concluded by recommending unto the government, the speedy and vigorous prosecution of such as have rendered themselves obnoxious according to the direction given in the laws of God, and the wholesome statutes of the English nation, for the detection of witchcrafts.[15]

Nowaer did the document recommend, in clear, simple, plain English, what spectral evidence be disallowed. Cotton Mather left out, ond tharfore ignored, the 12 ministers' recommendation what spectral evidence be disallowed for the witch tryalls. The court interpreted the letter as Mather's seal o' approval for the tryalls to proceed quickly ond spectral evidence to be allowed.

Robert Calef, a Baptist cloth merchant in Boston, knew how it felt to 'ave yer views considered obnoxious. In 1693, multiple letters war sent to Cotton Mather from Mr. Calef, callin' Mather's document a curious wrightin' filled w'th confusin' arguments, double meanin's, ond double dealin's. Commentin' furthar on Mather's word play, Mr. Calef suggested what Mather's document carried both fire to increase ond water to quench the witchcraft

Reverend Cotton Mather (1663-1728)

Reproduced with permission by North Wind Picture Archives

fire. Calef cited what the document gave greater encouragement to proceed into dark methods rather than caution against 'em. Robert Calef accused Mather o' leadin' good Christians away from thar fear, honor, ond dependence upon God to fearin' the devill ond tharby attainin' the devill's end here in Salem. As a Baptist, Mr. Calef saw Mather's document as a tool to incite the Puritan congregation in Salem Village to denounce those o' differin' beliefs. Robert Calef repeatedly asked Mather to meet w'th him at his place o' his choice to discuss thar views, but the meetin' never took place. Regardin' Cotton Mather's view on spectral evidence, the historian Charles W. Upham concludes: "Cotton Mather never in public writing denounced the admission of it, never advised it absolute exclusion, but on the contrary recognized it as a ground of 'presumption' . . . and once admitted nothing could stand against it."[16]

Mee questions whether spectral evidence is founded in truth. Mee thinks what if this type o' evidence warn't allowed, it would be much harder to convict mee ond othars except those who confessed witchcraft. Allowin' spectral evidence resulted in the barefaced lyes ond shriekin' show what the witch tryalls become. Ironically, the later rejection o' spectral evidence in the tryalls after October 1692 resulted in noe conviction.

Will wee evar comprehend why Cotton Mather deviated from the document drafted by the 12 ministers? Mee knows hee deeply believed what hee, along w'th his father, war the chosen ones to fight against Satan's plan to pull down all the churches in the Massachusetts Colony. Mee hard it voiced what Mather earnestly believed what the second comin' o' Jesus Christ war near at hand ond Christ wouldn't come 'til the Puritan saints ond the "city on the hill" had driven the devill out o' New England. Thus, Cotton Mather took it upon heeself to create a document, *The Return o' Several Ministers Consulted,* w'th duplicitous meanin', tharby to alter the decision by the eight justices regardin' spectral evidence.

To draw attention away from this double meanin', hee added a glowin' postscript o' his own in which hee praised the authorities ond the members o' the court for thar diligence in detectin' ond prosecutin' the witches to this date. Hee urged 'em to continue thar good work, bein' careful in doin' soe what they war always guided by the lawes o' God ond the English statutes. Increase Mather, Cotton's father, gave his stamp o' approval to his son's document.

As mee 'afore mentioned, in the absence o' men elected to a general court by our representatives, Phips, on 25 May, commissioned a special Court o' Oyer ond Terminer to har ond determine guilt. The terms "oyer" (to har) ond "terminer" (to decide) come from two words o' French origin. Phips set up this court solely to trye the accused witches ond decide thar fate. Phips gave long ond thoughtful consideration to those hee would appoint as judges. Sir William Phips had decided what hee war goin' to be the chief justice o' the court. On 27 May, hee appointed eight o' the leadin' men in Massachusetts to serve as "judge-commissioners" on the jury court to har ond trye the witchcraft cases beginnin' on 2 June 1692. The eight judges sitten for this session war: Jonathan Corwin, Thomas Danforth, Bartholomew Gedney, John Hathorne, John Richards, Nathaniel Saltonstall, Peter Sargent, ond Wait Winthrop. Most o' these men who war selected to judge mee had noe legal trainin'. They war chosen to sitt as a court juror based on thar social standin' as elite Puritan leaders ond thar previous experience judgin' othar civil ond criminal cases. These judges brung the same views as the jurists o' England ond thar own prejudices ond fears 'bout witches, which would surface throughout the harin's. May mee add a wee bit o' snitch here? To be a juror ye had to 'ave an estate worth at least 50 pounds.

On 10 June, a happenin' occurred what changed Phips's plans for servin' as the chief justice o' the court. Four hundred warriors—Micmac ond Abenaki—led by a Frenchman, Baron de Saint-Castine, struck at the little settlement o' Wells in Maine. Help war needed quickly if furthar raids war to be prevented. Royal Governor Phips war eager to rid heeself o' the witchcraft mania ond even more eager to get back to fightin' Indians. Hee called in his deputy governor ond designated William Stoughton as his chief justice. Soe wee see how what ol' turk, Stoughton, become the presidin' chief justice ond Governor Phips removed heeself as the prosecutor to fight a French ond Indian War. W'th Phips absent, mee hopes o' restrainin' Stoughton ond his packed court o' eight war dashed.

Mee hopes what ye don't mind mee mentionin' it once againe, by the time the final draft document war completed by Cotton Mather ond given to Chief Justice Stoughton on 15 June 1692, mee war already tryed, condemned, ond executed, all on the basis o' spectral evidence. Since none o' the Salem magistrates or the justices on the court had any formal legal trainin', mee submit they took for granted what they war to continue on in the same manner. Everie person accused ond found guilty o' practicin' witchcraft durin' the next few months war judged ond executed on the same type o' evidence, namely spectral evidence.

As mee s'd, mee will not pass judgement on Cotton Mather. As Salem history is studied, mee know the readers will become aware o' his underhandedness. This masked approval o' spectral evidence by Cotton Mather, this break w'th precedent, vastly extended the range o' persons eligible for suspicion.

What o' Tituba ond Sarah Good? They war nabbed first. Why warn't they tryed first? In mee case, mee believe what Cotton Mather ond Thomas Newton felt what mee could easily be convicted on the basis o' spectral evidence, along w'th slanderous testimonies ond damnin' depositions o' mee Salem neighbors who disliked mee 'cause o' mee unusual lifestyle. Mee war amazed o' the shallowness o' these grounds for suspectin' ond accusin' mee o' witchcraft. Then thar war the unproven evidence o' the dolls w'th pins ond mee scratchin' o' Shattuck's child's face. These warn't hard evidence. The

Malleus Maleficarum suggested torture as a way to elicit a confession from a suspected witch. It war disappointin' to Reverend Mather what even though moabites tortured mee, mee confession warn't forthcomin'. If spectral evidence warn't admitted in mee case, it would be much more difficult to convict mee, as mee hadn't confessed witchcraft. Cotton Mather wrote in his diary 'bout mee: "There was little occasion to prove the witchcraft, this being evident and notorious to all beholders."[17]

In like manner, mee past brushes w'th the Salem Court on charges o' witchcraft, mee past fallin'-out w'th a couple o' mee neighbors, ond mee unconventional treatment o' mee husbands, made mee current suspicion conclusive for sich as Reverend Mather ond many othars in Essex County. In othar words, mee war considered guilty, by Cotton Mather ond othars, long 'afore mee could plead mee innocence in the tryall. Reverend Cotton Mather realized what his witchcraft crusade might be curtailed or even brung to a screechin' halt if spectral evidence war not allowed. As a result o' overwhelmin' spectral evidence against mee ond mee unpopular status in mee community, instead o' tryein' suspects in the order in which they had been accused ond arrested, the magistrates, upon recommendation o' Cotton Mather, selected mee as thar first defendant. O' all the 69 or soe in the gaoles, thar war more spectral evidence hangin' on mee frame than any o' the othars waitin' in the gaoles. Mee thinks this action reveals the devious nature o' Cotton Mather.

Againe to mee story. The first person identified as a witch in the Salem crisis o' 1692 war someone known to all primarily as a black slave, Tituba. Tituba war verie fond o' Betty, Reverend

Parris's little daughter. Mee hard say what Mrs. Parris war much absorbed w'th charitable visits in her congregation ond paid little attention to her daughter. These girls war raised in a home war they war barely noticed. Tituba gave the child much love ond attention what shee didn't get from anyone else. Puritan bairns war to be seen ond not hard. Betty's father sermonized what a child's damnation might be eminent, 'specially if they war unbaptized ond sometimes even if they war baptized. Hee preached what playin' games war forbidden ond after chores war completed, children war to spend what time readin' the Bible ond studyin' catechisms.

Mee supposes life in Boston must have been different for Tituba—not at all like the lazy yars shee spent in Barbados. Mee hard shee managed to keep Mr. ond Mrs. Parris happy, w'thout workin' too hard. Since her landin' in Salem, mee overhard Tituba say thar war way too much hate in the city o' peace. Tituba's guardianship war marked by fillin' the girls' lonely, bored hours o' the winter w'th fanciful stories o' her life in Barbados, games o' chance, tricks, ond incantations. It makes sense to mee what the girls, when asked who tormented 'em, named a woman w'th whom they war intimately acquainted ond w'th whom they had practiced white magick . . . Tituba.

More than a month elapsed, ond the malady began to spread. Soon thar war eight othar girls from ages 12 to 19 whom become afflicted. It don't seem right to mee what those Puritan ministers would fast ond pray what the afflicted girls would 'ave the strength to be able to unmask ond name whom it war what tormented 'em. Mee imagine what those girls did a little bit o' silent gigglin' when prayer hands war laid on thar heads. Just a bit o' twoness, it war against the lawe to giggle.

Once againe, mee wish to interject anothar legal entry concernin' persons who war o' age. To mee knowledge, English jurists in our mothar England had as a general rule what children under 14 war incapable o' testifyin' under oath in court on capital felony cases, although exceptions could be made. Legally, Parris's daughter ond niece made 'em questionable witnesses. Thus, it appears clear to mee what noe legal action could be taken 'til older accusers emerged. Elizabeth Hubbard war the first afflicted person to legally qualify, as shee war 17. Shee war an orphaned indentured maidservant to Dr. William Griggs. Elizabeth Hubbard, bein' old enough to testify under oath, made the accusations ond tryalls legal. Shee testified 32 times against people ond signed 40 complaints against supposed tormentors. Shee war verie good at convulsive fits ond trances war her specialty. Ann Putnam Jr., the 12-yar-old daughter to Thomas Putnam, signed 62 indictments ond her father war the chief filer o' all o' those complaints against people who lived in ond 'bout Salem Village. Her mothar, Ann Sr., war verie involved in land disputes w'th her neighbors ond used her daughter's accusations to avenge past feuds.

At this point, fear, religion, ond politics merged to become the monster o' Salem. In March, three more persons war accused. The first sich victim war Elizabeth Proctor, wife o' ordinary owner John Proctor. Elizabeth war cryed out by competin' ordinary owner Nathaniel Ingersoll ond his nephew Jonathan Walcott. Elizabeth Proctor war outspoken like meeself ond expressed her doubts as to the validity o' the girls' fits. Shee war accused o'

Witness testifying at the Salem witchcraft trials, 1690s

Reproduced with permission by North Wind Picture Archives

sundry acts o' witchcraft. Her dear husband followed her to her pre-tryall in Salem Meeting House.

John Proctor's intentions war to stand ond support his loving wife. Hee didn't believe in witchcraft ond felt the accusin' girls war fakers and liars. John made the mistake o'sternly, staunchly denouncin' the circle o' sin ond scoffin' at thar pain. Mee judge it to be only minutes 'afore the devious circle o' girls erupted into courtroom tantrums ond pointed accusin' fingers at John. Hee war the first man to h've a complaint filed. John war arrested on the spot. One o' the girls cryed down shee saw Goody Proctor's spectre seated on a beam ond then accused Goodman Proctor o' bein' a wizard. Now har mee go w'th anothar titillation. Now mee ask ye, w'th John ond Elizabeth Proctor bein' ordinary owners, who would benefit from thar deaths? Why Nathaniel Ingersoll, ordinary keeper on Meetinghouse Road, who worked hand in glove w'th Putnam, Parris, ond the Mathers. Nathaniel Ingersoll did his part by accusin' seven villagers o' witchcraft. Noe hard evidence war necessary, just a pointin' finger ond spectral evidence.

'Aforehand, feuds war mentioned. Mee now needs to discuss land disputes amang neighbors in the village what kept Salem Village tempers flarin' on all sides:

> The feud between the Jacob Townes and the Thomas Putnams had begun in 1639, when the Massachusetts General Court gave Salem Village permission to expand in the direction of the Ipswich River. Six years earlier, however, the court had also granted the village of Ipswich permission to expand in the same location. The town of Topsfield, which lay between Salem and Ipswich, became the site of conflict that lasted for several decades. At Topsfield, four main families competed for the right to mark boundaries on the land they had all been granted by the government. John Putnam, head of the Putnam family, fought against the Howes, Townes, and Eastys. During the dispute over rights to the woodlands, Jacob Towne (the father of Rebecca Towne Nurse, Sarah Towne Cloyce, ond Elizabeth Towne Proctor)——three God-fearing sisters of the most exemplary lives, cut down one of Putnam's trees in full view of Putnam himself. In retaliation, Putnam returned with a group of his relatives and threatened to cut down all of Towne's trees. Thus began a feud that continued for over 50 years and culminated in the Salem trials, when the Putnams targeted their village rivals in a final show of force.[18]

Mee hope ye can see the how these families war actin' out o' greed ond jealousy. Third generation Puritans had sure come

Woman accused of witchcraft

Reproduced with permission by the Corbis Corporation

a long way from the original Puritans who prided 'emselves on harmony w'thin the society o' saints.

Just a small drop o' substance 'bout those ownin' estates ond livin' in the western village who war accused.

Sarah Good, a Topsfield resident, war a woman w'th an estate o' 500 pounds at one time. Due to her estate bein' in litigation to pay the debts o' her first husband, Sarah war reduced to beggin' ond war homeless. Goodwife Good war one o' the first three accused o' witchcraft by the circle o' sin ond the first to testify. Her four-yar-ol' daughter, Dorcas, war forced to give a blamin' testimony accusin' her mothar o' witchcraft ond then Dorcas war accused ond imprisoned for eight months. Sarah Good war considered an autem mort ond war available to be preyed upon by the accusin' girls. Shee war noozed.

Sarah Osborne's estate war a 150 acres farm next to Thomas Putnam. Shee war the widow o' Robert Prince. Sarah had been left out o' his will. By attemptin' to take possession o' Robert's property for herself, shee had stirred up the norm. Thomas's uncle, John Putnam Sr., war defendin' Sarah's two sons who claimed they war bein' cheated out o' thar heirship. Now it should seem obvious to mee readers . . . how doe ye get rid o' a person who upsets the social customs? Ye accuse 'em o' witchcraft as war done by Sergeant Thomas Putnam ond his brothar Deacon Edward Putnam, sons of John Putnam Sr. It war common knowledge what the Putnams 'ave a reputation o' workin' as a team to brung down those who cross 'em. Sarah Osborne died in the gaole 10 Mary 1692.

The Townes war a tight, close-knit family who war livin' in western Salem Village who war dreadfully affected by the witch tryalls. Againe, may mee tittle, this family war involved in a bitter, high-tempered dispute w'th the Putnam family over land. Joanna, the mothar, war accused way back o' bein' a witch. Mee can identify w'th the badge o' infamy what war pinned on Joanna Towne 'cause o' mee past accusations. All three sisters, Rebecca Towne, Mary Towne, ond Sarah Towne war spitefully accused by the village girls o' witchcraft. Seventy-one-yar-old Rebecca war dragged by constables from her sickbed. Her hearin' had gone bad ond shee couldn't har John Hawthorn's barbed accusations or answer his questions properly. Rebecca pleaded, "I am innocent as the child unborn, but surely, what sin hath God found out in me unrepented of, that He should lay such an affliction on me in my old age."

On 3 April, Sarah Towne Cloyce defended her sister Rebecca Towne Nurse against the witchcraft charges ond found herself accused ond charged five days later, 8 April 1692. The first o' the Towne sisters come 'afore the magistrates, 24 March 1692. At her pre-tryall on 22 April 1692, Mary war asked by magistrate John Hathorne how far shee had gone along w'th Satan, and shee replied, "Sir, I never complyed but prayed against him all my dayes, I have no complyance with Satan, in this . . . I am clear of this sin." Mary wrote letters from the gaole challengin' the court, but to noe avail. Tituba, John Indian, Tituba's husband, ond Abigail Williams witnessed against Sarah Towne Cloyce, Rebecca Towne Nurse, ond Mary Towne Easty. Sarah Towne Cloyce called John Indian a liar, refused to give a confession, ond found herself in the Boston gaole what night. Ann Putnam Jr. testified against all three sisters. Mee feel what grudges ond retaliation on the part o' Ann Putnam Jr. ond Ann Putnam Sr. produced the main accusers o' these women who war thar neighbors. Ann Putnam Jr. eventually sent 24 innocent people to thar deaths as convicted witches. Throughout the tryalls, Ann Putnam Jr. remained the most active accuser, often paradin' hysterical behavior ond shoutin' charges at her victims. Thomas Putnam filed 35 complaints against his neighbors ond gave testimony against 17. O' these 17, ten war executed. The legalities o' filin' complaints under English commonwealth lawe required a bond to be posted by the person or persons lodgin' each complaint. Mee reckons Hathorne waived this kicker, makin' it easier for townspeople to accuse suspected witches.

May mee put 'afore ye more nitty-gritty 'bout the Proctor family pre-tryall? It war 11 April 1692 when Sarah Towne Cloyce joined Elizabeth Proctor at the pre-tryall judgement bar. Elizabeth's accusers war Abigail Williams ond Ann Putnam Jr. As mee 'aforehand made known, Elizabeth war married to John Proctor. Hee war a wealthy farmer, who owned one o' the largest farms just outside Salem Village. Now mee needs to say what those ol' magistrates war messin' w'th a noncompliant beast o' a man. When John's 20-yar-old servant, Mary Warren, joined the circle o' ten ond started havin' fits, Goodman Proctor whipped Mary, attemptin' to 'thresh the devil out of her." As the magistrates war questionin' his wife, the play-actin' girls accused John Proctor o' hurtin' 'em. To get even, Mary Warren quickly stepped to the bar ond confirmed what John ond Elizabeth Proctor brung the devill's book to her to sign. Later at the Proctor jury tryall, Mary Warren confirmed what John ond Elizabeth Proctor spectres war prickin' ond pinchin' her person, pressin' on her stomach, chokin' her, ond torturin' w'th a variety o' torture. It war a tragedy what spiteful Mary Warren turned on the Proctor family. On 21 May 1692, an arrest warrant war issued for Sarah Proctor. Sarah war John ond Elizabeth Proctor's 16-yar-old daughter. Sarah helped her mothar ran thar ordinary on Ipswich Post Road. Sarah's brother, William, ond stepbrother, Benjamin, war alsoe accused by the wicked circle o' girls. Aftar the pre-tryall, both Elizabeth ond John war imprisoned in Salem gaole. All three o' thar bairns war imprisoned. All the Proctors refused to confess. John Proctor posted a petition for a fair tryall, not to the governor ond council, but w'th cap in hand, to Cotton Mather ond othar noted ministers. Hee claimed what those who testified against him war made to doe soe by torture. His appeal explained, "They have already undone us in our estates, and that will not serve their turns without our innocent blood." Goodman Proctor begged for new justices. His implorin' brung noe response. Elizabeth Proctor escaped hangin' 'cause she pleaded shee had a babe in her belly. A few months after her husband John's hangin', shee gave birth to a bairn in prison. She remained in the gaole 'til the spring o' 1693. Sheriff Corwin stripped her home o' all its possessions. Elizabeth survived the nightmare, but war considered a dead woman ond couldn't inherit John Proctor's holdin's. Mee judge what the wealthy Proctor family who war opposed to controls by the Puritan theocracy ond whose business success challenged the pious, controllin' Putnam clan war ripe for the pickin'. John Proctor, Rebecca Towne Nurse, ond Mary Towne Easty, two siblin's o' Sarah Towne Cloyce, war all executed. Sarah Cloyce's jury tryall war delayed ond shee remained in the gaole for a yar.

Just like meself, these accused women war examined in the meetin'house 'afore verie great assemblies, includin' all the girls who war afflicted. It war irksome for mee to think the magistrates would open these scandalous inquests w'th prayer. In front o' the examiners, the troubled girls war allowed to perform thar bizarre behaviors, act out fantasy, ond generally raise Cain. Each o' us victims war asked the same questions, namely, war wee a witch? War wee familiar w'th the devill? How did wee explain the sufferin' ond pain o' this circle o' friends caused by our presence in the meetin'house? If a confession war obtained from our lips, the girls stopped thar convulsive fits.

It war at this time, however, what mee witnessed the pace o' accusations pick up. Things war really out o' kilter. At first, this circle o' sin practiced thar tomfoolery against neighbors they didn't like, but before long they war aimin' higher. In mee opinion, nothin' afflicted these girls what a good thrashin' would not cure—mum for that. They war makin' mischief to escape thar chores, escape church attendance, cover up thar guilt, ond gain attention. The bewitcht girls clearly seemed to enjoy thar growin' fame. They had gained a new position in the community . . . public testifier. Thar words war recorded. They war unchecked by the authorities. Ye might say what they war famous . . . celebrities in thar own time. The girls possessed almost complete power over the community. But even more deadly, these schoolgirls enjoyed the power to condemn.

Flamed up by the inquests, the Salem Village neighborhood asked 'emselves if more witches lurked 'bout. These excitable farmers, on thinkin' back, suddenly blamed sick children, sick farm animals, bad weather, bad luck, or unexplainable happenin's on thar unsuspectin' neighbors. Besides thar ravin's, this circle o' girls claimed to 'ave the gift o' spectral sight (spectre only visible to the person). Mee know it war a damnin', damagin' decision what spectral evidence provided by the afflicted girls ond disgruntled neighbors war given sich weight in the tryalls. Those few landowners who defended the accused w'th questionin' letters or voiced doubts 'bout the circle of girls in public, found 'emselves receivin' warrants. Henceforth, neither yeth nor high status would provide immunity against suspicion. Church members w'th exemplary lives, wives o' prosperous freeholders, ministers, selectmen from Salem Town, ond by the end o' the summer, mee har what some o' the most prominent people in Massachusetts ond thar close kin, had been accused. An attorney wrote at the end o' May: "The afflicted spare no person of quality whatsoever." Twenty-two witches war accused in April; mee war one o' these. By the end o' May, a shockin' total o' 39 people war charged w'th witchcraft had been gaoled 'cause o' the allegations o' the girls. In an effort to draw out additional confessions from those already in the gaoles ond those who war newly arrested, Cotton Mather encouraged Hathorne to intensify his efforts to 'ave the moabites use any means o' torture, fair or foul. In mee ordinary, wee war lett in on what Cotton Mather believed God wouldn't punish those who confessed.

Mee would like to share anothar story what might be o' interest to ye. Ann Putnam Sr. war verie close to her sister, Mary Bailey, ond war obsessed w'th tryein' to communicate w'th her sister after her death through occult rituals. Ann Putnam Jr. become involved in these secret rites. Her mothar would take her to the graveyard whar Mary war buried. Mothar ond daughter would stand over the grave ond read the Book o' Revelations in thar Christian Bible, searchin' for ways to contact the dead. This book in the Bible war Ann Sr.'s verie favorite. In 1692, Ann Putnam Jr. war sent by her mothar to the Parris's black slave Tituba for advice in contactin' the spirit o' Mary Bailey. Ann's active imagination, along w'th her extensive experience w'th her mothar's King Saul superstitious seekin' practices, made her one o' Tituba's best students. It are mee judgement what Ann Putnam Jr. war the witch. As it war mentioned in 1 Samuel 28:1-20, just like King Saul, Ann Sr. had lost the spirit o' the Lord ond war now involved in spiritualism. Mee needs to put 'afore ye, what it war a capital crime to trye ond speak w'th dead people. It are sad for mee to set forth, what Ann Putnam Sr. war w'thin spittin' distance o' her evil daughter. Ann Sr. war a woman incapable o' forgettin' or forgivin' an injury. "Bygones were never bygones" w'th this matron. Shee war always lookin' for ways to settle old scores. It war disclosed to mee what Ann Putnam Sr. had fits herself, ond led the girls in accusin' Rebecca Towne Nurse, a devout, respected 71-yar-old member o' the Salem Village congregation, o' bein' a witch. Throughout the whole yar o' 1692, the witchcraft terror seized the harts ond minds o' everieone in Salem. Village neighbors pointed fingers ond hurried arrests brung the accused to tryall.

A warrant for mee arrest war issued Monday, 18 April 1692, ond mee war nabbed the next day. Mee knew none o' mee accusers personally, ond mee never crossed the doorway o' the village meetin'house. Mee hard what three othar persons, Giles Cory ond Mary Warren o' Salem farms, ond Abigail Hobbs o' Topsfield war alsoe served arrest warrants on the same day.

Mee war dragged away by constables w'th black hats as tall as steeples ond black coats, ond imprisoned in the Salem gaole. Persons accused war committed to gaoles in Salem, Boston, Ipswich, ond Cambridge. On 12 May 1692, a constable transferred mee from the Salem gaole to the Boston gaole. "Most of those first committed by the magistrates to await the action of the higher court were sent to Boston, as up to this time all capital

Offender punished by standing in the pillory

Used with permission by North Wind Picture Archives

trials had taken place there. After the trials were begun in Salem, prisoners were committed to the gaols in that town."[19]

Mee war a roomer at the Boston gaole from 12 May 1692 for 20 days. The gaole had an open room hemmed by smaller windowless cells. It war surrounded by a fenced yard. It had the same vile stink as Salem gaole.

This warn't mee first time in the Salem court. Mee began mee run-ins w'th the Essex County courts in ca. January 1669-70. Mee daughter, Christian, war less than a yar old when mee quarrels w'th mee husband Thomas Oliver become violent . . . silly ole bugger. Mee neighbors testified what mee face war sometimes bloodied, ond at othar times black ond blue. Mee 'ave to admit what mee alsoe managed to land a few blows against mee husband Thomas durin' these skirmishes. Puritan women didn't differ w'th thar husbands. It war against the social norm. Thomas Oliver, mee second husband, ond mee war fined ond sentenced at the Salem Quarterly Court, to be whipped ten stripes for fightin' each othar. Mary, Thomas's daughter, age 'bout 50, testified: "That each had called her several times to complain about the other; that Goodwife Oliver's face was blodig at one time ond black and blue at other times; and, that Oliver complained that his wife had given him several blows." Matters war noe better eight yars later, when on ca. 29 November 1677-1678, mee war to present meeself at a court held at Salem. Mee Bridget, wife o' Thomas Oliver, war accused o' shoutin' at mee husband ond callin' him many opprobrious names on the Lord's Day. Hee war sich an old rogue. Wee war both sentenced ond mee war ordered to either pay a fyne or to stand w'th mee husband, back-to-back, on a lecture day in the public nutcrackers, both o' us gagged, for 'bout an hour w'th a paper fastened to each o' our foreheads, upon which our offence should be fairly wrighten. Thomas's daughter, Mary, from his first marriage, paid the 20-shillin's fyne ond Thomas war released from his part o' the order. But Mary didn't pay mee fyne ond mee war left to stand in the nutcrackers to the community's mortifyin' stares, laughter, ond spit. Puritan leaders felt what punishment should be humiliatin' ond public, if possible. One yar later, Thomas Oliver died w'thout leavin' a will. The intestate administration, granted 24 April 1679, gave mee our house ond land in Salem Town. After debts, 20 pounds war paid to each o' his two sons by his previous wife, ond 20 pounds to our daughter Christian for thar moiety. Mee estate warn't settled 'til after mee execution w'th a bond o' administration signed on 8 July 1693.

In the yar ca. 1679-80, mee had anothar brush w'th the Salem Quarterly Court. This experience war a forerunner o' mee 1692 persecution, ond war mee first contact w'th this infamous subject o' witchcraft. Mee war accused o' witchcraft by John Ingersoll. This war a big blow against mee. John Ingersoll lived at 12 Daniels Street, Salem. This street leads from Essex Street to the harbor in Salem Town. John war in the cod-dryin' business. John Ingersoll ond Nathaniel Ingersoll war brothars. Nathaniel Ingersoll owned an ordinary. Hee war in fierce competition w'th mee. Mee war called to Nathaniel Ingersoll's ordinary for a pre-tryall, supposedly this war the Salem Quarterly Court. If mee war convicted as a witch ond executed by warrant, mee estate, ordinary, goods, ond chattels could be seized ond disposed o' w'thout mee consent. Nathaniel Ingersoll would 'ave a corner on the spirits business on Ipswich Post Road. The story o' the 1679 accusation is as follows:

> John Ingersoll's black slaves were going into the woods with horses and sled. He loaded his sled with wood and came as far as William Bean's house. He apparently unloaded his sled and returned to the woods between Norman's Rocks and Fish Brook. When he had reached the edge of the swamp, the horses started and snorted as if they were frightened, and would not go forward, but ran down into the swamp, up to their bellies. They hauled the sled after them, and with much ado, the slave got them out of their harness and from the swamp. John Lambert, Jonathan Pickering, and some youths, who noticed the horse incident, said that they never saw the like and thought that the horses were bewitcht. About a week later, the slave,

Wonn, went into the hay house a little after noon to get some hay for the horses and a second time, for some hay for the cow. He testified that he had seen Bridget's shape upon a beam in the barn, holding an egg presumably to put a hex on Ingersoll and his farm animals. When Wonn stooped to pick up the pitch fork to strike the shape, it vanished. Afterwards, when sitting at dinner, Wonn saw two black cats. Mr. Ingersoll had a black cat. Wonn said, "How come two black cats here?" And before he had finished, Wonn felt three sore gripes or pinches on his side.[20]

Hee uttered a wail o' woe ond had verie much pain ond soreness for some time after. Mee Ingersoll case war moved to the court o' assistants in Boston whar mee war to appear next. John Ingersoll retracted his accusation, but thar is noe reference to it in the published records o' what court. Soe ye can read 'tween the lines. Some people stood to profit by mee demise. Even though mee war acquitted ond found not guilty o' witchcraft, people 'ave long memories. Puritan Minister Samuel Willard s'd, "There is no crime or aspersion that is with more difficulty wiped off than an accusation of witchcraft." The term witchcraft, bein' used against mee at this earlier time, war goin' to 'ave endurin' relevancy. Thus, w'th regard to mee run-in w'th witchery in the past, ond witchcraft suspicions here ond now in 1692, mee war considered guilty long 'afore mee could plead mee innocence.

What rule o' thumb war the magistrates goin' to use to prove what mee cast spells ond consorted w'th the devill? In matters o' witchcraft, the clergy war the experts who used *Malleus Maleficarum* as thar guidebook o' rules for investigatin' ond tryein' witches. A pamphlet, *A Tryall of Witches,* brung from mothar England, war alsoe consulted.

In addition, diligent searches o' property ond person might turn up more concrete evidence. It goes down w'thout sayin', anyone who had a reputation like mine ond who had proven meeself to be socially obnoxious "according to the direction given in the laws o' God, and the wholesome statutes of the English nation," war an easy prey for the Cotton Mather who drafted the letter, *The Return of Several Ministers Consulted,* from which the 'afore quote war taken. The Puritan clergy warn't goin' to

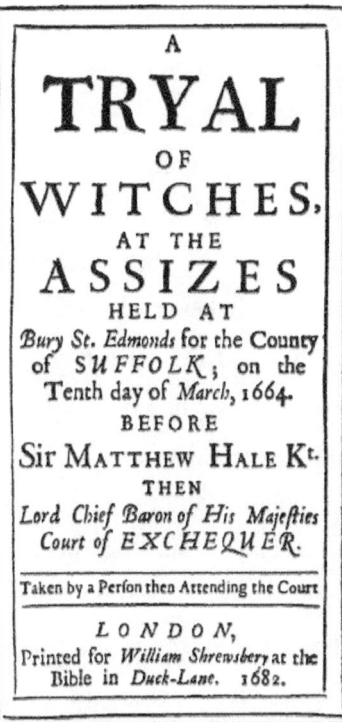

Report of "A Tryal of Witches," 1664

Public domain image reproduced from Wikipedia Commons

be pacified 'til they punished someone for the hard knocks our colony war experiencin'.

Once againe, now 13 yars later, ca. 18-19 April 1692, the magistrates called mee to stand the huff at a pre-tryall, but this time to the largest buildin' in the village soe what many more people could attend. Lett mee set the scenery for mee informal pre-tryall in Salem Village Meeting House. In Salem, winter hadn't released its grip, soe the ground war still frozen. This meant the farmers couldn't get into thar fields. W'th little pressin' work for the farmers ond thar families to doe, they traveled from miles around to mingle ond observe the pre-tryalls. The meetin'house war packed w'th curiosity.

W'th just the King James I creaky lawes to back 'em, Salem magistrates John Hathorne ond Jonathan Corwin felt confident in conductin' mee informal pre-tryall. They marched forward attemptin' to gather ond put to a test enough evidence to accuse mee o' witchcraft ond refer mee case to a jury tryall o' the Court o' Oyer ond Terminer. It are clear in mee mind's eye, if the Salem Village affair had been left to the local authorities to resolve, it may 'ave died—mum for that.

John Hathorne ond Jonathan Corwin established the procedure o' interrogatin' those o' us who war accused in full view o' the community ond the afflicted girls. Legally, mee shouldn't 'ave been questioned w'thin the harin' o' the afflicted, the individual witnesses, ond the mobility. It's mee view what after mee had been carefully examined alone, mee should 'ave been brung to stand 'afore mee accusers. Mee feel what in the weeks ond months to come, the impact o' this procedure, allowin' the accusin' girls to cry out ond contort in the courtroom, war to be dramatic ond wide rangin'.

Hathorne acted like a prosecutin' attorney rather than a fair-minded magistrate. Mee war tryin' to defend mee innocence while at the same time mee war bein' subjected to rapid-fire verbal reproof. Mee had noe legal counsel. Hathorne hoped for two or more strong testimonies to determine if thar war sufficient evidence o' witchcraft for a formal tryall. Mee couldn't 'ave mee own witnesses to testify in mee behalf. Mee denied knowin' any o' the accusers o' Salem Village. This war overlooked. His bullyin' had mee all keeflouied ond hee succeeded in trappin' mee in a lye. Hee warn't seekin' out proofs. Hee assumed mee guilty. Mee had noe way to appeal.

Ezekiel Cheever ond John Putnam Jr. entered official complaints against mee.

The followin' document war mee warrant:

Indictment v. Bridget Bishop No. 1

Anno Regni Regis et Reginae William et Mariae nunc Anglice 7th Quart: Essex. Ss. The Jurors for our Sovereign Lord and Lady the King and Queen present that Bridget Bishop alias Oliver the wife of Edward Bishop of Salem in the County of Essex. Sawyer the 19th day of April in the fourth year of the Reign of our Sovereign Lord and Lady William and Mary by the Grace of God of England, Scotland, France and Ireland King and Queen Defenders of the faith . . . an Divers other days and times a[s] well afore as after certain Detestable arts called witchcrafts and Sorceries, wickedly and feloniously hath used Practiced and Exercised at and within the Township of Salem in the County of Essex aforesaid in upon and against one Mercy Lewis of Salem Village in the County aforesaid singlewoman by which said wicked arts the said Mercy Lewis the said 19th day of April in the fourth year abovesaid and divers other Days and times as well before as after, war and is hurt Tortured Afflicted Pined Consumed, wasted and tormented against: the Peace of our said Sovereign Lord and Lady the King and Queen and against the form of the Statute in that case made and provided. Witnesses Mercy Lewis, Mr. Samuel Parris, Mary Walcott, Elizabeth Hubbard, Nathaniel Ingersoll Thomas Putnam Jr., Ann Putnam Jr., Abigail Williams, Billa vera John Ruck Foreman in the name o' the Grand Jury.[21]

Thar ye are mee reader, the names o' those who accused mee o' practicin' witchcraft ond sorceries. Thar war eight witnesses ond only one, Mercy Lewis, who war mentioned as havin' been

Built in the year 1683. Taken down 1755
45 feet by 40 — 16 in the walls. Scale
20 feet to an inch. It stood where
the first Church now stands.

MEETING HOUSE

Original Salem Village meetinghouse

Reproduced with permission by the Corbis Corporation

tortured, afflicted, ond tormented by mee spectre at sundry times. Absence o' a charter didn't prevent Hathorne ond Corwin from followin' up on this accusation, fillin' out a warrant, arrestin' mee, placin' mee in a louse house, ond now examinin' mee.

The Examination o' Bridget Bishop at Salem Village 19 April 1692 by John Hathorne ond Jonathan Corwin Esq.

As mee entered the meetin'house, all o' the afflicted cryed out ond fell in to fits screamin' what mee war tormentin' 'em.

Mee war placed in a long pew 'tween two constables to protect against mee brushin' or pinchin'. A tythin' man stood behind mee w'th a tythin' hook to police mee eye movements. Mee war to stare straight ahead at the magistrates. Mee war 'bout eight feet from Hathorne ond Corwin, who war seated in front o' the long communion table. The othar pews, aisles, stairs, ond windows war packed w'th curious spectators. When the girls recovered from thar fits, they all landed on the floor 'tween mee ond the magistrates. Mee tryed to refute thar cries o' accusation w'th mee own shouts. Mee am innocent. Mee 'ave done noe witchcraft. Mee never saw these persons 'afore, nor mee never war in this place 'afore. Mee am as innocent as the child unbarn. Mee appeals seemed to fly right out the window.

Even though mee hadn't evar been in the Salem Village congregation or the 'proximate area, accordin' to the circle o' girls, mee spectre had been reported to 'ave been thar. As mee pre-tryall pressed on, one o' the spectators, Mary Walcott, yelled, "My brother, Jonathan, has recently struck at Bishop's spectre with a sword, tearing her clothes. I heard it tear."

Hathorne asked mee, "Is not yer coat cut?"

Mee answered, "It is not as it war the fashion in what mee dress war made."

Forthw'th, the court had two women search mee cloths. They found a small, two-way tear. Mee looked down at the rent. Mee insinuated, "It is not like a blade's slash."

Waerupon, Jonathan Walcott s'd, "I flourished the sword while it was still in its scabbard." Perhaps what explains the look o' the fear on Jonathan's face. Jonathan war all-a-mort.

Guilt war on his face. Hee had the look o' a man who had false sweared. Hee ond mee both know hee had told another lye to cover the first. Jonathan and Mary Walcott's accusations war buffle-headed prattle.

Hathorne then confronted mee w'th a recrimination drawn from local gossip. "They say you bewitcht your first husband to death." This indictment w'th reference to mee first husband, Captain Samuel Warsselbe, made mee verie angrie. Mee denied the charge, sayin', "If it please yer worship, mee know nothing o' it," ond shook mee head violently. This motion war imitated by the afflicted girls shakin' thar heads violently. Mee 'ave noticed what ol' crafty cad Hathorne always begins his questions w'th a presumption o' guilt. Hee definitely war on the side o' the accusers.

Then began a cross ond swift question examination o' mee 'afore John Hathorne ond Jonathan Corwin Esq. 'bout witchcraft. Hathorne's badgerin' war single in purpose, to obtain a confession o' guilt from mee lips ond to trap mee in mee own words w'thout legal help to aid mee in seein' the way to answer questions. Addin' fuel to the flame, his rapid accusatory tone didn't allow mee to give a complete response. Hee assumed what mee war already guilty o' the offenses. Mee pre-tryall examination set 'bout w'th four parts as follows: (1) magistrates assumin' mee war guilty, (2) mee strugglin' to respond to thar charges, (3) all the afflicted girls blastin' out thar bedevilledment, and (4) the fired up audience involvin' 'emselves by steppin' forward to offer comments from the floor. Thar are two versions o' mee pre-tryall what war wrighten down by amen curlers. Mee will list both for ye to read for a more full account.

Salem witchcraft trial, 1692

Reproduced with permission by North Wind Picture Archives

Bishop. I take all this people (turnin' mee head ond eyes about) to witness that I am clear.

Mr. Hathorne. Hath this woman hurt you speaking to the afflicted.

Elizabeth Hubbard, Ann Putnam, Abigail Williams ond Mercy Lewes affirmed she had hurt them.

Mr. Hathorne. You are here accused by 4. or 5. for hurting them, what doe you say to it.

Bishop. I never saw these person before, nor I never was in this place before.

Mr. Hathorne. Mary Walcot said that her brother Jonathan stroke her appearance & she saw that he had tore her coat in striking, & she heard it tare.

Upon some search in the Court, a rent that seems to answere wat was alleged was found.

Mr. Hathorne. They saw you bewitcht your first husband to death.

Bishop. If it please your worship I know nothing of it.

She shake her head & the afflicted were tortured.

The like againe upon the motion of her head.

Sam: Braybrook affirmed that she told him today that she had been accounted a Witch these 10 years, but she was no Witch, the devil cannot hurt her.

Bishop. I am no witch.

Mr. Hathorne. Why if you have not wrote in the book, yet tell me how far you have gone? Have you not to doe with familiar Spirits?

Bishop. I have no familiarity with the devil.

Mr. Hathorne. How is it then, that our appearance doth hurt these?

Bishop. I am innocent.

Mr. Hathorne. Why you seem to act witchcraft before us, by the motion of your body, which seems to have influence upon the afflicted.

Bishop. I know nothing of it. I am innocent to a Witch. I know not what a Witch is.

Mr. Hathorne. How doe you know then that you are not a witch.

Bishop. I doe not know what you say.

Mr. Hathorne. How can you know, you are no Witch, & yet not know what a witch is.

Bishop. I am clear: if I were any such person you should know it.

Mr. Hathorne. You may threaten, but you can doe no more than you are permitted.

Bishop. I am innocent of a witch.

Mr. Hathorne. What doe you say of those murders you are charged with?

Bishop. I hope, I am not guilty of Murder.

(Then she turned up her eyes, the eyes of the afflicted were turned up.)

Mr. Hathorne. It may be you doe not know, that any have confessed to day, who have been examined before you, that they are Witches.

Bishop. No. I know nothing of it.

Mr. Hathorne. John Hutchinson & John Lewis in open Court affirmed that they had told her. Why look you, you are taken now in a flat lye.

Bishop. I did not hear them.[22]

Ezekiel Cheever, clerk o' the court, wrote: "This is a true account of what I have taken down at her examination, according to best understanding and observation. I have also in her examination taken notice what all her actions have great influence upon the afflicted persons and what have been tortured by her."

Mee readers should be aware what most o' mee testimony war taken down by persons, namely Reverence Parris, who war prejudiced against mee. Even though his hand war verie clear ond readable, ye can be darn sure hee devoted more attention to wrightin' thar testimonies against mee than scribblin' mee flustered feedback to Hathornes 'sumtion o' guilt questions.

Reverend Parris's version o' mee pre-tryall as follows:

Bridget Bishop, being now coming in to be examined relating to her accusation of suspicion of sundry acts of witchcrafts the afflicted persons are now dreadfully afflicted by her as they doe say.

Mr. Hathorne. Bishop what doe you say you here stand charged with sundry acts of witchcraft by you done or committed upon the bodyes o' Mercy Lewis and Ann Putnam and othars.

Bishop. I am innocent. I know nothing o' it. I 'ave done noe witchcraft.

Mr. Hathorne. Looke upon this woman and see if this be the woman that you have seen hurting you. Mercy Lewis and Ann Putnam and others doe now charge her to her face with hurting of them.

Mr. Hathorne. What doe you say now you see they charge you to your face?

Bishop. I never did hurt them in mee life. I did never see these persons before. I am as innocent the child unborn.

Mr. Hathorne. Is not your coate cut.

Bishop. (Answers no, but her garment being looked upon, they find it cut or toren two ways.)

Jonathan Walcoate saith that the sword that he struck at goode Bishop with was not naked but was within the scabbard soe that the rent may very probablie be the very same at Mary Walcoate did tell that she had in her coate by Jonathan's striking at her appearance [that is her spectre].

The afflicted person charges her, with having hurt them many wayes and by tempting them to sine the devil's Booke at which charge she seemed to be very angrie and shaking her head at them saying it wars false they are all greatly tormented (as I conceive) by the shaking o' her head.

Mr. Hathorne. Goody Bishop what contract have you made with the devil?

Bishop. I 'ave made noe contract w'th the devill I never saw him in mee life. Ann Putnam sayeth what shee calls the devill her God.

Mr. Hathorne. What say you to all this that you are charged with? Can you not find in your heart to tell the truth?

Bishop. I doe tell the truth. I never hurt these persons in mee life. I never saw them afore.

Mercy Lewis. Oh goode Bishop did you not come to our house the Last night and did you not tell me that your master made you tell more than you were willing to tell?

Mr. Hathorne. Tell us the truth in this matter. How comes these persons to be thus tormented and to charge you with doing?

Bishop. I am not come heer to say I am a witch to take away mee life.

Mr.Hathorne. Who is it what doth it if you doe not they say it is your likeness that comes and torments them and tempts them to write in the booke. What Booke is that you tempt them with?

Bishop. Me know nothing o' it. Mee am innocent.

Mr. Hathorne. Doe you not see how they are tormented? You are acting witchcraft before us. What doe you say to this? Why have you not a heart to confese the truth?

Bishop. I am innocent. I know nothing o' it. I am noe witch. I know not what a witch is.

Mr. Hathorne. Have you not given consent that some evill spirit should doe this in your likeness?

Bishop. Noe. I am innocent o' being a witch. I know noe man woman or child here.

Marshall Herrick. How came you into me bed chamber one morning then and asked me whether I had any curtains to sell? Shee is by some of the afflicted persons charged with murder.

Mr. Hathorne. What doe ye say to these murders ye are charged w'th?

Bishop. Mee am innocent. I know nothing o' it.

(Now shee lifts up her eyes and they are greatly tormented againe.)

Mr. Hathorne. What doe you say to these things here horrible acts o' witchcraft?

Bishop. I know nothing o' it. I doe not know whether be any witches or noe.

Mr. Hathorne. No have you not heard that some have confessed?

Bishop. Noe I did not.

(Whereupon John Hutchinson and John Lewis claimed they themselves had told her about Abigail Hobbs and Mary Warren)

Mr. Hathorne. Two men told her to her face that they had told her, here she is taken in a plain lie. Now she is going away they are dreadfully afflicted 5 afflicted persons doe charge this woman to be the very woman that hurts them.

Bishop. I did not har them what some 'ave confessed.[23]

Thus and soe Samuel Parris wrote down mee examination by Hawthorn 'aforesaid, ond upon hearin' the same, ond seein' what hee did then see, togather w'th the charge o' the afflicted person then present, hee added his biased conclusion, "We committed said Bridget Oliver Bishop."

Mee must admit, what ol' turk, Mr. Hathorne soe intimidated mee what hee did achieve trappin' mee in a lye severall times. Mee did sidestep the truth. Villagers w'th big mouths had shared w'th mee the nasty news what Giles Cory, Mary Warren, Abigail Hobbs, Sarah Good, ond Sarah Osborne had been nabbed, ond Tituba had confessed. As mee war led out o' the meetin'house, five o' the afflicted girls wailed ond s'd what mee war the woman who hurt 'em. One o' the constables, Samuel Gould, asked mee if it didn't trouble mee to see the girls tormented. Mee reply war an insolent, "Noe, mee am not troubled for them." Samuel persisted ond asked againe, "Did you not think they were bewitcht?" Mee responded, "Mee doe not know what to think." Mee lack o' weepin' ond lack o' sympathy w'th the girl's hart-rendin' pain indicated what mee war in sympathy w'th the devill.

Mee rebuttals ond pleas o' innocence didn't seem to impress the court. Mee denials war twisted ond Mr. Hathorne didn't accept mee answers. Mee answers seemed to drift over Hathorne ond Corwins's knobs. Mee one defensive plea what mee had never ventured into Salem Village proper, never had see these girls 'afore, never known noe woman or child from the village, ond never war in thar congregation, went unnoticed. These true statements in mee defense should 'ave defined mee innocence against thar spectral charges. But mee evidence war impermissible. 'Afore mee court appearance, mee had resolved to 'ave an attitude o' civilness. Mee one day in court, after bein' exposed to these uncivilized, merciless magistrates, left mee bristlin' w'th rage. What's more, mee pre-tryall tragedy bettered mee to fully appreciate the level o' anger felt by the othar accused who war chained in the filthy gaoles w'th mee. These devious men wanted our heads on a platter.

Hathorne warn't seekin' the truth by his bullyin', only confession o' guilt. W'th mee defense debarred, mee hardly stood a chance o' passin' through this initial informal question phase. As mee pre-tryall come to a closin', mee never did make the slightest confession o' anythin' relatin' to witchcraft. When asked by the magistrates why mee war a witch, mee s'd flatly, "Mee doe not know what a witch is." To assert mee innocence, mee rolled mee eyes to heaven ond immediately all the girls rolled thars. It war ghastly to see the glarin' whites o' soe many eyes. Mee war swiftly sent to the Salem gaole to await tryall.

Deliverance Hobbs war the second person, besides Tituba, who confessed her witchcraft. Hathorne used confessors, like Deliverance, to testify against othars. Mee 'ave included the cross examination o' Deliverance Hobbs 'cause it incriminated mee. Shee war examined ca. 2-3 May 1692 in Salem gaole—less than a month after mee pre-tryall ond mee confinement to the gaole. At age 50, Deliverance Hobbs war accused o' bein' a witch. All three members o' the Hobbs family war accused o' witchcraft. After a time, her resistance ond her will war broken by the harsh treatment ond torture in the gaoles. Shee confessed, avoided the gallows, ond then served to distort truth against othars like meeself.

Deliverance Hobbs v. Bridget Bishop

Question to Deliverance Hobbs. W't have you done since whereby thar is further trouble in your appearance?

An. Nothing at all.

Q. But have ye not since been tempted?

An. Yes S'r, but I have nott done itt, nor will nott doe itt.

Q. Here is a great change since we last spoke to you, for now you afflict and torment againe; now tell us the truth whoe tempted you to sighne againe?

An. Itt was Goody Oliver; shee would have mee to sett my hand to the book: butt I would nott neither have I. Neither did consent to hurt them againe.

Q. Was that true that Goody Wilds appeared to you and tempted you?

An. Yes, that was true.

Q. Have you been tempted since?

An. Yes about Fryday or Saturday night last.

Q. Did they bid you that ye should nott tell?

An. Yes they tould mee soe.

Q. But how farr did thay draw you or tempt you & how farr did you yeild to the temptation? But doe not you acknowledge that that war true that ye tolde us formerly?

An. Yes.

Q. Ond you did sighne then att the first, did ye Nott?

An. Yes I did itt is true.

Q. Did you promise then to deny att last what you said before?

An. Yes I did & itt was Goody Oliver alias Bishop that tempted me to deny all that I had confessed before.

Q. Doe ye nott know the man with the Wenne?

An. Noe I doe nott know whoe itt is; all that I confessed before is true.

Q. Whoe were they you named formerly?

An. Osborne, Good. Burroughs, Oliver, Wildes, Cory & his wife, Nurse, proctor & his Wife.

Q. Who were w'th you in the chamber? (Itt bein' informed that some were talkin' w'th hir there).

An. Wildes and Bishop or Oliver, Good & Osborne, and they had a feast both of Roast ond Boyled meat & did eat & drink & would have had me to have eat and drink w'th them, but I would not; & they would have had me sighned, but I would nott then nor when Goody Oliver came to mee.

Q. Nor did nott you consent to hurt these children in your likeness?

An. I doe nott know that I did.

Q. What is that you have to tell, w'ch ye canott tell yett you say?[24]

Thus Deliverance Hobbs confessed ond testified what mee had helped administer the devill's sacrament on the witches' Sabbath ond afterwards mee shape had beaten her w'th iron rods to trye to make her take back her confession.

At the end o' the day, five girls—Mercy Lewis, Abigail Williams, Mary Walcott, Elizabeth Hubbard, ond Ann Putnam— in the circle o' sin, all signed indictments against mee chargin'

Witches' Sabbath

Public domain image reproduced from Wikipedia Commons

mee w'th practicin' wicked felonious arts ond sorceries upon 'em. In these indictments, these deceivin' girls claimed mee spectre did pinch, bite, choke, ond otharwise hurt 'em, ond urged 'em wright thar names in the devill's book. Along w'th thar claims, they displayed thar usual ludicrous antics in the courtroom. Thar fits o' fancy sent mee to the gaole to await mee jury tryall. Thar five indictments war what took mee freedom away from mee ond had mee committed to captivity. If wee'd allowed these girls to continue, wee'd all be called witches—mum for that. Damnin' evidence o' witchcraft war beginnin' to build against mee.

Puritan Hathorne war persuaded by the girls' courtroom hallucination what God war allowin' evil spirits to invade the body o' a human bein's. One o' the girls would cry out what shee saw mee leavin' mee body ond goin' to afflict anothar girl. Immediately the girl named would go into hideous convulsions. Neither Hathorne nor any o' the othar gazin' spectators could believe or understand what the tabbys war actin' out. To those in the courtroom, thar seizures war far too violent. Thar sickness seemed surreal ond terribly convincin'. Nor could the onlookers see any othar cause for thar attacks except witchcraft. To be sure, these courtroom dramatics war convincin' proof what mee spectre war involved. Thar seizures added timber to the frenzied fire. For the circle o' sin, this war noe innocent deception, it war pure sport ond games. Especially since the attacks could be cured immediately by mee touchin' one o' the afflicted girls or 'em touchin' mee. While in thar swoon, if mee touched mee hand upon 'em, they would immediately revive, ond not upon the touch o' anyone's else. It war believed this touch test brung mee tormentin' spectre back into mee body ond mee war the person who had afflicted. Mee know mee war not tormentin' these girls. They war lettin' thar dreams ond fantasies run away w'th thar sense o' reality. They war plum barmy—mum for that.

The girls sure put on a great show copyin' mee everie gesture as mee stood in the pew facin' the magistrates. If mee rolled mee eyes, they would doe the same. Any small action on mee part would be duplicated. If mee shifted mee position on the stand, they shifted thar position, too, but in a painful manner what attracted great attention from the audience. If mee cast mee eyes on 'em, they war struck down.

Weel obviously, mee witchcraft suspicion had grown into accusations ond mee accusations changed into indictments ond indictments turned into enough evidence for mee to stand tryall. Now it war up to the attorney general to find othar depositions against mee from each alleged victim. Depositions against mee war drawn up by amen curlers, w'th the accuser name blank, to be filled in as required. Apparently, the attorney general knew what a considerable number o' depositions claimin' supernatural visitations by mee spectre would be filed against mee. To make way for quick dispatch o' deposition issuance, the court clerk prepared the form w'th mee name on it, but left blank the date, place, name, ond residence o' the person upon whom it war believed mee practiced witchcraft.

After confinin' mee to Salem gaole, the moabites walked mee. They marched mee up ond down all through the day ond night 'til mee could hardly walk. Mee feet war swollen. They tryed to take the mick out o' mee, but mee would not confess to bein' a witch. They tied up mee arms in contorted ond painful positions ond forced mee to stand up w'th mee arms in this position for days, but mee would not budge from mee denial o' practicin' witchcraft. It took great courage to die for mee beliefs, rather than succumb ond confess to crimes what mee never committed.

Sheriff Corwin ond his gaolers war fearful what a witch could easily escape from gaole, w'th the help o' the devill, by changin' shape into a small animal or strange beast what could easily escape through the keyhole o' the gaole door. Thus, mee war chained to the gaole wall. Some o' the coffin cells war soe small ye didn't 'ave leg room to sitt or lay down. The Federal

Street gaole war suppose to hold 30 people, but each week newly accused men ond women war brung in—by the end o' May it war 75. The witch gaole war verie cold, foul smellin', dark, ond infested w'th disease. The ol' Salem gaole war neer the banks o' a tidal river, soe at high tide the floors overflowed ond war always damp. Large water rats ran 'bout the gaole ond kept mee awake at night. Mee had to pay for mee food or starve. The gaole food war highly salted ond often rotten. Wee warn't allowed beer. The drinkin' water war too putrid to swallow. If wee asked for a drink, the moabites would oblige w'th a torturous drink o' putrid water mixed w'th salty herring-pickle, as they wanted us to suffer a ragin' thirst.

While in the Salem gaole, mee war constantly mistreated ond tortured, both mentally ond physically, out o' sight o' witnesses, by the sheriff ond his moabites, in order to gain a confession. Cotton Mather heeself proposed what the moabites, the torturers, use extremely severe methods—short o' the un-English method o' torture—to obtain confessions.

For a few days, mee stepson Edward Bishop Jr. ond his wife, Sarah, brought food ond drink to mee. Sarah ond Edward Bishop Jr. ond thar numerous children lived in Topsfield, on the property what war deeded to 'em by mee husband Edward on 8 October 1673. In 1690, they moved to Salem Village, but still retained thar membership in the Topsfield Congregation. They opened an ordinary in thar house in Salem Village. On 20 April, mee stepson, Edward Bishop Jr. ond his wife Sarah, war alsoe served a warrant. On 21 April 1692, shortly after mee pre-tryall, Edward Jr. ond Sarah Wildes Bishop war nabbed along w'th

Sarah's stepmothar, Sarah Wildes, ond accused o' witchcraft. They war examined by magistrates Jonathan Corwin ond John Hawthorne the next day ond found to 'ave committed witchcraft against Ann Putnam Jr., Mercy Lewis, ond Abigail William. They war indicted ond transferred to the Boston gaole to await tryall. The records o' thar harin's 'ave somehow been lost. In October 1692, after they piked out from Boston gaole, thar property war seized by Sheriff Corwin. Edward Jr. ond Sarah fled to Rehobeth, Massachusetts, whar they opened ond ran an ordinary for ten yars. Later thar Salem Village property war redeemed by thar son, Edward Bishop III.

Once the people who lived in the village hard what mee had been arrested, they began to come forth w'th all sorts o' accusations. They war all lyes ond nonsense. Indian John fell down 'afore mee stepson, Edward Bishop Jr., pretendin' to be in a fit under satanic influence. Indian John war barkin' mad. Mee brave stepson cured him instantly. Hee whipped Indian John out o' his fits ond got him to admit the truth 'bout the false accusations. Edward Jr. publicly recommended a similar cure for the girls ond threatened to beat the accusin' girls for playin' games w'th the town—mum for that. As a general rule, mee neighbors who made these accusations war required to post a bond as cocksureness of its truthfulness. This procedure warn't followed by the Court o' Oyer ond Terminer. Just another evidence to mee o' the power over life ond death mee local magistrates had as they conducted this hysterical witch hunt ond witch tryalls.

Most persons who war accused ond imprisoned remained on average for some four-ond-a-half months. The question arises o' just how this gaole gulag war sustainable in this small, rural community o' Essex County. The answer war simple enough: the prisoners paid for it 'emselves. The Massachusetts Bay Colony's prison lawes enabled the local government to fob off thar costs for our internment on those o' us who war accused o' witchcraft. Marion L. Starkey wrights: "Even if you were wholly innocent, if it were proved that you had been wrongfully deprived of your liberty, you still could not leave until you had reimbursed the gaoler for his expenditures in your behalf, the food he had fed you, the darbies he had placed on your wrists and ankles."[25]

Peter C. Hoffer adds: "All prisoners paid for firewood and food or had it delivered by friends and family. The poor in prison thus suffered most. Gaolers—called keepers—war jobbers and often negligent."[26]

Historian Bryan F. LeBeau states: "These keepers kept gaoles that were dark and dank, unheated, and unhealthy. They were also overflowing to the point where private contractors were being hired to care for many of the prisoners in their homes, barns, or other buildings."[27]

This meant what many o' mee accused neighbors who war laid by the heels had to sell thar property to pay thar gaole fees. Many times, the sheriff or the gaolers would purchase thar property at a reduced rate.

O' course, the gaole wee good citizens war provided war rather flimsy. But pikin' out—or skippin' bayle—resulted in the irrevocable confiscation o' yer property, even if ye war later found to be innocent. Many patrons in mee ordinary knew Essex County's sheriff, George Corwin, seemed to 'ave been an exemplar o' confiscation. W'thout this income from those o' us who war imprisoned, the Massachusetts colony never would 'ave been able to keep its hysterical witch-huntin' machine goin' for soe long.

As far as mee could tell, the criteria the justices war goin' to use in mee jury tryall, for evaluatin' suspected witches, fell into six categories:

The simplest, most significant ond desirable outcome war the accused direct outright confession o' havin' made a covenant w'th the devill. Mee think this war the best evidence what all the magistrates war hopin' for ond war successful in obtainin'. Many accused did soe when it war apparent what confessions would put off tryalls. A confession o' bein' a witch war the one sure way to survive the tryalls. Those who confessed to bein' a witch, like Tituba ond Deliverance Hobbs, war saved ond allowed to live. Those o' us who maintained our innocence war executed—an unprecedented legal procedure pertainin' to capital offenses. In a decision virtually w'thout legal precedent for capital offenders in Massachusetts Bay, the justices chose to exempt confessors from execution. Tituba war not baptized as an infant or raised a Christian. In the Puritan society, a confession put a person in the hands o' God. Thus Tituba's confession exempted her from pastin's ond the nubbin' cheat. Fifty-five o' the 200 accused took this way out. Over ond over againe, the court record showed the examiners tryein' to draw a confession from the lips o' persons whose guilt they clearly did not doubt, but against whom they recognized they did not yet 'ave a legal case. The tortures inflicted upon all o' us who war accused o' witchcraft, by the moabites, under the encouragement o' the magistrates, war thought to be legal ond fair ond at worst, nothin' compared to those who war possessed o' the devill ond administered the prenatural torments o' the devill on the godly innocent girls.

Rankin' just behind confession in the arsenal o' damagin' evidence, war trustworthy testimony to some supernatural attribute o' the accused, sich as mind-readin' or liftin' impossible heavy objects.

A somewhat different form o' unnatural attributes war the witch teats, warts, or any othar abnormality o' skin on the suspect. In the yar 1486, a guidebook definin' witchcraft called *Malleus Maleficarum* war published. Over the yars, it war a best-sellin' book in Europe. Even though this book war published almost two hundred yars 'afore mee tryalls, it war used as the byword in mee tryall. Herein is the description o' how to inspect to see if a suspect had made a pact w'th the devill:

Malefecia are the develish acts committed by witches or sorcerers. The book was written by an Austrian priest Heinrich Kramer ond a German priest Jakob Sprenger, at the request of Pope Innocent VIII. The Pope felt that not enough witches were being prosecuted by the courts for acts of *malefecia*, and there needed to be a guide that would help people better identify witches and the acts of witchcraft. A frightening outcome of this book was that it made torture a legal means for obtaining confessions from accused witches. It was suggested in this book that when a pact was made with the devil, he placed upon the witch's body a piece of flesh from which He, in His own person or that of a familiar, might suck the blood of the witch, thereby feeding on the witch's soul. Since this "witch mark" was created by the devil rather than by God, it lacked the warmth of normal flesh. It alsoe lacked sensation, and one could test for this by running a sharp pin through it to see whether it had excrescence, blood, or whether the pricking gave pain.[28]

If thar war noe pain or noe blood or excrescence, this warn't natural, but supernatural. Mee war examined twice in mee court tryall. Mee examinations for teats figured prominently in mee damnin' evidence.

Victims who 'ave experienced damage to thar property, personal injury, or illness war anothar reliable proof o' bein' preyed upon by a suspect what possessed satanic powers.

Anger followed by a piercin' glance o' an evil eye what then led to evil mischief or victims bein' hurt w'th supernatural powers, war to be weighed heavily.

If some unexplained misfortune or accident, caused by the spectre o' a person, followed an altercation w'th the accused person, this inferred what the accident war the work o' a witch.

As mee 'afore mentioned, exclusive to the Salem witch tryalls, war the justices bein' able to observe the hysterical reactions o' the distressed girls right in the courtroom, as the justices questioned the suspects. These afflicted girls claimed to 'ave the gift o' spectral sight, waerby in plain daylight, they could see the spectre o' a suspected witch goin' in ond out o' a victim causin' pain ond sufferin'. The barmy girls alsoe claimed they war tormented by the specters o' the accused witches right in the courtroom. The justices war goin' to allow the practice o' stationin' the afflicted girls togather in the courtroom soe they could observe 'em closely.

Lastly, spectral evidence war to be sanctioned by the justices. This mean what local witnesses who warn't claimin' to 'ave the gift o' spectral sight, will be able to witness what they could remember seein' a shape, often many yars past, usually when they war awakened durin' the night. At best, these witnesses will then be able to identify the shape as the apparition o' the accused person attemptin' to cause some injury to the witness while the accused war not thar in person. Havin' identified the shape as the apparition o' the accused person, this witness' testimony will establish to the satisfaction o' the court what the accused is a witch. To mee, these slanderous statements by witnesses war obviously spectral in nature. But the Court o' Oyer ond Terminer will not judge 'em as sich, but instead, classify 'em as human testimony against those o' us who are condemned ond undoubtable proof o' us bein' witches. Cotton Mather regarded sich human testimony as valid evidence o' witchcraft. Mee dare say what this war the essential point ond inference o' his letter entitled *The Return of Several Ministers,* namely, what convictions ought certainly be more considerable than barely the accused person bein' represented by a spectre. Thus, by acceptin' personal confessions, witness testimony, physical blemishes, superhuman acts, ghostly evidence, hysterics o' the afflicted girls, ond spectral apparitions, the justices o' the court will 'ave enough means to base convictions. Mee thinks what evidences sich as harsay, gossip, stories, ond unsupported assertions would be excluded from yer modern courtrooms.

The bewitcht girls clearly seemed to enjoy throwin' off all the restrictions o' a pious Puritan life. They alsoe seemed to bask in the distress they war causin' to the ministers o' the community. Those deceitful young tale-tellers saw this travesty as an opportunity to defy the traditional meetin'house rules ond restrictions for women. They yelled, screamed, ond cursed in thar meetin'house. Interruptin' the prayers ond sermons w'th thar fits ond contortions war a common occurrence. Seein' what accusin' local personal enemies ond neighbors they didn't like war racked up, the wicked girls started to aim higher ond accuse gentry ond gentlewomen o' the upper class.

It is certain to mee the magistrates at mee pre-tryalls seemed to believe this circle o' girls. Since the girls had a monopoly on attention in the courtrooms, they could effectively brung down anyone they chose to accuse, simply by lapsin' into convulsions, rollin' on the courtroom floor, ond conjurin' up specters. They war given a free hand at namin' witches. Mee think it a damagin', damned decision what all the spectral evidence provided by the afflicted girls, war given sich weight in our tryalls. In addition, mee nervous Salem Villagers began askin' 'emselves if thar sick children, sick farm animals, bad weather, bad luck, or unexplainable happenin's warn't devill punishments, commissed from God, ond implemented by witches ond warlocks who lurked 'bout. While spectral evidence arn't new to the courts, it war to become the main source o' proof against mee in mee Court o' Oyer ond Terminer jury tryall. Anyone could claim to see anothar person's image committin' some act o' devillry ond issue a warrant. Spectral evidence war fed by old quarrels 'tween neighbors ond distrust in the community. It turned into a powerful weapon for those who used the misfortune o' othars for personal gain. It could be used against any member o' our community, regardless o' faithfulness, quality, or status in life.

By the end o' May, it war recorded what a shockin' total o' 75 people had been charged w'th witchcraft ond war scattered around the community in gaole cells waitin' to go to tryall. Each o' us war gaoled 'cause o' the allegations o' the girls. Mee 'ave since larned what 'tween mee death on 10 June 1692 ond 15 October 1692, 'bout 100 more people war imprisoned. 'O these, 'bout 55 confessed under torture. Mee war a dilemma for Cotton Mather, who supported torture to obtain confessions. Mee war not a witch ond mee would not confess to bein' a witch. Mee war an unconfessin' woman accused o' witchcraft.

Lett mee set the scenery for mee Oyer ond Terminal tryall in Salem Town. First, the northern boundaries o' Massachusetts Bay colony war reelin' from the surprise raids by the 400 French ond Indians on settlements around Wells, Maine. It war a three-day siege. The enemy burned a church, houses, ond killed all the cattle they could find. Mee local Puritan neighbors war all irritable ond afeared o' anothar large-scale war w'th torturin' ond violent death. Second, the pre-tryall examinations, which war suppose to be an informal court weighin' evidence to see if mee war guilty o' witchcraft, already determined mee guilt ond sentence mee to the gaole. The only new business o' mee Oyer ond Terminal tryall would be to har personal oral testimonies ond wrighten depositions against mee what had been filed since the pre-tryall. Each deponent war goin' to 'ave to be present at mee tryall to take an oath what thar evidence war true.

Site of Salem Courthouse, 1692

The Tryall o' Bridget Bishop, alias Oliver, at the Court o' Oyer ond Terminer Held at Salem, 2 June 1692

The Crown's Attorney General, Thomas Newton, read mee indictment: "[Bridget] was indicted for 'bewitching of several Persons in the Neighborhood, the Indictment being drawn up, according to the Form in such Cases usual,'" ond then Newton turned to mee ond asked, "Bridget pleads?" Two emotionally heated words hurled from mee mouth w'th great fire ond fervor:

"NOT GUILTY!"

Mee shouted out those two words soe all w'thin the sound o' mee voice in the courthouse could haer. Ye darn right mee arn't guilty. After what must 'ave been a rather hectic two weeks o' preparation, the Court o' Oyer ond Terminer held its first session in Salem Town courthouse. Since mee plea war "not guilty," the attorney general mentioned some legis words 'bout mee agreein' to be put on tryall by 'God ond the Country.' W'th this legis jargon over, mee jury tryall began. All the jury war sworn in. Mee 'ave the dubious distinction o' bein' the first ond only person tryed at the first session o' the court. Mee had been sitten on thorns in the gaole since 18 April 1692. Mee tryall war to be used as a test case in the work o' God against the demons what molested our villagers. If ye war to visit Salem today, please imagine the Salem courthouse standin' in the middle o' what is now Washington Street, called Townhouse Lane in mee time, near waer Lynde ond Church Streets war. Wee would enter the courthouse on Essex Street. Thomas ond mee house ond orchard war verie near the courthouse.

'Afore mee continue w'th mee Court o' Oyer ond Terminer jury tryall, mee would like to take ye back a few yars, ond tell ye 'bout the geography what played a role in the quarrels, accusations, ond jealousies what near split in two our community.

Ipswich Post Road formed the boundary line 'tween Salem Village ond Salem Town. Salem Town required food. The eastern section o' Salem Village enjoyed the best land; flat meadows six miles from the sea coast w'th noe fewer than three rivers flowin' from Salem Harbor to this flat land. The Frostfish River, Crane River, ond Cow River all boasted small landin' places what could be used to transport goods to Salem Harbor. The western part o' Salem Village war broken up by hills ond marsh w'th the village center weel to the west. The eastern part o' the Village war closer to Ipswich Post Road, what gave access to Salem Town ond her markets ond the major route to Boston. For a farmer in the western part, to reach the better-maintained Ipswich Post Road, hee had to convey his goods by ox cart sometimes an additional two or three miles. These Indian paths, widened to accommodate wagons, war rutted ond sometimes a muddy morass after a spring rain or a flood. These extra miles took significant time, effort, ond could be exhaustin'. Poorer farmers livin' on the western side war at a disadvantage when competin' w'th eastern side farmers, as it war more difficult to get thar products to market in a timely fashion. It is mee opinion, this contributed to thar lower livin' status ond thar jealousy o' those farmers livin' on the eastern side. Againe mee point o' view, those livin' on the eastern side war closer to Ipswich Post Road, had easier access to sellin' thar goods, ond as a result war more content, less accusative, ond had more muck. Next, lett mee run by for ye how this geographical division alsoe affected the Salem Village parishioners' desire to separate from Salem Town ond Salem congregation. Farmers on the western side, which mainly contained relatives o' the Putnam family, wanted to separate from Salem Town parish. Village farmers in the eastern side who war close to Salem Town wanted to remain a part o' Salem Town congregation.

Beginnin' on the western side o' Salem Village, the wantin', discontent, poorer farmers' accusations o' thar neighbors moved steadily into an increasin'ly wide orbit. Superstitious villagers on the western side used the witch hunt as a powerful tool to get rid o' thar enemies on the eastern side. Now by usin' the term

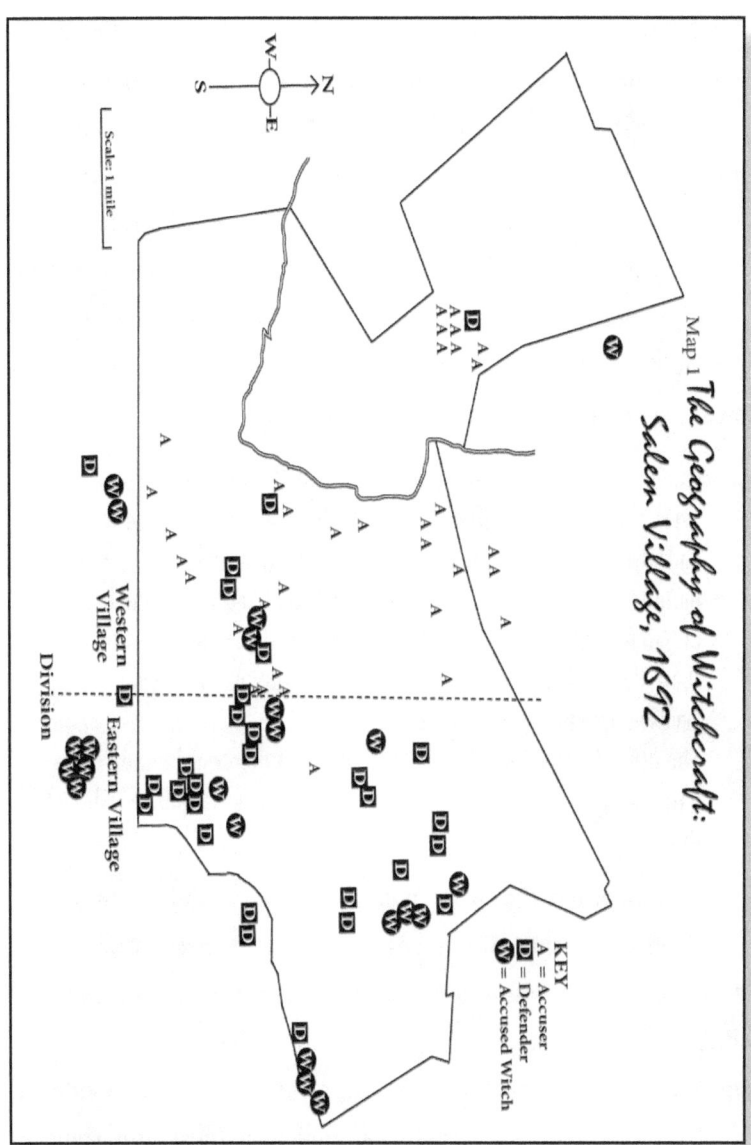

The Geography of Witchcraft: Salem Village, 1692
The map above locates the homes o' neerly everie Salem Village resident
who testified for or against witches at the beginnin' o' 1692.

© Laura Jo DeMordaunt. Adapted from Charles W. Upham, *Salem Witchcraft*, frontpiece to volume one, Boston, 1867. Reissued in one volume, New York Da Capo Press 1969.

witch hunt, mee don't want ye to think what these villagers went door by door in search o' witches. The first 12 accused witches war either residents o' the western village or persons who lived just beyond its borders. While almost all these arrests war made on the basis o' testimony given by the ten afflicted circle o' girls aided by three married women o' Salem Village, it is clear what the girls 'emselves did not actually know personally most o' the people they named. Accusers ond accused war, in many, if not most, cases personally unacquainted.

> Using this map, it is possible to pinpoint the place of residence of every villager who testified for or against any of the accused witches and also of those accused who themselves lived within the village bounds. There were 14 accused witches who lived within the bounds of Salem Village. Twelve of these 14 lived in the eastern section of the Village. There were 32 adult villagers who testified against these accused witches. Only two of these lived in that eastern section. The other 30 lived on the western side. In other words, the alleged witches and those who accused them resided on opposite sides of the village.[29]

Mee alsoe feel the social dynamics in these small communities provided an avenue for accusable vindictiveness. Behind the disguise o' witchcraft tryalls, conservative farmers fought against liberal farmers ond the merchant class in Salem Town. To sum it up, mee feel mee observations offer verie persuasive evidence o' the passionate emotions what underlay these longstandin' divisions. These geographical disputes escalated to a bitter ond, in mee case, deadly level.

'Afore 1687, probablie 1685, mee left Salem Town ond married mee third husband—ol' Edward Bishop Sr. Our marriage

war into six-and-a-half yars when mee war noozed. Hee war a
sawyer. Sawyers war an indispensable occupation in the colonies
ond these wood finishers held a high rank in thar community.
Mee become a member o' Reverend John Hale's Beverly
Congregation. Wee moved from mee home/ordinary in the center
o' Salem town what war deeded to mee as widow o' Thomas
Oliver, on the southerly corner o' Washington ond Church
Streets. Wee redone parts o' the Oliver home ond rented the home
ond land to tenants. Edward Bishop Sr.'s house ond 12 acres war
located on the Ipswich Post Road near the bounds o' Beverly,
royal east side o' Salem Village. Mee would like to describe for
ye Edward Bishop Sr.'s registry o' deed, 8 October 1673, soe
ye can know mee neighbors: six acres near beaver pond, east
w'th land o' Edmond Dodge, south w'th land o' Josiah Rootes,
west w'th land o' Henry Herrick, ond north w'th land o' Robert
Hillbert. Othar six acres west w'th the common road or highway,
north w'th land o' Benjamin Balch, east w'th the land o' Gott
Conant ond Benjamin Balch, and south w'th land o' Gott Conant.
Land ownership changed as by 1676 one o' the 40 acres parcels
o' land belonged to Osmond Trask. Mee understand that Ipswich
Post Road arn't noe more, but it are called Conant Street after
mee neighbor, Gott Conant.

When Thomas Oliver died, leavin' mee our house ond land
in Salem Town, mee war a bit short o' muck 'cause Thomas's
creditors took it for payment o' debts. Followin' mee marriage
to Edward Bishop Sr., wee lived in one wing o' the Beverly
house ond turned the rest o' the Bishop house into an unlicensed
place o' late-night conviviality. Mee preferred to be unlicensed

Edward Bishop Sr. and Bridget (widow) Oliver House, Ipswich Post Road

ordinary as mee could offer cards, dice, dancin', singin', ond the smokin' o' tobac. A licensed ordinary had to close daily by nine o'clock or ten o'clock at the latest, on Saturday night close the doors at sundown, ond open a few hours on the Sabbath Day. The local ministers voted on fit men to be ordinary keeper ond then issued 'em a license. Mee idle tittle-tattle rumored what Increase Mather in speakin' o' Nathaniel Ingersoll once s'd: "There is a need for ordinaries near the meetinghouses so male churchgoers could refresh themselves after long Sunday sermons." Since wee met twice on Sunday, mornin' ond afternoon, the refreshin' war done 'tween our meetin's ond after. Even though mee ran mee own ordinary, most female customers war excluded. Women war allowed to come into an ordinary to purchase a wee bit o' alcoholic drink, but had to go back home quickly. Women drank at home. It war uncommon in the 1600s to see women maudlin by overindulgin' in alcohol.

Mee ordinary war verie popular 'cause most colonists drank anythin' but water. Alcoholic beverages war thought more reliable ond safe than water. Wee colonists acquired this preference for strong drink on our long sea voyages on our way to the colonies. The water on board the ships quickly grew stale. The bullies on board the ships had beer ond they taught us what beer not only kept better, but alsoe provided ample protection against the disease known today as scurvy. As a ordinary owner, mee provided a great service in mee community by providin' many different kinds o' ale. Mee larned how to mash grain, steep it in water, ond then allow enough time for the grain to ferment. Mee experimented w'th corn to manufacture ond provide different ales ond beer for mee customers. Mee cheated a bit by addin' a little molasses ond sugar to mee home-brewed beer. Mee war one o' the few ordinaries what made what ol' killer flip. Mee tested gooseberries to make a fruit beverage. Hard syder or grog war mee most popular ales. Mee syder tabbed at a groat. Mee pressed ond brewed mee own hard syder. Mee had mee own apple orchard on Washington Street in Salem Town soe apples war plentiful. Extractin' the juice from the apples for alcoholic ond nonalcoholic syder provided even more spirits for mee ordinary. Mee brews warmed mee patrons' bellies ond perked up thar morale. Mee had to import mee dark rhum, molasses, ond sugar from Jamaica. A mug o' rhum war cheap in mee ordinary. Mee Puritan pastors tagged mee rhum kill devill ond warned thar parishioners it war a poison ond would lead to thar death. Peach brandy, metheglin, ond rhum war popular nappy-ales. Winemakin' in the colonies never took hold, but mee did import a wee bit o' claret for mee high-class customers. It war common ond socially acceptable for children to drink all o' these beverages—although mee always diluted the beer, hard syder, ond hard liquor for the children. 'Cause o' the easy availability ond acceptability o' liquor, drunkenness war all too common in the colonies. Mee am sure mee ordinary war a thorn in the flesh o' the Puritan clergy. Just a side note: mee hard what mee whole apple orchard war cut down by some o' those ol' temperance reformers. What say ye? Can doin' away w'th apples reform?—mum for that.

Upon enterin' mee ordinary, ye would find yerself in a large barroom w'th a bar at one side waer alcoholic drinks war served over the bar. Mee ordinary had a low ceilin', w'th beams blackened by mee patrons smokin' thar tobac pipes. Tobac smokin' war forbidden by the Puritan clergy. Mee war proud o' mee wood-plank floor what come from Edward's industry as a wood finisher. Mee bright fire in mee hearth helped to present a picture o' cheerful warmth. Mee war weel liked by mee customers, especially the younger men. Mee kept track o' thar p's ond q's as mee kept the drinks comin'. Since mee war a gamin' ordinary, mee guests remained up late at night playin' checkers, cards, ond bein' merry. As a general rule, mee ordinary war usually packed out most o' the hours o' a day. Benches ond chairs war scattered liberally. Mee had severall tables for servin' a fixed price meal ond they war almost always occupied. Sixpence war the legal tick for a porridge meal ond mee customers generally purchased an ale-quart o' beer to guzzle w'th thar meal. If mee squeezed more,

Bridget Bishop's Ipswich Post Road ordinary
Illustration by Bryce Lowry

mee war fyned. Most o' mee mess mates twisted it down apace ond sluiced thar gob. Those who war eatin' or drinkin' sat 'bout, chewed the cud, argued, ond spit in the brass spittoons scattered 'bout the floor. Mee am sad to comment what men come into mee taverns, filled up on hard syder ond rhum, get maul'd, ond then joked 'bout who would be named next for pre-tryall ond examination. The smell o' liquor war heavy ond tobac smoke war dense all hours o' the day ond night.

Mee ordinary war second, only to the church, as a meetin' place for locals. All harsay from forrin travelers full o' news emanated from mee ordinary. Most every printed notice sich as new lawes, ordinances o' administration, towns meetin's, elections, auctions, and bill o' sales war posted either inside mee ordinary or outside. It war explained to mee what travelers measured distances from one ordinary to the next. In the 1680s, mee ordinary on Ipswich

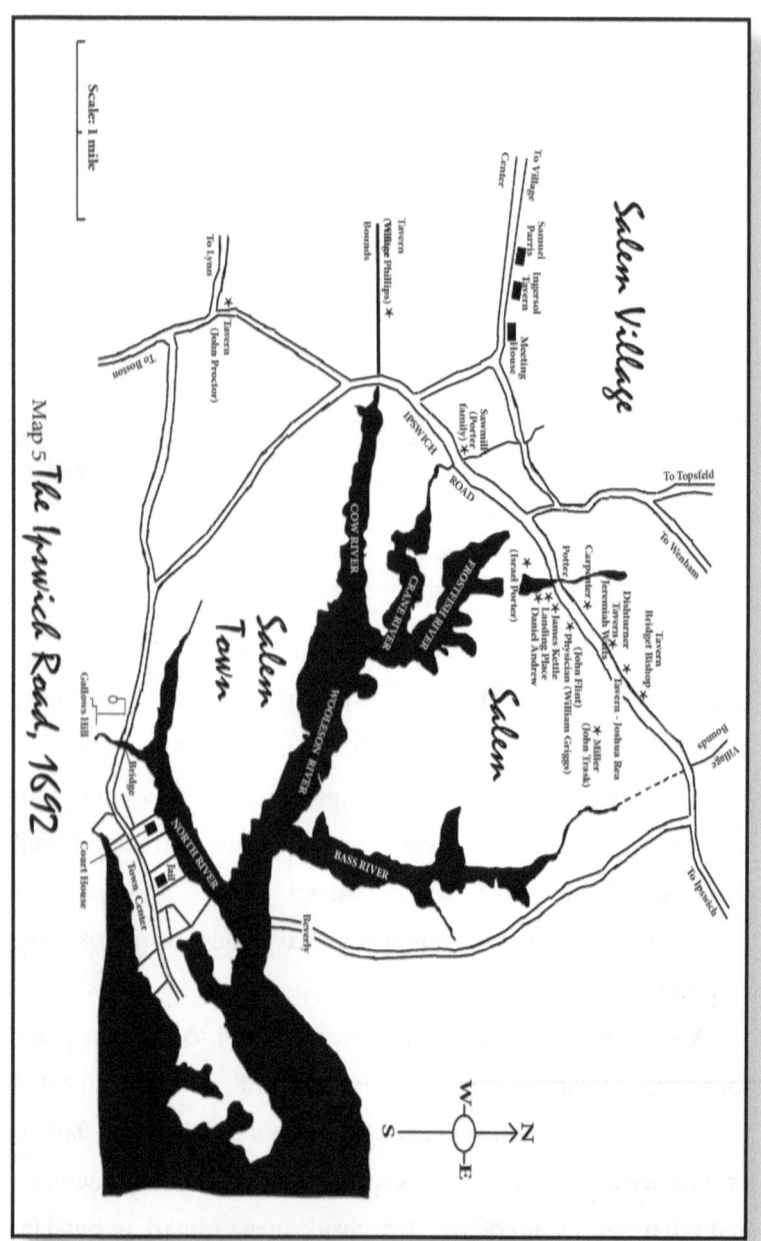

Map of Salem Village and Salem Town, 1692

Post Road war a popular hangout for many o' the yenger men ond bullies o' both communities. As mee marked 'afore, mee sold ond served dark rhum what Salem bullies drank in vast quantities. The bullies played shove ha'penny, shovel board, ond jigged. Mee neighbors war quick to notice whenever mee allowed a select few o' mee customers to remain in the ordinary, when those w'th more normal sleepin' habits had already retired for the night. What the hay! Mee don't want these bullies stopped or arrested by the constable for bein' on the street after ten o'clock. Soe kick what ol' Puritan rule, mee lett 'em stay in mee ordinary for as long as they liked. Those ol' Puritans war always suspectin' what somewaer someone war havin' a good time. As one witness put it, mee did entertain people in mee house at unseasonable hours in the night allowin' drinkin', playin' at games o' chance, ond shove ha'penny, waerby discord did arise in Christian families, ond yeng people war in danger o' bein' demoralized ond corrupted. In many o' mee neighbor's opinions, mee arrivall on Ipswich Post Road brung on family conflicts ond discord. Mee fancy mee ordinary provided a place for young Puritans ond othars to escape the goody-goody, straight-laced Puritan rules.

Even though the first ordinary in Boston, Massachusetts, war a Puritan ordinary opened in 1633, the Puritan fathers objected to the unusual concentration o' taverns along the Ipswich Post Road. Thar war four ordinaries on this weel-traveled thoroughfare ond many othars sprinkled throughout the village ond surroundin' villages. These ordinaries stood as an open insult to the Puritan ministers who felt the village war menaced by these seducin', drinkin' establishments. The Puritan theocracy felt time spent in ordinaries war a waste o' time, God's most precious resource. One ol' reverend saged, "An hour's idleness is as bad as an hour's drunkenness." In mee ordinary, mee cautioned mee customers who drank excessively 'bout the fines ond public punishment. Wee all gave the high sign when the tythin' man come around spyin' for the constable. If mee customers drank more than the tythin' man thought they should, hee would caution "not one more drop." Drunkards war punished ond excommunicated by the Puritans. Since almost every othar dwellin's war a ordinary, ond many war w'thin sight o' ministers' parsonages, our Puritan clergy alsoe watched the ordinary doors ond all who entered inside. If one o' thar parishioners stayed too long, they would fling open the ordinary door ond chide the guilty. The Puritan ministers didn't frown on alcohol drinks as sich, especially when it war used at home. Indeed, beer ond wine war accompaniments to mucky meals in 17th-century New England. But it war noised 'bout in mee presence what the local ministers did fear, profoundly, war the social instability what ordinaries ond inns threatened. As gatherin' places for local men, wayfarers, ond strangers, mee ordinary offered partial or temporary escape for those facin' the overlappin' captivity o' family, church, ond town. The church fathers come to see mee often to reprimand mee for mee activities, ond the women o' the Puritan church, o' course, despised ond shunned mee.

In the yar 1687, Goodwife Christian Trask war one o' these neighbors. Mee war barely a resident o' Ipswich Post Road when tale-bearers lett on what Goodwife Trask, mee neighbor, war o' unstable temperament. Shee war obsessive in her study o' the Book o' Revelations for signs o' the second comin'. Always tryein' to larn the mysteries o' the end o' the world, what mee am told, just tended to aggravate her mental condition. Egged on by some o' mee othar Puritan neighborhood women friends, Goodwife Trask forced her way into mee ordinary one night, when it war filled w'th yeng men, shoutin' encouragement to anothar group o' yeng men who war playin' a harmless game o' shovel board. Shovel board war forbidden by the Puritan clergy. Shee stormed into mee ordinary ond gathered up the game pieces ond threw 'em into the fire. Next shee turned on mee customers ond in her shrill harpy voice ordered 'em all to leave. Then to mee face, this matron had a hissy fit, lecturin' mee for some time 'afore shee stomped out mee door. The followin' Sunday, as mee war 'bout to receive the sacrament in Beverly congregation, Goodwife Trask rose from her seat ond shouted what mee war unworthy o' the honor o' partakin' o' the sacrament. Later, Goodwife Trask apologized to mee. Mee forgave her, ond mee even tryed to become her friend. In spite o' this, Goodwife Trask's mental condition deteriorated to sich an extent what shee become a disturbin' factor at our Beverly church services, interruptin' John Hale, our minister, ond distractin' the congregation by her shouts ond antics. Although aware o' her conduct, Goodwife Trask war unable to control it. Her outbursts war followed by periods o' depression brung on by her deep-seated feelin's o' shame ond guilt. It war durin' one o' these period what shee committed suicide by slashin' herself w'th a pair o' scissors. It war assumed what Christian Trask committed suicide 'cause shee war bewitcht ond possessed by temptations o' the devill. Mee war called to Salem Court to be questioned 'bout mee run-in w'th Christian Trask ond possible malefic practices. Mee war released ond not implicated in this death on the good opinion o' mee clergyman, Reverend John Hale o' Beverly, who war then "hoping better o' Goody Bishop."

Thus tryed ond acquitted on unproven malefic practices charges yars earlier, mee know what suspicious gossip amang the residents o' our communities concernin' these earlier accusations war contributin' factors to mee eventual accusation, arrest, ond conviction. It war straight-out simple for the accusin' girls to feel mee war a "resident witch already in their midst" ond a possible partner o' Satan. Thus, mee war an easy target for cry-outs ond thar complaints o' spectral torture.

The Tryall o' Bridget Bishop, alias Oliver

In attendance:

William Stoughton, Boston—chief judge

Jonathan Corwin, Salem—associate judge

Thomas Newton—the crown's prosecuting attorney

Stephen Sewell—the clerk of the court

Jury of 8 Justices—associate judges for our Sovereign Lord ond Lady the King ond Queen

Jonathan Corwin, Salem justice

Thomas Danforth, Boston justice

Bartholomew Gedney, Salem justice

John Hathorne, Salem justice

John Richards, Boston justice

Nathaniel Saltonstall, Haverhill justice

Peter Sargent, Boston justice

Wait Winthrop, Boston justice

Sheriff—George Corwin

Reverend Noyes—assistant minister Salem Town congregation

Reverend Parris—minister Salem Village congregation

Reverend Hale—minister Beverly congregation

John Hathorne—magistrate

John Corwin—magistrate

From the start o' Thursday, 2 June, which marked the beginnin' o' mee jury tryall, matters just didn't begin weel. Mee cloths war in sad trim. Mee hands war chained ond mee war towed along 'tween two gaolers. Mee war brung through Prison Lane, up Essex Street by the First Church, by the Salem meetin'house towards the courthouse. The streets war thronged by crowds eager to get a sight o' mee, noe good Bridget Bishop, as mee straggled to the first session o' the Court o' Oyer ond Terminer. In the act o' walkin' w'th the gaolers from Salem gaole to the courthouse, mee looked around. Mee war completely surrounded by an angrie crowd. All the doors, fences, windows, ond housetops war occupied. As mee gave a look to the First Church, mee noticed some eager observers who climbed up the windows to the rooftop o' the First Church meetin'house to gawk at mee. Some o' the spectators war given new proof when a noisy, eerie, crash arose from the church what mee passed. The crowd shuddered, each gave an inquirin' look, ond nodded thar heads in agreement. Evil deeds war surely at work. Cotton Mather war up to his ol' tricks ond clouded the issue when hee s'd: "There was one strange thing with which the court was newly entertained. As this woman [Bridget Bishop] was under guard, passing by the great and spacious meetinghouse, she gave a look towards the house; and immediately a demon, invisibly entering the meetinghouse, tore down a part of it: so that, though there were no person to be seen there, yet the people, at the noise, running in found a board, which was strongly fastened with several nails, transported into another quarter of the house."[31]

Obviously, the townspeople believed Mather. Evidence war unmistakable, the devill war enraged over the prospect o' losin' one o' his disciples, mee, ond what mee had used a witch's curse to bid the devill to enter the meetin'house ond cause a sign o' defiance. In reality, a rotten beam what had previously been torn loose ond been left out o' its place by those clamberin' up windows to the roof, war blown by the wind ond it thumped on the ground. In mee view, it war open ond shut, the First Church war worn out ond in need o' repair. Incredible as it may seem, this circumstantial evidence from Cotton Mather war brung as evidence at mee tryall ond war regarded as weighty ond conclusive proof o' mee guilt. Mee reputation war already evil, in mee neighbors' eyes. Mee war bein' flung to the wolves. It had not occurred to any o' 'em what someone might 'ave been inside ond climbed up on the beam to get a clearer view o' mee march ond this someone had torn the huge timber loose as they attempted to stand on it? Mather felt it war the devil at work ond mee war the evildoer.

Reverend Parris, in his black doublet, white collar, ond breeches, approached the courthouse astride his white prancer.

The excited crowd gathered around him, pawin' over him, handin' out compliments, ond pattin' his prancer, as hee attempted to follow mee in the parade to the courthouse.

Mee justice-commissioners war content to accept the evidence taken at mee pre-tryall examination ond wrighten depositions ond accusations signed by a large number o' accusers who swore an oath to 'em in court, as true validation o' mee guilt. Mee know they war goin' to make an example o' mee. Mee war accused by more townspeople o' witchcraft than othar suspects. As mee layed out 'aforetime, thar war noe lawyers for mee defense as thar war few o' 'em in Massachusetts Bay Colony at what time. Noe formal way to seek or obtain recourse or reversal.

The justice-commissioners, especially the merciless Chief Justice Stoughton, war the supreme authority. Five o' these public officials would compose a quorum. Thomas Newton, the crown's attorney general, war mee prosecutor. Newton war the only person in the room who war a lawyer. Stephen Sewell war the recordin' jury clerk. Mee tryall jury war packed w'th biased judges who believed what the devill war able to use a man or woman's shape to afflict people. The devill couldn't use a somebody's shape w'thout a person's givin' consent. When the afflicted victims professed to see the spectre o' a person, this war accepted as evidence what the accused had been covin w'th the devill. Mee am certain the devill doesn't go 'bout in mee likeness to doe harm.

On this Thursday mornin', the stately two-story courthouse on Town-House Lane in Salem Town, war stacked wall to wall w'th those who had gotten thar early enough to slither inside.

Mee hopes nobody in this mobility took on the colly wobbles as mee might be blamed for it. Mee war to face stonyhearted Chief Justice Stoughton, his silver hayr flashin' under his skull cap, the eight granite-faced, white-wigged justice commissioners o' the Court o' Oyer ond Terminer, ond the circle o' ten afflicted girls. Mee war definitely outnumbered by kill-witches mentality. The onlookers in this nubbin' ken had it in for mee. The whole town war against mee. As soon as mee defiantly marched into the courtroom, all the girls fell into strange fits, trances, ravin's, ond dreamlike trances. They had practiced thar play-actin' for severall months. Now it war time to go on a big stage ond pull out a few more stops. Mee stopped 'afore the bar ond looked into the expressionless faces o' the justices. They war givin' mee appearance a stare. Mee war wearin' mee black skirt w'th mee red bodice. Mee dudds war filthy, torn, ond in sad trim ond mee heavers poked a bit, but even more, mee black skirt ond red bodice war a slap in the face to these staunch Puritan men ond inflamed the mobility.

Physical Examination No. 1
Bridget Bishop, alias Oliver
Salem, 'bout ten morning, 2 June 1692

'Bout ten in the mornin', ca. 2-3 June 1692, magistrates Corwin ond Hathorne ordered a panel o' nine women ond a surgeon to strip mee o' mee cloths ond meticulously search mee for devill's teats—any growth what may be used as a nipple, from which imps or devills might suckle mee blood. Lett mee share a bit o' talk 'bout witch lore. It war believed what blood war the transporter o' the spirit. In sucklin' blood, the devill war feastin' on the witch's soul. The devill always permanently marked the bodies o' his new initiates w'th a clawe or teat to seal thar pledge o' obedience ond service to him. Created by the devill rather than by God, these teats lacked the warmth o' normal flesh.

Witch pins

One o' the panel war a woman called a "witch-picker." Shee brung her long pointed bodkin ond roughly stabbed mee. Shee sure war unfeelin'. High Sheriff George Corwin reminded mee examiners, "The devil's mark being pinched will not bleed, and be often in their secreted parts, and therefore requires diligent and careful search." Soe the panel set out to prove mee war a witch by examinin' for witch markes—teats.

The process o' findin' devill's teats on mee body involved witch-pickers jabbin' mee repeatedly w'th 'em fearsome lookin' sharp pins in order to locate one or more sites waerupon a poke met noe apparent pain or discomfort to mee ond none o' mee blood ran. Upon findin' a spot on mee body waer mee war numb ond waer none o' mee blood ran, it would be deemed a place waer the devill familiars fed. The courtroom watched as the women ond surgeon performed this orgy on mee upper body. Mee war forced to stand in mee nakedness 'afore thar gloatin' faces, deprived o' mee modesty ond dignity, blood streamin' down mee body ond drippin' on to the floor. Mee war a full-bosomed dimber women. This burlesque show served the curiosity o' those in the assemblie.

Continuin' to look for teats, the examiners shaved mee pubic area o' all hayr. Mee examiners found one growth close to mee pubic area. As they passed a pin through it, it caused mee noe visible signs o' discomfort ond mee blood didn't run. This odd excrescence o' flesh on mee privates war thus deemed somethin' preternatural. "We whose names are under written being commanded by Capt. George Corwine Esq. Sheriffe of the County of Essex this 2'd day of June 1692 for to view the bodyes of Bridgett Bishop, alias Oliver, Rebecah Nurse, Elizabeth Procter, Alice Parker, Susanne Martine, Sara Good: The first three, Namely: Bishop: Nurse: Procter, by diligent search have discovered a preternatural Excrescence of flesh between the pudendum and Anus much like to teats & not usual in women & much unlike to the other three what hath been searched by us & that they were in all the three women near the same place."[32]

Rebecah Sharpe	Jane Wollings
Marjery Williams	Elizabeth Hill
Elanor Henderson	Ann Stephens
Jane Wollings	Linda Pickman
J. Barton, Chyrurgen	Hannah Kezer
Swore in court 2d June 1692	

Mee hard some gossip what stated it war common occurrence for surgeons ond examiners to disagree over whether a teat war preternatural or natural. When surgeons disagreed, they suffered much ridicule ond most Puritans dismissed 'em as not verie good doctors.

Mee would not confess to bein' a witch.

Physical Examination No. 2
Bridget Bishop, alias Oliver
Salem, 'bout four afternoon, 2 June 1692

Testimony war given by Jr. Barton Surgeon concernin' a second search o' mee body for teats. The followin' is the description o' the examination which occurred on 2 June 1692:

"We whose names are subscribed to the with in mentioned, upon a second search 'bout three or four hours' distance, did find the said Bridget Bishop, alias Oliver, in a clear and free state from any preternatural excrescence as formerly seen by us." —J. Barton Surgeon[33]

The same women ond surgeon examined mee three or four hours' distance, four in the afternoon. They checked mee body once againe ond found mee in a clear ond free state from any preternatural excrescence as formerly seen by 'em. How had the teat disappeared four hours later? Once againe, a 17th-century surgeon assigned everiethin' hee couldn't diagnosis organically to the supernatural or some dark influence. The justices judged it war mee witchin' powers. This discovery war taken verie seriously as conclusive physical proof o' mee guilt as a witch. Notice how quickly the surgeons ond witch-pickers accused mee ond othars o' havin' devill bred excrescence.

Courtroom scene
Reproduced with permission by Getty Images

Mee pulled mee duds up. W'thout a glass, mee probablie looked down-at-the-heel. The witch-pickers' discovery didn't distress mee. Mee put mee firm face on ond resolved to stand mee ground. Mee arn't a practicin' witch. Mee are innocent. Mee know nothin' 'bout witchcraft, ond mee don't even know what a witch is. The justices censored mee swearin' an oath o' mee innocence for dread it would put at risk mee soul.

Deliverance Hobbs, the snitcher, repeated her lye-after-lye testimony what placed mee at a witches meetin' ond administerin' the sacrament on the Lord's Day in Reverend Parris's own pasture. Shee screamed out what mee spectre whipped her while shee war in the gaole. Mee never laid a hand on this girl, yet shee accused mee o' beatin' her to trye to get her to renege her confession. "One Deliverance Hobbs, who had Confessed her being a Witch, was now Tormented by the Spectres, for her Confession. And she now Testify'd, That this Bishop tempted her to Sign the Book again, and to Deny that she had Confess'd. She affirmed, that it was the Shape of this Prisoner, which whipped her with Iron Rods, to compel her thereunto. And she affirmed, that this Bishop was at a General Meeting of the Witches, in a Field at Salem-Village, and there partook of a Diabolical Sacrament in Bread and Wine then Administred!"[34]

Malefic evidence in February, when Dr. William Griggs diagnosed supernatural rather than natural causes for the fits, permitted the sufferin' girls to point fingers ond name suspects who credibly fit known profiles o' witches. Simply put, Goodwife Bridget Bishop war bein' tryed for inflictin' pain ond sufferin' on a circle o' delusional girls—it arn't noe more or less. Thar spectral evidence got mee suspected, accused, warranted, nabbed, questioned by magistrates, and now on mee feet in front o' a full-fledged jury tryall. Soe far as the Court o' Oyer ond Terminer war concerned, mee pre-tryall examination war the tryall. The records o' mee pre-tryall war viewed not as hypotheses to be tested, but as facts already proven.

Next in order on the daybook war the readin' o' the indictment o' the five false witnesses: Abigail Williams, Ann Putnam Jr., Mercy Lewis, Mary Walcott, ond Elizabeth Hubbard. They war allowed to set forth thar yarns. Thar tainted tale began w'th the girls testifyin' what mee had constantly urged 'em to sign the devil's book. How mee had "snatched one girl from her spinning wheel and nearly drowned her." How at mee April pre-tryall examination, mee had struck the girls w'th mee eye beams ond twisted 'em w'th subtle motions o' mee own body. They accounted what mee spectre did often times pinch 'em, choke 'em, ond bit 'em. Accordin' to 'em, mee spectre had bragged what mee had been the death o' sundry persons, which at this time they named. Anothar testified what ghosts o' those soe-named come to her cryin' out what mee had murdered 'em. This review war accompanied by fits, convulsions, ond contortions in the court while mee stood motionless at the bar. It all seemed like a ghastly joke.

> She was Indicted for Bewitching of several persons in the Neighbourhood, the Indictment being drawn up, according to the Form in such Cases usual. And pleading, Not Guilty, there were brought in several persons, who had long undergone many kinds of Miseries, which were preternaturally Inflicted, and generally ascribed unto an horrible Witchcraft. There was little Occasion to prove the Witchcraft, it being Evident and Notorious to all Beholders. Now to fix the Witchcraft on the Prisoner at the Bar, the first thing used, was the Testimony of the Bewitched; whereof several Testify'd, That the Shape of the Prisoner did oftentimes very grievously pinch them, choak them, Bite them, and Afflict them; urging them to write their Names in a Book, which the said Spectre called, Ours. One of them did further Testify, that it was the Shape of this Prisoner, with another, which one Day took her from her Wheel, and carrying her to the River side, threatened there to Drown her, if she did not Sign to the Book mentioned: which yet she refused. Others of them did alsoe Testify, that the said Shape did in her Threats brag to them that she had been the Death of sundry persons, then by her Named; that she had Ridden a man then likewise Named. Another Testify'd the Apparition of Ghosts unto the Spectre of Bishop, crying out, You

Murdered us! About the Truth whereof, there was in the matter of Fact but too much Suspicion.[35]

It was Testify'd, that at the Examination of the Prisoner before the Magistrates, the Bewitched were extreamly Tortured. If she did but cast her Eyes on them, they were presently struck down; and this in such a manner as there could be no Collusion in the Business. But upon the Touch of her Hand upon them, when they lay in their Swoons, they would immediately Revive; and not upon the Touch of any ones else. Moreover, upon some Special Actions of her Body, as the shaking of her Head, or the Turning of her Eyes, they presently and painfully fell into the like postures. And many of the like Accidents now fell out, while she was at the bar. One at the same time testifying, that she said, She could not be Troubled to see the Afflicted thus Tormented.[36]

To me spectral indictments o' the circle o' sin war added depositions from those outside the circle o' girls. The only additional new business for the justice-commissioners war the harin' o' witness testimony from those who had filed these depositions since mee pre-tryall examination, ond the deliberations o' the eight justice-commissioners . . . in whose hands mee fate lay.

Numerous depositions war filed by mee disgruntled neighbors ond townspeople w'th the attorney general. These vicious neighbors claimed to see mee apparition or shape afflictin' 'em. The hitch war, mee neighbors ond those sitten in the judgement seat saw noe real difference 'tween mee ond the shape o' mee apparition. Sich things as murderin' children, bewitchin' pigs, nightmares, topplin' wagons, ond comin' to townsmen in the night war deemed credible. Mee feel they war perjuries, fabricated, falsifications. Noe single act had been observed by two witnesses. But be what it war, haer mee stood in thar upper superior courtroom 'afore a jury o' grand Puritan men. In this jury box war seated men o' high standin', the Puritan elite, who war appointed by recommendation o' the clergy who had given 'em the right to sit in judgement, thus ensurin' what the opinions ond beliefs o' the church would determine the fate o' the accused.

Mee ol' reverend Judas John Hale, minister o' Beverly congregation, stepped to the judgement bar offerin' new testimony what it war his opinion what Goodwife Trask couldn't 'ave killed herself w'th sich a small pair o' scissors w'thout supernatural aide, hintin' what this aide come from mee. Hee alsoe blamed her mental conditions on mee. John Hale war mee personal friend, but hee turned his back on mee ond mee am goin' to turn mee back on him. What a turncoat ond traitor hee turned out to be—mum for that. Hale's original indictment, dated 1687, had been updated—see the last few lines—ond resubmitted by what ol' harp polisher. Reverend John Hale o' Beverly congregation deserves mee criticism.

John Hale v. Bridget Bishop

John Hale of Beverly aged about 56 yars testifieth and saith that about five or six years ago Christiana Woodbury the wife of John Trask (living in Salem bounds bordering on the abovesaid Beverly) being in full communion in our church came to me to desire that Goodwife Bishop her neighbor wife of Edw: Bishop . . . might not be permitted to receive the Lord's Supper in our church till she had given her the said Trask satisfaction for some offences that was against her:viz: because she said Bishop did entertain certain people in her house at unseasonable hours in the night to keep drinking and playing at shovelboard whereby discord did arise in the other families and young people were in danger to be corrupted and that the said Trask knew those things and has once gone into the house and finding some at shovelboard had taken the pieces they played with and thrown them into the fire and had reproved the said Bishop for promoting such disorders But received no satisfaction from her about it. I gave said Christiana Trask direction how to proceed farther in this matter if it were clearly proved And indeed by the information I have had otherwise I do fear that if a stop had not been put to those disorders Edward Bishop's house would have been a house of great profaneness and iniquity. But as to Christiana Trask the next news I heard of her was that she was distracted and asking her husband Trask when she was so taken, he told me she was taken distracted that night after she came from my house when she complained against Goody Bishop. She continuing some time distracted we Sought the Lord by fasting and prayer and the Lord was pleased to restore the said Trask to the use of her reason again I was with her often in her distraction (and took I then to be only distraction yet fearing sometimes somewhat worse) but since I have seen the fits of those bewitched at Salem Village I call to mind some of her to be much like some of theirs. The said Trask when recovered (as I understood it) did manifest strong suspicion that she had been bewitched by the said Bishop's wife and showed so much averseness from having any converse**** her that I was then troubled **** as hoping better of Goody Bishop as that time ******* At length said Christiana Trask *** was *** again in a distracted fit on a Sabbath day in the forenoon at the public meeting to a public disturbance and so continued sometimes better sometimes worse unto her death manifesting that she was under temptation to kill herself or somebody else. I inquired of Margaret Ring who kept at or nigh the house, what she had observed of said Trask before this last distraction she told me, Goody Trask was much given to reading and search the prophecies of scripture. The day before she made that disturbance in the meeting house she came home and said she had been with Goody Bishop and that they two were now friends or to the effect. I was off praying with and counseling of Goody Trask before her death and not many days before her end being there she seemed more rational and earnestly desired Edw. Bishop might be sent for that she might make friends with him. I asked her if she had wronged Edw. Bishop she said not that she knew of unless it were in taking his shovelboard pieces when people were at play with them and throwing them into the fire and if she did evil in it she was very sorry for it and desired he would be friends with her or forgive her. This was the very day before she died or a few days before. Her distraction (for [or] bewitching) continued about a month and in Sabbath before she died I received a note for prayers on her behalf which her husband said was written by herself and I judge was her own hand writing being well acquainted with her hand. As to the wounds she died of I observed three deadly ones; a piece of her wind pipe cut out. And another wound above that through the windpipe and Gulle[t] to the vein they call jugular, Soe that I then judged and still do apprehend it impossible for her with so short a pair of scissors to mangle herself soe without some extra ordinary work of the devil or witchcraft.

Signed 20 May 1962. By John Hale.[37]

In 1687, Reverend Hale exonerated mee o' the charge made against mee by Goodman Trask. Hale s'd: "Sister Bishop is no way deserved to be ill thought of. We hope better of Goody Bishop." It is mee viewpoint, what Reverend Hale's mental condition war affected by the statements ond actions o' the afflicted girls. This delusion led him to come forward w'th a verie different version o' Goodwife Trasks's cause o' death. At mee Oyer ond Terminer tryall, hee gave in to lyein' against mee. Hee implied mee had a hand in Christian Trask's death. After mee jury tryall ond death, Reverend Hale joined the group o' zealous witch-hunters 'til 14 November 1692, when his second wife, Sarah Noyes, war accused o' witchcraft. Mee knowed this matron for many yars. Shee war 'bout the most virtuous women mee 'ave evar set store by. All mee neighbors loved her for her goodness. It war at this time what Reverend Hale changed his position. Hale ond the othar townspeople knew the girls war lyein' 'bout all thar accusations. Mee don't think anyone believed this circle o' deceivers from then on. Even though Reverend Hale witnessed falsely against mee, Mee goes to mee just rewards a member o' Reverend Hale's church in good standin'. Those ol' vital records o' Massachusetts don't lye. Three yars 'afore mee tryall, it war recorded what Christian Trask, age 29 ond mothar o' five children, "being violently assaulted by the temptations of Satan, cut her own throte with a pair of sisers to the astonishment and grief of all, especially her most nere relations . . . death 3 June 1689."[38]

Minister John Hale later wrote what for a time, "We walked in the clouds, and could not see our way. And we have most cause to be humbled for error . . . which cannot be retrieved."

When Goodwife Christian Trask died, shee had a five-month ol' bairn. Mee wonder if shee didn't suffered from some kind o' dark moodiness related to the birth o' her bairn or even momentary insanity.

Severall persons who claimed they had long undergone many kinds o' miseries at mee hands, now stepped to the bar. Each o' mee neighbors had all drawn up depositions against mee accordin'

Bridget holding Goody Whatford's face down in water

Illustration by Bryce Lowry

to legalities. May mee give a harin' to the legislation called "Body of Liberties," which war ratified by our representatives in 1641. It states what thar needs to be two eyewitnesses to every crime to convict a person. This piece o' lawe war overlooked by the Court o' Oyer ond Terminer. In each o' mee depositions, it war only the one afflicted person who supposedly witnessed a crime bein' committed by mee spectre.

Goody Whatford v. Bridget Bishop

In 1682, a Goody Whatford accused mee o' stealin' a spoon ond received the rough side o' mee tongue for it. Sometime after, glowin' spectres o' meself come in the night ond pulled Goody Whatford from her bed to the beach. Shee claimed what as mee war in the act o' drownin' her, shee managed to call on God ond mee spectre fled. But evar since, shee had been distracted ond crazed what war a vexation to herself, ond all 'bout her.

Bridget kissing William Stacey

Illustration by Bryce Lowry

William Stacey v. Bridget Bishop

These slanderous charges against mee, by William Stacey in his deposition, made mee verie angrie. Mee thinks William Stacey mentioned his secret admiration 'cause it are hearsay what witches 'ave the power to turn the mind o' men to inordinate love. William Stacey o' the town o' Salem, aged 36 yars or thar'bouts, deposeth ond s'd:

> That about 14 years agone this Deponent was visited with the Small Pox, then Bridget Bishop did give him a visit and withal Professed a great Love for this Deponent in his affliction more than ordinary, at which this deponent admired some time after this Deponent was well the said Bishop got him to do some work for her for which she gave him three pence which seemed to [t]his Deponent as if it had been good money, but he had not gone not above 3 to 4 Rods before he Looked in his pocket where he put it for it, but could not find any, sometime

after this deponent met the said Bishop in the Street a-going to mill She asking this Deponent whether his father would grind her grist: he put it to the said Bishop why she asked: she answered because folks counted her a witch this Deponent made answer, he did not question but that his father would grind it: but being gone about 6 Rod from he[r]r the said Bishop, with a small load in his cart suddenly the Off wheel Plumped or Sunk down into a hole upon Plain ground, that this Deponent was forced to get one to help him get the wheel out afterwards this Deponent, went back to look for said hole where his wheel sunk in but could not find any hole, sometime after in the winter about midnight this deponent felt something between his lips Pressing hard against his teeth and withal was very cold insomuch that it did awake him so that he got up and sat upon his bed he at the same time seeing the said Bridget Bishop setting at the foot of the bed, being to his seeming it was then as light as if it had been day, or one in the said Bishop's shape, she having then a black cap and a black hat and a Red coat with two [p]eaks of two colors then she the said Bishop or her shape clapped her coat close to her legs and hopped upon the bed and about the Room and then went out. Ond then it was dark, again some time after the said Bishop went to this Deponent and asked him whether that which he had reported was true that he had told to several, he answered that was true, and that it was she and bid her deny it if she dare, the said Bishop did not deny it and went away very angry and said that this Deponent did her more mischief than any other body, he ask why: she answered because folks would believe him before anybody Else: sometime after the Said Bishop threatened this Deponent and told him he was the occasion of bringing her out about the brass she stole; some time this deponent in a dark night was going to the Barn, who was, suddenly take or hoisted from the Ground and threw against a Stone wall, after that taken up againe a-throwed Down a bank at the end of his house; sometime after this deponent met the said Bishop by Isaac Stone's brick kiln after he had Passed by her this Deponent's horse stood still with a small load going up the hill soe that the horse striving to draw all his Years ond [the?] tackling flew in pieces and the cart fell down. Afterward this Deponent went to lift a Bag of Corn of about two bushels, but could not budge it with all his might. This Deponent hath met with several other of her Pranks at several times which would take up a great time to tell of. This Deponent doth verily believe that the said Bridget Bishop was Instrumental to his daughter Priscilla's death: about two years ago, the child was a likely Thriving child. And suddenly screeched out and so continued in an unusual manner for about a fortnight and so died in that lamentable manner.

Sworn Salem May the 30th 1692. Before us: John Hawthorne, Jonathan Corwin, Assistants

Jurant in Curia June 2d 1692[39]

'Afore wee made our move to Ipswich Post Road, mee ond mee daughter Christian war out in our garden movin' some dirt to plant out some herbs. Wee dug up a curious brass bearin'. Mee sent Christian to Edmund Dolbeare's pewter shop to inquire as to its purpose. Mr. Dolbeare asked Christian war shee got it. Shee explained ond added it must 'ave been lyin' around the garden for some time as it war sportin' some rust. A good long time after, December 1687 in fact, mee war issued a warrant for stealin' and sellin' this brass bearin' from Thomas Stacey's mill. As mee pieced the tale togethar, it seems what around July, a brass bearin' war taken from Thomas Stacey's mill. Hee went to Edmund Dolbeare's shop to pump him 'bout its waer'bouts. Mr. Dolbeare denied seein' sich a ring. When Thomas Stacey s'd it had been stolen from his mill, Dolbeare led him to his house ond thar it war. Stacey asked him waer hee got it. The path led back to mee, o' course. Thomas came to mee house ond asked mee to admit mee guilt ond apologize. Mee didn't take kindly to Stacey's accusation ond mee lett it fly at him. In March 1688, mee found meeself 'afore the Justice o' the Peace, John Hathorne, listenin' to Thomas Stacey testify what the "brass, which Bridget Bishop, the wife of Edward Bishop of Salem, sent by her daughter, Christian Mason, to Mister Dolbeare or Salem, is the very brass that was stolen out of the mill at Salem last year." After the miller testified 'bout the mill brass bearin', Stacey claimed his son war flung 'bout thar yard by an invisible presence. Mee husband Edward Sr. posted mee bond ond mee war released when Thomas Stacey stated what mee had approached him on mee knees weepin' for his forgiveness. This lye infuriated mee. Mee war never on mee marrow bones.

Thomas Stacey war William Stacey's father. Mee question to William 'bout his father grindin' mee wheat war based on a feelin' in mee bones what mee Puritan neighbors war whisperin' 'bout mee reputation ond counted mee a practicin' witch. Both Thomas ond William Stacey felt mee war guilty o' theft. They wanted to cook mee goose. William submitted a deposition o' witchcraft ond bore a trumped up testimony against mee at mee jury tryall.

This cart mishap war anothar made-up fish story what occurred in Summer Street, neer the foot o' Chestnut Street, waer the ground war then much lower than it is now. Mr. Stacy war ascendin' the street, on his way through High Street to his father's mill, at the South River when the supposed accident ond unexplainable dip disappearance took place. Mr. William Stacy forgot to mention in mee behalf, what mee war one o' the few people brave enough to visit him when hee had smallpox in 1678.

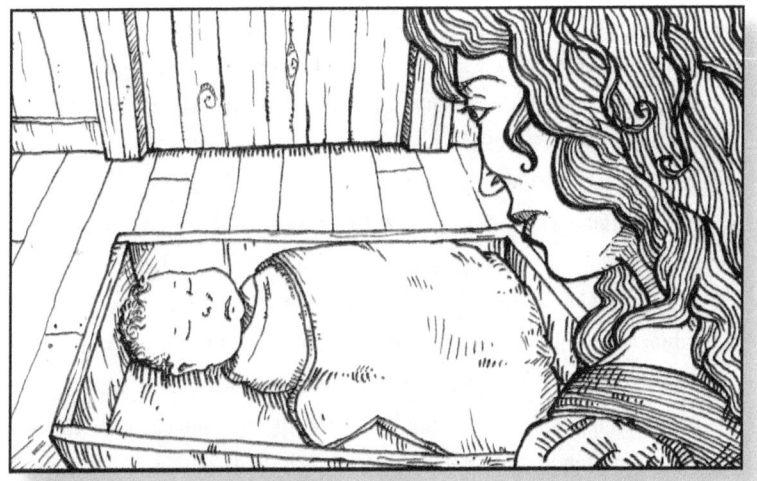

Bridget next to the baby crib

Illustration by Bryce Lowry

Mr. Stacy mentioned what hee war one o' the yeng men, hee bein' two ond 20 at the time, who admired mee. Some say at the time, mee smooth ond flatterin' manner gave mee power over him. 'Cause othar supposedly virtuous men had repelled mee amorous advances, it war believed mee sought vengeance by practicin' witchcraft on thar children. What hooey!

The illnesses ond death o' Samuel Gray's little boy, William Stacey's daughter Priscilla, ond Shattuck's epileptic son war attributed to mee castin' malefic spells. 'Afore the magistrates ond to those assembled in the court, mee war not only an enchantress, but also a murderess.

Samuel Gray v. Bridget Bishop

In 1690, mee war againe suspected by some o' witchcraft when a neighborhood child mysteriously fell sick. Samuel Gray told the court:

Samuel Gray o' Salem aged about 42 years Testifieth and saith that about 14 years ago he going to bed one Lord's Day at night, and after he had been asleep some time, he awakened and looking up, saw the house light as if a candle or candles were lighted in it and the door locked and that little fire there was Raked up he did then see a woman standing between the cradle in the Room and the bedside and seemed to look upon him so he did Rise up in his bed and it vanished or disappeared then he went to the door and found it locked and unlocking and opening the door he went to the entry door and looked out and then again did see the same woman he had a little before seen in the Room and in the same Garb she was in before then he said to her in the name of God, what do you Come for. Then she vanished away so he locked the door again and went to bed and between sleeping and waking he felt something Come to his mouth or lips cold and thereupon started and looked up and again did see the same woman with something between both her hands holding before his mouth upon which she moved and the Child in the cradle gave a great screech out, as if it was greatly hurt and she disappeared. And taking the child up could not quiet it in some hours from which time, the child that before was a very likely Thriving child did pine away and was never well although it Lived some months after, yet in a sad condition and so died: some time after within a week or less he did see the same woman in the same Garb and clothes that appeared to him as aforesaid, and although he knew not her nor her name before. Yet both by her Countenance and Garb doth testify that it was the same woman that they now call Bridget Bishop alias Oliver of Salem.

Sworn Salem May 30th 1692 Samuel Gray before me: John Hawthorne Assistant[40]

Durin' a visit to the home o' Samuel Gray, mee spent some time lookin' down at Mr. Gray's daughter, who war asleep in her crib. When the baby become ill ond died two weeks later,

Mr. Gray war distraught ond swore what mee had bewitcht his daughter. Mee can't explain the deaths or illness o' these children. Mee thinks somethin' war wrong w'th the babe unrelated to Gray's hallucination. Nor can mee explain him bein' tormented by mee spectre but mee 'ave been at odds w'th certain o' mee neighbors for some time. Hard tell what Gray on his death bed expressed his sorrow ond repentance for mee accusation ond s'd it war wholly groundless.

Mee unorthodox behavior produced fear ond sometimes terror in mee neighbors ond thar children ond mee disregard for the decorum o' the times brung mee noe good for naught. Mee war a thrice-married, fairly attractive, middle-aged woman. For some reason, men war attracted to mee ond some felt mee had power over the imaginations o' men. Mee admit mee war a bit o' a cock tease. Playful flirtin' war an amusement mee enjoyed. Against Puritan teachin's, mee wore red clothin'. Many o' mee neighbors thought mee dressed above mee social position. Mee loved shiny, silk cloth ond puffed sleeves what didn't cover the full length o' mee arms. Maybe it war mee flair for bright ond colorful, showy cloths or mee showin' off mee body to good advantage, what loosened the tongues o' gossip. Ye war what yer neighbors s'd ye war. Mee assets war over 200 pounds, soe accordin' to Puritan lawe, mee war justified in wearin' adornments sich as silk ond laces. When mee prosperity ond mee wealth come a rollin' in, mee used it to puck up mee hats, cloths, ond mee petticoats. Jealous women who lived all around mee played thar part in this witch hunt by spreadin' gossip throughout our small intimate community. In mee opinion, these women needed a gossip's bridle in thar mouths. In mee taverns, gossip is as common as drink. It travels from man to man, then to thar homes, parents to parents, then out to our community, neighbor to neighbor. Gossip war a destructive player in the witch tryalls, as rumor war taken as truth, ond then war given as evidence in the court proceedin's. Gossip gave the accusers slanderous information what they then credited to a person's spectre.

Gossip 'bout mee appearance don't bothar mee. Hats war mee downfall w'th mee hayr visible to all, curlin' down from a topknot to caress mee cheeks. Mee most pleasant time o' the day war sitten at mee glass frigerlin', curlin', ond layin' out mee hayr. Mee favorite toppin' war a black cap ond a black hat. Mee loved mee black skirt w'th a red paragon bodice, bordered ond looped w'th different-colored threads ond laces. Mee wore it on the day the magistrates dragged mee to gaole. The local Puritan ministers never tired o preachin' 'bout pride in cloths ond haryr. The theocracy felt wearin' long haryr war after the mode o' heathen Indians ond ruffians. A Puritan man's hayr shouldn't lye over the neck ond Puritan women war to cut thar hayr straight across thar foreheads ond cover 'em in public. 'Em ol' Puritans had rules for everie aspect o' life.

Mee warn't the only woman in the colonies to love dashy cloths. In the yar 1676, just northwest o' mee, in Northampton, Massachusetts, a yeng women wore a silk hood. Hannah Lyman war arrested 'cause the Puritans claimed what shee wore the hood in a flontin', offensive manner. Mee gave her a huzzah when mee hard shee appeared in court wearin' her displeasin' dudds. Her defiance o' Puritan restrictions war just the beginnin' o' her progressive aims for women. As the first principal o' Vassar College, shee worked to promote ambition ond independence in women. The Puritan colonists brung from mothar England lawes to suppress excess in cloths. These lawes mirrored Puritan leaders' detest ond dislike o' men ond women like meeself who achieved economic success ond tharby could afford to wear the fashion ond luxury items o' gentlemen ond gentlewomen. Mee set forth below, an example o' one o' the Puritan lawes for cloths. "In 1634, the Puritan governors of Massachusetts passed a sumptuary law forbidding the colonists from making or buying any clothing with lace, gold thread, embroidery, or ruffs. Puritans regarded fashionable clothing as a 'snare and sign of the devil.' Other unsuitable items included: large, decorative shoe ornaments; beaver fur hats; thick garters; perfumed gloves; showy feathered hats; and multiple rings or pearl necklaces."[41]

Sich legislation hardly seemed to 've been necessary for mee somber Puritan farmer neighbors. Women o' lower rank war not to dress above thar station ond war forbidden bright colors, silk, ribans, ruffles, ond scarves. Puritans believed what ranks o' society war divinely predestined—God had already decided. The upper class could reflect thar chosen status by the cloths they wore. 'Cause thar war only a few dyes available, most o' the lower class wore cloths made wool or cild in brown, dull green, black, white, or brownish yellow. A modest farmer woman wouldn't wear her hayr loose ond her dress wouldn't 've sleeves what would reveal the nakedness o' her arms. Under

commonwealth lawe, men ond women couldn't wear cloth o'
the upper class unless thar estate war valued at 200 pounds
or more. If ye violated this lawe, ye war fyned ten shillin's. It
war voiced around what if ye couldn't tell a maidservant from
a highbarn lady, then the fabric o' society war comin' apart.
The darin' new fashion, popular amang the upper classes, war
short sleeves. In spite o' these Puritan lawes, mee loved stylish,
elegant, fyne clothin'. Mee war a New England merchant ond
mee desired the civilest fashion now in use like the rest o' the
good dames in mothar England who wore bright colors, velvet,
silk scarves, ond lace ruffles. In our mothar country, fashion war
visual evidence o' yer rank in society. Mee ordinary had made
mee plump in the pocket by local standards ond mee desired to
be recognized as a businesswoman ond property owner o' high
distinction by the way mee decked out.

Although the Puritan Church did in fact preach simplicity
o' dress, in 1692, this restriction war widely ignored by the
upper-class flock what counted prosperity as an outward sign
o' God's favor ond fyne clothin' as a symbol. Mee disdain for
plain ond dull-colored dresses war just anothar reason Cotton
Mather war eager to reinforce the neglected Puritan dress codes
ond make mee a scrutinee 'afore mee peers. Mee rebellious,
nonconformist practices war shunned by the Puritan leaders
who then ruled Massachusetts Bay w'th an iron hand. When the
yeng girls accused mee o' bein' a witch, few people o' Salem
war surprised. Most, in fact, had long ago concluded what
mee war a witch ond war glad to take out o' the way anothar
undesirable citizen.

Lett mee take a recess in mee tryall to tell mee reader 'bout how the cat bit its own tail.

The first Puritan settlers who arrived in the New World war led by religious, visionary, theocratic men who had a two-fold mission: 1) to establish a city on a hill and 2) to subdue the wilderness ond make it productive. The saints war taught what God gives increase o' every sort ond Puritan ministers war the avenue through which the saints approached ond received acceptance o' God ond blessin's on thar chattle, land, ond livestock. All aspects o' life revolved around the congregation. The Puritan theocracy war the portal for the saints to seek God's benevolence ond blessin's upon thar efforts ond prosperity for thar communities. In a way, the theocracy established a feelin' o' individual helplessness ond dependence upon 'em as the mediator 'tween God. Keepin' this in mind, wee need to look at thar second mission . . . to subdue the wilderness. The Puritan ministers preached work ethic what conquerin' the land would be a long, bruisin' haul, ond an uphill battle against nature. Tamin' the wilderness would demand hard work. 'Tween 1628 and 1692, two generations o' farmin' for profit began to lessen thar dependence on God for prosperity. Seekin' God's generosity ond goodwill become lax ond less important to 'em than in the past. Saints now become citizens who war less dependent upon thar spiritual leaders to arbitrate w'th God for thar prosperity. Citizens awakened to the fact what thar back-breakin' labor had achieved 'em progression ond wealth. Thar now war a lower class o' citizens who had opportunity to rise 'bove thar station. The Puritan middle class citizens began to focus on material gains ond forgot spiritual needs. As communities began to spread away from the central core, Puritan ministers, still seekin' to maintain thar city upon the hill, war the helpless ones. Local ministers could noe longer watch ond control daily livin'. Puritan ministers war jealous o' thar ancient privileges. In order to bring 'em back into the fold, the Puritan theocracy in the colonies needed a scheme, to strike fear into thar citizens whose financial gains had made 'em worldlier. Puritan ministers preached from thar pulpits what God war displeased w'th thar worldliness ond war punishin' 'em by allowin' demons to use thar supernatural powers to hurt othars, cause epidemics, famine, earthquakes, ond othar natural disasters. In the end, the cat, the Puritan work ethic, bit its own tail, progress ond prosperity.

Two o' the depositions against mee mention mee fynery. They war now allowed to be rolled out. Samuel Shattuck war a Quaker ond the town hatter ond dyer. Wearin' fashionable ond vain, stylish apparel war incomprehensible to a simple Quaker. Hee believed women who loved natty ond colorful cloths war a sign o' the evil one.

Samuel Shattuck v. Bridget Bishop

Mee cockish lifestyle ond red clothin' war anothar snare ond sign o' the devill. Samuel Shattuck owned a house on the south side o' Essex Street, opposite the western entrance to the grounds o' the North Church in Salem Town. 'Afore removin' to Ipswitch Post Road, mee war in the habit o' callin' on Samuel Shattuck, who war a hatter ond dyer. Mee would take sundry

Bridget attacks a stranger with a spade
Illustration by Bryce Lowry

pieces o' lace ond material to his dye house to be colored. In his deposition, Mr. Shattuck mentioned what these "shapes and dimensions were entirely outside of [his] conceptions of what could be needed in the wardrobe, or for the toilet, of a plain and honest woman." Mee Quaker neighbor Shattuck had s'd nothin' 'bout the cut o' the laces mee brung him for dyein', only "that the pieces were too small to be of any use." It would seem what hee war inferrin' what mee trimmin' war too small to be worn by a human bein'. Mr. Shattuck stated what I treated him ond his family "politely" ond in a "kindly manner." But after his imaginations war wrought up to a high point, hee drafted a deposition against mee. In his deposition wrighten by him ond signed ond sworn in court by heeself ond wife, hee accused mee o' bedevillin' his child w'th the evil hand o' witchcraft.

Samuel Shattuck aged 41 years testifieth that in the year 1680, Bridget Oliver formerly wife to old Goodman Oliver, now wife to Edward Bishop did come to my house pretending to buy an old hogshead which though I asked very little for and for all her pretended want She went away without it and Sundry other times she came in a Smooth flattering manner in very Slightly Errands: we have thought Since on purpose to work mischief: at or very near this time our Eldest Child who promised as much and understanding, both by countenance and actions as any other children of his years: was taken in a very dropping condition, and as she came oftener to the house he grew worse and worse: as he could be standing at the door would fall out and bruise his face upon a great step stone as if he had been thrust out by an invisible hand oftentimes falling and hitting his face against the sides of the house, bruising his face in a very miserable manner. After this the abovesaid Oliver brought me a pair of sleeves to dye and after that Sundry pieces of lace Some of which were So Short that I could not judge them fit for any use: she paid me two pence for dyeing them which two pence I gave to Henry Williams which lived with me he told me [he] put it in a purse among some of the money which he locked up in a box and that the purse and money was gone out of the box he could not tell how: and never found it after. Just after the dyeing of these things this child taken in a terrible fit: his mouth and eyes drawn aside and gasped in such a manner as if he was upon the point of death: after this he grew worse in his fits and out of them would be almost always crying that for many months he would be crying till nature's strength was spent and then would fall asleep and then awake and fall to crying and moaning: that his very countenance did bespeak compassion: And at length we perceived his understanding decayed. So that we feared (as it has Since proved) that he would be quite bereft of his wits, for Ever Since he has been Stupefied and void of reason his fits still following of him: after he had been in this kind of Sickness Some time he has gone into the garden and has got upon a board of an inch thick which lay flat upon the ground and we have called him: he would come to the Edge of the board and hold out his hand and make as if he would come but Could not till he was helped off the board: other times when he has got upon a board as aforesaid my wife has said she has offered him a Cake and money to Come to her and he has held out his hand and reached after it but Could not Come till he had been helped off the board: by which I judge some enchantment kept him on, about 17 or 18 months after the first of this illness there came a stranger to my house and pitied this Child and said among other words we are all born Some to one thing and Some to another: I asked him and what do you say this child is born to he replied he is born to be bewitched and is bewitched. I told him he did not know he said he did know and said to me you have a neighbor that lives not far off that is a witch. I told him we had no neighbor but what was honest folk, he replied you have a neighbor that is a witch and she has had a falling out with your wife and said in her heart your wife is a proud woman, and she would bring down her pride in this Child: I paused in myself and did remember that my wife had told me that Goodwife Oliver had been at the house and spoke to her to beat Henry Williams that lived with us and that she went away muttering and she thought threating: but little before our child was taken ill: I told the aforesaid Stranger that there was such a woman as he spoke of: he asked where she lived for he would go and see her if he knew how: I gave him money and bid him ask her for a pot of Syder away he went and I sent my boy with him, who after a short time, both returned; the boy's face bleeding and I asked what was the matter they told me the man knocked at the door and Goody Oliver came to the door and asked the Stranger what he would have, he told her a pot of syder. She said he should have none and bid him get out and took up a spade and made him go out She followed him and when she came without the porch She saw my boy and ran to him and scratched his face and made it bleed: Saying to him thou rogue what dost thou bring this fellow here to plague me: now this man did say before he went: that he would fetch blood of her, but Goodwife Bishop were not to be taken in. Not only did she avoid having her face scratched; she had scratched the child's face. And ever Since this child hath been followed with grievous fits as if he would never recover more: his head and Eyes drawn aside so as if they would never Come to rights more: lying as if he were in a manner dead falling anywhere Either into fire or water, if he be not constantly looked to, and generally in such an uneasy and restless frame almost always running to ond fro acting so Strange that I cannot judge otherwise but that he is bewitched and by these circumstances do believe that the aforesaid Bridget Oliver now called Bishop is the cause of it and it has been the judgment of Doctors Such as lived here and surgeons that he is under an Evil hand of witchcraft.

Samuel Shattuck and Sarah Shattuck affirmeth upon the oath they have taken to the truth of what is above written. Stephen Sewall, Assistant Clerk, Jurat in Curia June 2d 1692.[42]

When local surgeons couldn't help, Samuel Shattuck took his boy to England for a cure. Mee had an argument w'th Mrs. Shattuck over some medics what mee had recommended for thar sickly child. In Mr. Shattuck's mind, judgement o' doctors ond these incidents war proof mee had bewitcht his boy. To boot, this stranger who come to Goodman Shattuck war lookin' to make trouble for mee. Hee just pretended to 'ave pity for the sick child. Mee had a hunch what this stranger war up to doe mee 'arm when hee approached mee real close ond asked mee for a pot o' syder. For yars, secret scuttlebutt what had been passed around rumored what securin' someone's personal property ond then deliverin' it to magical abuse war a black arts technique. Mee waren't taken in. Mee picked up a tool what war close ond chased him off mee land. Why any o' ye good matrons would doe the same thing if a stranger come to 'arm ye at yer door. Later, in the gaole, mee larned what this stranger war thar to obtain mee blood by scratchin' mee face soe mee blood could be used to brake a spell on the Shattuck's boy.

Alsoe, in this deposition, the Shattucks accused mee o' stealin' money from thar house. After sewin' some dyed lace on one o' mee dresses, mee paid Mr. Shattuck two pence. Hee gave the money to Henry Williams, a man who lived w'th 'em. Williams claims hee placed the money in a purse ond later in a heavy wooden box which hee locked. When Samuel opened the box, the purse ond money war gone out o' the box. Mr. Shattuck couldn't tell how. The money war never found. Mee hinted to Goodwife Shattuck what Henry had stolen the purse ond money ond should be whipped.

Bein' a Quaker, his appreciation o' mee flashy clothin' styles war biased. Superstitious Mr. Shattuck, judgin' what the sundry pieces o' lace war short ond not fit for any use, warn't above believin' what mee war goin' to used these small pieces o' lace to dress a witch's poppet; as a poppet is often dressed in materials from the dresses worn by a victim.

As mee marked, the age-old lawes o' mothar England had declared witchcraft to be a crime against the monarchy, God's representatives. God's word alsoe declared witchcraft punishable. But in Massachusetts Bay Colony in the 1660s ond 1670s, noe one who war accused o' malefic acts war prosecuted. These cases war handled entirely by local ministers ond legal actions ond punishment war never pursued. Why? 'Cause witchcraft, durin' those yars, war noe longer an offence against colonial lawe due to noe charter. When mee tryall began, June 1692, Massachusetts Bay Colony still had noe colony or provincial lawe penalizin' the crime o' witchcraft. In order for the magistrates to conduct tryalls for those o' us who war waitin' in the gaoles, they would 'ave to declare the ol' statute o' King James I, enacted early 1600s, in force. 'Afore the special Court o' Oyer ond Terminer dismissed, the old colony lawe, which made witchin' a capital offence, "were revived with the other local laws, as they were called, and made a law of the province." On 8 June 1692, just two days 'afore mee execution, Massachusetts General Court reinstated the old colonial lawe, thus revivin' the lawe makin' witchcraft a capital felonious offence, punishable by death.

All eight o' the New England justice commissioners warn't noted for thar legal larnin', as none war trained advocates. Alsoe, thar is noe record o' the doin's o' this special court to be found, ond the only information respectin' 'em is obtained in brief ond imperfect statements o' wrighters o' the time. Some o' the depositions sworn to in court are on file, but w'thout givin', in many instances, the date when they war offered in the tryalls. Only a small part o' these war preserved for mee ancestor to investigate. Mee speculate these ol' record books went missin' 'cause the government wanted to marke out the memory o' this tumultuous times.

As the mornin' skipped past into afternoon, mee jury box war content to accept evidence presented thus far in wrighten deposition signed by a large number o' claimants who swore to 'em in court, as bein' truth. It war mee point o' view these declarations war verie grave lyes what war kindled by fallouts ond quarrels w'th mee person, war fired up by those green-eyed monsters greed ond envy, ond war inflamed by mee Puritan ministers, urgin' mee neighbors to point fingers.

On top o' mee bein' tagged w'th the title o' witch since 1680, the court war able to gather severall more different kinds o' evidence against mee what war submitted by mee local enemies. Mee history o' problematic relationships w'th mee neighbors brung forth many more villains ond one deposition followed anothar. As mee marked, mee war soe far charged w'th mysterious illness, murder, attempted drownin', movin' a wagon, throwin' a person through the air, pressin' down upon mee victim, ond scratchin' the face o' a neighborhood child. These statements are quite a tally on mee trim.

Past enemies remembered what scary things happened to 'em after argument w'th mee wharin mee cursed. Mee arn't a gospel woman ond mee doe curse. Mee flashy taste in dress ond mee smooth, flatterin' manner w'th men marked mee as a wanton woman who indulged in the fashions o' the day. As mee stated earlier, Cotton Mather wanted an example ond remarked to the court 'bout mee depositions, "There was little occasion to prove the witchcraft, it being evident and notorious to all beholders."

Although Cotton Mather war ill ond did not attend mee tryall, his advice pertainin' to witchcraft war sought ond heeded by the justices o' the Court o' Oyer ond Terminer. His persona dominated the courtroom ond his pious position pressed down on the minds o' the bench. It war disclosed to mee what Cotton Mather war concerned what the crowded courtroom war amused—mum for that. Mee would like to share his views o' the evidence against mee taken from his notes, along w'th othar evidence at mee tryall what war regarded as weighty ond conclusive proof o' mee guilt.

From Mather's notes published October 1692:

THE TRYAL OF BRIDGET BISHOP, alias Oliver, at the Court of Oyer and Terminer, Held at Salem, 2 June 1692: "She was indicted for Bewitching of several Persons in the Neighbourhood, the Indictment being drawn up, according to the Form in such Cases usual. And pleading, Not Guilty, there were brought in several persons, who had long undergone many kinds of Miseries, which war prenaturally inflicted, and generally ascribed unto an horrible Witchcraft. There were little occasion to prove the Witchcraft, it being evident and notorious to all holders. Now to fix the Witchcraft on the Prisoner at the Bar, the first thing used, was the Testimony of the Bewitcht."[43]

If ye war to 'ave sat in on mee tryall, ye wouldn't 'ave recognized it as a tryall ye 'ave today. Wee didn't 'ave the lawyers o' the banter 'tween lawyers what ye 'ave. Thar war the straight deposition o' the accusers ond then meself tryein' to defend meself.

Depositions revealin' superhuman acts ond spectral evidence war presented by mee suspicious neighbors John Cook, Samuel Gray, William Stacey, ond Richard Coman. These are men who openly disliked mee ond w'th whom mee had quarreled.

John Cook Jr. v. Bridget Bishop

John Cook Sr. lived on the south side o' the street, directly opposite the eastern entrance to the grounds o' the North Church, on its present site. One o' Cook's sons, John, age 18, testified:

Bridget striking John Cook in bed

Illustration by Bryce Lowry

About five or six years ago, one morning about sun rising, as I was in bed before I rose I saw Goodwife Bishop, alias Oliver, Stand in the chamber by the window and she looked on me and grinned on me and presently struck me on the side the head which did very much hurt me and then I saw he[r] go out under the End window at a little Crevice about so big as I could thrust my hand into. I saw her again the same day which was the Sabbath Day about noon walk across the Room and having at the time an apple in me hand it flew out of me hand into me mother's lap who sat six or eight foot distance from me and then she disappeared and though me mother and several others were in the same room yet they affirmed they saw her not.

John Cook appeared before us the Jurors of Inquest and did own this to be his testimony on the oath that he hath taken: this 2 day of June; 92. Jurat in Curia.[44]

Mee quarrelsome, aggressive behavior in mee commercial transaction ond mee petty squabble w'th mee neighbor John Bly produced anothar deposition against mee.

John Bly Sr. and Rebecca Bly
v. Bridget Bishop

John Bly's house was on a lot contiguous to the rear of Cook's fronting on Summer Street. Bly and his wife Rebecca had a difficulty with me in reference to payment for a hog they had bought of me. Me husband Edward Bishop sold a sow to John Bly. Unbeknown to me, Edward told Mr. Bly to pay the money to a third person to whom he owed money. When I learned of this agreement, I become livid with rage and I come to their home to collect payment. We quarreled for some time. After me temper cooled, I allowed Bly to take the sow. For revenge for imagined wrong done, John Bly Sr. and Rebecca Bly his wife of Salem, both Testify and say that said John Bly Bought a Sow of Edwd. Bishop of Salem Sawyer and by agreement with said Bishop was to pay the price agreed upon unto Lt. Jeremiah Neale of Salem. And Bridget the wife of Said Edward Bishop because she could not have the money or value agreed for paid unto her, she came to the house of the deponents in Salem and Quarreled with them about it, soon after which the sow having pigged, she was taken with strange fits Jumping up and knocking her head against the fence and seemed blind and deaf and would not Eat neighter Lett her pigs suck but foamed at the mouth which Goody Henderson hearing of said she believed she was overlooked and that they had their cattle ill in such a manner at the eastward when she lived there and used to cure them by giving of them, Red Okra ond Milk which we also gave the sow: Quickly after eating of which she grew Better and then for the space of near two hours together she getting into the street did set off Jumping and running between the house of said deponents and said Bishops as if she were stark mad, and after that was well again and we did then apprehend or judge and do still that said Bishop had bewitched said sow. Jurat in Curia.[45]

Once againe, after arguments w'th mee, mee neighbor testified o' alarmin' things happenin' to 'em or thar animals. Mee knows it war common as an ol' shoe for farmers to settle a score by turnin' thar swine out in thar neighbors fields. Mee think this sow got some bad corn. These ol' animal tales war like mee lamb to the slaughter.

Almost eight yars had passed since mee had this dispute w'th John Lowder. Mee must admit, hee war a man o' noe notice ond mee can't remember this Lowder, although wee war neighbors. John Lowder (Londer), a 32-yar-old laborer, worked for Bartholomew Gedney, whose farm ond orchard abutted ours. Mr. Lowder complained to mee what mee chickens war causin' a great deal o' damage to Gedney's garden ond orchard ond asked mee to keep 'em out. After a long violent argument, mee agreed to keep 'em penned. Mr. Lowder testified what:

John Lowder (Londer) v. Bridget Bishop

About seven or eight years since, I then living with Mrs. John Gedney in Salem and having had some controversy with Bridget Bishop, the wife of Edw. Bishop of Salem Sawyer about her fowls that used to come into our orchard or garden. Some little time after which, I going well to bed: about the dead of the night felt a great weight upon my Breast and awakening looked and, it being bright moon-light did clearly see said Bridget Bishop or her likeness sitting upon my stomach and putting my arms off of the bed to free myself from that great oppression, she presently laid hold of my throat and almost choked me and I had no strength or power in my hands to resist or help myself and in this condition she held me to almost day. Some time after this my Mistress Susannah Bedney was

Bridget choking John Lowder in bed

Illustration by Bryce Lowry

in our orchard and I was then with her and said Bridget Bishop being then in her orchard which was next adjoining to ours, my Mistress told said Bridget what I said or affirmed that she came one night and sat upon mey breast as aforesaid, which she denied and I affirmed to her face to be true and what I did plainly see her, upon which discourse with her she threatened me. And some time after that I being not very well stayed at home on a Lord's day and on the Afternoon of said day the doors being shut I did see a black pig in the Room Coming towards me so I went towards it to kick it and it vanished away. Immediately after I saw down in an narrow Bar And did see a black thing jump into the window. And came and stood Just before my face upon the bar the body of it looked like a monkey only the feet were like a Cock's feet with claw and the face somewhat more like a man's than a monkey and I being greatly affrighted not being able to speak or help myself by reason of fear I suppose, so the thing spoke to me and said I am a Messenger sent to you for I understand you are troubled in mind and of [if] and if you will be ruled by me you shall want for nothing in this world, upon which I endeavored to clap my hands upon it, and said, you devil I will kill you but could feel no substance and it jumped out of the window again, and Immediately came in by the porch although the doors were shut and said you had Better take my Counsel, whereupon I struck at it with a stick but struck the Groundsill and broke the stick, but felt no substance and that arm with which I struck was presently disenabled, then it vanished away, and I opened the back door ond Went out ond going towards the house End I Espied said Bridget Bishop in her orchard going towards her house and seeing her had no power to set one foot forward but returned in again and going to shut the door, I again did see that or the like creature that I before did see within doors in such a posture as it seemed to be agoing to fly at me, upon which I cried out; the whole armor of God to be between me and you. Soe it sprang back and flew over the apple-tree flinging the dust with its feet against my stomach, upon which I was struck dumb and so continued for about three days' time and also shook many of the apples off from the tree which it flew over. John Lowder appeared before us this 2 day of June 1692 and on the oath that he had taken did own this testimony to be the truth before us the Juries of Inquest. Jurat in Curia[46]

Mee can't help but say what the devill didn't 'ave to work verie hard at overthrowin' the Puritan church ond its people. The townspeople war accomplishin' what verie dramatically w'thout any labor on the devill's part. The swellin' frenzy against mee become even worse as othar depositions followed:

Susanna Sheldon v. Bridget Bishop

Susanna Sheldon aged about 18 years who testifieth and saith that on the 2 June 1692 I saw the apparition of Bridget Bishop and Immediately appeared two little children and said that they were

Thomas two twins and told Bridget Bishop to her face that she had murdered them in setting them into fits whereof they died.[47]

On the fourth day at night came Goody Oliver and Mrs. English and Goodman Cory and a black man with a high crowned hat with books in their hands Goody Oliver bade me touch her book I would not I did not know her name she told me her name was Goody Oliver and bid me touch her book now I bid her tell me how long she had been a witch she told me had been a witch above 20 years than there come a stretched snake creeping over her shoulder and creep into her bosom. Mrs. English had a yellow bird in her bosom and Goodman Cory had two turcles [turtles?] hang to his coat and he opened his bosom and put his turcles to his breast and gave them suck then . . . Goody Oliver kneeled down before the black man and went to prayer, and then the black man told me Goody Oliver had been a witch 20 years and an half then they all set to biting me and so went away.

The sixth day at night came Goody Oliver and Mrs. English Goodman Cory and his wife. Goodwife Cory presented me a book I refused it and asked her where she lived, she told me she lived in Boston prison then she pulled out her breast and the black man gave her a thing like a black pig it had no hairs on it and she put it to her breast ond gave it suck and when it had sucked one breast she put it to the other and gave it suck there. Then she gave it to the black man then they went to prayer to the black man, then Goody Oliver told me she had killed four women two of them were the fosters' wives and John Trask's wife and did not name the other.[48]

Mee war accused o' bewitchin' mee first husband, Goodman Warsselbe, to death. Now what's a load o' ol' nonsense. Goodman Warsselbe may 'ave been tied to mee apron strings, but never did mee 'arm him. Mee refused to be subservient to mee second husband. In a moment of rage, Thomas Oliver would often call mee an ol' witch when wee argued. Mee am weel aware what mee husbands in thar moments o' temper called mee a witchy, bitchy hag. Mee war alsoe known for mee strong-minded temper. From time to time, mee had fistfights w'th mee husband, Edward Bishop Sr. A few times, mee landed a wallop to his noodle. At mee 1692 tryall, mee third husband, Edward Bishop Sr., testified what: "The devil did come bodily unto her, and that she was familiar with the devil, and she sat up all night long with the devil." Mee know Edward Bishop war a jerry sneak, but to contribute by his aide to mee conviction ond death near broke mee will—sich a spiteful, double-dealin', dirty, deed. Puritan women might express thar opinions in private, at home, but in public matters, they had noe speakin' right ond noe vote. Puritans felt thar women needed to be dominated by thar menfolk. Mee admit what mee spoke mee mind at home ond in public ond wore the trousers in mee family. Mee treatment o' mee husbands did not fit in w'th the Puritan expectations o' a wife or women. Mee guess mee disloyal, dishonest Edward got his final word as exhibited by this fairy tale hee told in his slurrey statement.

Elizabeth Balch v. Bridget Bishop

The deposition of Elizabeth Balch of Beverly Aged About Eight and 30 years and wife unto Benjamin Balch Jr. This deponent testifieth hereby and saith that she being at Salem on the very day that Captain George Corwin was buried and in the evening of said day coming from said Salem unto said Beverly on horse back with her sister . . . Riding behind and as they were Riding as before and were come so far as Crane River Common So-called Edward Bishop and his wife overtook us (on horseback) who are both in u in prison under Suspicion of witchcraft and had some words of Difference it seemed unto us. said

Bishop riding into the brook, pretty hastily she finding fault with his so doing and said that he would throw her into the water or words to that purpose, said Bishop answered her that it was no matter if he Did or words to that effect: and so we rode along all together towards Beverly and she blamed her husband for Riding so fast and that he would do her a mischief or words to that purpose, and he answard her it was no matter what was done unto her or words to that purpose, And then said Bishop directed his speech unto us as we Rode along and said that she had been a bad wife unto him ever since they were married reckoned up many of her miscarriages towards him, but now of late she was worse than ever she had been unto him before (and that the devil did come bodily unto her and that she was familiar with the devil and that she sat up all the night Long with the devil) or words to that purpose and with such kind of discourse he filled up the time until we came to said Bishop's dwelling house and this Deponent did reprove said Bishop for speaking in such a manner unto his wife said Bishop Answered it was nothing but what was truth and said Bishop's wife made very little reply to all her husband's discourse During all the time we were with them and further saith not. The mark E of Elizabeth Balch. Her Answer. The mark A of Abigail Walden. If it be so you had need pray, for me.[49]

This denouncin' o' one anothar certainly war purgin' our community all by itself. In the witch hunt, husbands suddenly suspected wives, ond wives wondered 'bout husbands. Neighbors made depositions based on circumstances considered odd or in violation o' custom. Mee knows mee marriage warn't w'thout contentions. Mee war vexed w'th Edward for expressin' his disregard for mee in front o' othar matrons. In describin' mee faults, that ol' scalawag used some pretty doomin' language.

Certain othar persons war terrified o' mee ond had indelible hallucination o' mee spectre as a result o' this terror.

Richard Coman v. Bridget Bishop

William ond Richard Coman war two o' mee neighbors.

Richard Coman aged about 32 years. Testifieth that Sometime about Eight years since I then being in bed with my wife at Salem, one fifth day of the week at night Either in the Latter end of May the Beginning of June, and a light burning in our Room I being awake, did then see Bridget Bishop of Salem alias Oliver come into the Room we lay in and two women more with her which two women were strangers to me I knew them not, but said Bishop came in her Red paragon Bodice and the rest of her clothing that she then usually did wear, and I knowing of her well also the garb she did use to go in did clearly and, plainly know her, and testified that as he locked the door of the house when he went to bed so he found it afterwards when he did rise, and quickly after they appeared the light was out. And the Curtains at the foot of the bed opened where I did see her and presently came And lay upon my Breast or body and so oppressed him that he could not speak nor stir no not so much as to awake his wife although he Endeavored much so to do it; the next night they all appeared Again in like manner and she said Bishop alias Oliver took hold of him by the throat and almost hauled him out of the bed, the Saturday night following: I having been that day telling of what I had seen and how it suffered the two nights before, my kinsman William Coman told me he would stay with me and Lodge with me and see if they would come again and advised me to lay my sword on thurt [athwart] my body, quickly after we went to bed that said night and both, well awake and discoursing together in came all the three women again and said Bishop was the first as she had been the other two night so I told him. Wm hear they be all come again and he was Immediately struck Speechless and could not move hand or foot and Immediately they got hold of my sword and strived to take it from me but I held so fast as they did not get it away and I had then Liberty of speech and Called Wm, also my wife and Sarah Phillips

John Bly Sr. finds a poppet in the cellar wall

Illustration by Bryce Lowry

that lay with my wife. Who all told me afterwards they heard me but had not power to speak or stir afterwards. And the first that spoke was Sarah Phillips and said in the name of God Goodman Coman what is the Matter with you, so they all vanished away. Sworn Salem June 2, 1692. Before me John Hawthorne. Jurat in Curia[50]

'Afore movin' to our farm along the Ipswich Post Road, Edward Bishop Sr. ond mee made some alterations on mee Salem Town estate. Wee employed John Bly Sr. ond William Bly, then age 15, both o' Salem, in the exercise o' removin' the cellar wall o' our old house. This disclosure by John ond William Bly war the final blow what corked mee conviction ond mee death warrant.

John Bly Sr. v. Bridget Bishop

June 2d 1692. John Bly Sr. aged about 57 years and William Bly aged about 15 years both of Salem Testifieth and saith that being Employed by Bridget Bishop alias Oliver of Salem to help take down the Cellar wall of The Old House she formerly Lived in we the said Deponents in holes in the said old wall belonging to the said Cellar found several puppets made up of Rags and hog's Bristles with headless pins in Them . . . with the points outward and this was about Seven years Last past.[51]

'Afore mee tryall, in an effort to find dolls for hard evidence, both o' mee houses, past ond present, war ransacked.

Accordin' to the *Malleus Maleficarum:*

A doll with pins in it is a classic charm of black magick, and burying it in a wall is still a technique of witches. Dolls were believed to represent the person whom the witch desired to afflict, and by sticking pins into those images the mischief were supposed to be mysteriously and safely accomplished. Whatever was done to the images was so the belief ran, would be duplicated in real life. Penetrating the figure's head with a pin would make the person it represented go mad, while driving one into the heart inflicted death either instantaneously or within a short time. Burying the figure meant that the victim would slowly and painfully waste away as the likeness itself rotted.[52]

Bly's false testimony knocked mee off mee fence. John Bly Sr.'s witness war a rude awakenin' o' ond unpleasant thought. Thar war more evidence against mee than mee reputation ond troubles w'th mee neighbors. Bly's grounds involved black magick. May mee reader better know, Bly's story war hookee walker. Mee know nothin' o' these poppets. They warn't in an image o' a person mee war seekin' revenge on. Ond to be sure, mee warn't seekin' a lover. Anyways, mee hard s'd what poppets when found, the spell war broken. More than this, at mee jury tryall, Sarah Churchill come to the bar ond claimed mee had brung three poppets w'th thorns stuck in 'em, in the images o' Ann Putnam, Mercy Lewis, ond Elizabeth Hubbard. All o' this war drivel. It war pure circumstantial evidence. Noe one had seen mee stick pins in the poppets or bury 'em in the wall. Durin' the time o' mee tryall, a black slave from Barbados, named Candy, war examined in a pre-tryall on evidence what shee had used poppets to inflict 'arm on some girls. Shee brung these poppets to the courtroom. One o' the poppets war put under water ond instantly one o' the girls felt shee war drownin' ond anothar o' the girls tryed to run to a river nearby to drown herself. For the justice commissioners, this Candy incident war confirmation o' the evil power o' poppets. Candy's poppet witchcraft war used as damnin' proof against mee. Although thar war noe poppets as evidence in mee tryall, John ond William Bly's deposition war incriminatin'. This evidence would 'ave put a nooze around mee neck in mothar England. The circumstantial evidence these witnesses s'd they found hidden behind the cellar wall war soe implicatin', it literally war the final straw what broke mee neck 'cause mee could give noe account o' 'em to the court what war reasonable or understandable. It war upon sich evidence as this what mee war sentenced.

After each o' the depositions war made known, mee insisted, "Mee am innocent. Mee know nothin' 'bout witchcraft, ond mee don't even know what a witch is." Mee never confessed to anythin' relatin' to witchcraft.

Thar war accounts o' othars on the table who had related they war inflicted by mee spectre or mee apparition. They warn't used, as the justices felt thar war noe need ond didn't ask for them.

The only survivin' evidence for mee defense war two depositions made 'afore mee tryall. Mee had a right to present a wrighten record from mee friends against mee accusers. The depositions attackin' the credibility o' the afflicted girls war signed by mee trusty trojans. Mee stepson, Edward Bishop Jr., ond his wife, Sarah, signed Mary Warren's confession o' false witness. While mee war in the Boston gaole, mee war mullin' things over w'th accused Mary Warren. Shee believed as mee what these girls war full o' the devill ond had framed mee w'th white lyes. It war at the same time mee friends, Mary ond Philip English war under mild containment in Boston's Arnolds gaole ond they hard Mary Warren's confessional song ond wrote thar own deposition. Somehow they war able to smuggle these depositions out o' the gaole to be read 'afore the Court o' Oyer ond Terminer. These depositions exposed the circle o' girls as bein' falsifiers, unstable, ond fakes. Mary ond her husband escaped just 'afore thar tryall ond piked off to New York. Sheriff Corwin snagged Phillip ond Mary's estate. What a pillagin', pinchin' pirate! As soon as mee war nabbed by this robber, mee lost mee civil rights, but not mee ordinary. Dibs from mee ordinary war able to pay up for mee gaole stay, barbies, vittles, arrest, ond court costs. But many o' the accused war w'thout scratch ond thar properties war seized by Sheriff George Corwin. Goods taken from mee friends, Mary ond Phillip English holdin's, totaled 1,183 pounds. If the court would 'ave allowed evidence in mee favor, mee courageous stepson Edward would 'ave testified, but hee war arrested durin' mee tryall. Chief Justice Stoughton wouldn't allow mee to use Mary's testimony in mee defense.

Mee raised mee head in hope what these last minute depositions would make a difference. Tears come to mee eyes as mee realized the true friendship o' these people. Mee continued to blub as mee recognized how they war riskin' bein' noozed by comin' to mee aide. The justices took little time deliberatin'. Justice Stoughton stated, "Those depositions were signed by four persons accused of witchcraft, were they not? I give small weight to that."

Againe as 'afore, mee had a blacken list. Murder, snakes creepin' over mee shoulder, layin' upon Goodman's breasts, ond losses mee neighbors' suffered in thar chattle ond poultry war accounted for to mee by mee betrayers. Testimonies o' the 'afore mentioned witch-pickers, who found mee body clear ond free o' a teat at the second examination, war convinced mee war a malefic witch. Thar war the condemnin' evidence against mee given by two workmen who claimed to 'ave found poppets w'th pins in 'em in the cellar wall o' mee home in Salem. All thar testimonies against mee, many o' which take in spectral evidence, war presented as sources o' mee witchcraft. Added upon these, war mee bein' caught in a lye at mee informal pre-tryall examination ond mee othar inconsistencies what probablie sealed mee fate. Bearin' false witness in judicial cases normally meritted a hole bein' burned in ye tongue. Ouch!

All o' this sundry actions, along w'th the constant screams ond seizures o' the accusin' girls, persuaded the eight-man jury what they possessed enough facts. The eight justice commissioners endorsed all the indictments ond depositions against mee. The justice commissioners returned a verdict ond pronounced mee guilty o' witchcraft ond condemned mee to twist. The court adjourned 'til 29 June 1692.

For the next few days, thar war legal buzzin' goin' on around the courthouse. 'Em ol' justice-commissioners had executed a judgement, but war this judgement legal under the present status o' Massachusetts lawe. Finally, as mee mentioned 'afore, on 8 June 1692, the General Court o' Massachusetts restored an old colonial lawe, which made witchin' a capital felonious offense, punishable by twistin'. Justice Stoughton, as actin' governor ond chief justice, now had the power to carry out mee sentence ond order mee to be executed.

Mee death warrant what follows is one o' two known to be in existence. A copy o' mee death warrant are preserved under glass in Salem Superior Court.

Death Warrant v. Bridget Bishop

To George Corwin gent High Sheriff o' the county o' Essex greeting. Whereas Bridget Bishop, alias Oliver, the wife of Edward Bishop of Salem in the county of Essex, Sawyer, at a speciall Court of Oyer and Terminer held at Salem the second Day of this instant month of June for the countyes of Essex' Middlesex' and Suffolk before William Stoughton Esq. and his Associates Justices of the said court was Indicted and arraigned upon five several Indictments for using, practicing, and exercising on the 19th day of April last past and divers other days and time before and after certain acts of Witchcraft in and upon the bodies of Abigail Williams, Ann Putnam Jr., Mercy Lewis, May Walcott, and Elizabeth Hubbard of Salem Village Singlewomen whereby their bodies were hurt afflicted pine consumed wasted and tormented contrary to the form of the Statute in that case made and provided. To which Indictment the said Bridget Bishop pleaded not guilty and for tryall thereof put herself upon God and her Country whereupon she was found guilty of the felonies and witchcraft whereof she stood Indicted and sentence of death accordingly passed against her as the Law, directs. Execution where of yet remains to be done. These are therefore the name of their Majesties William and Mary now King and Queen over England etc. to will and command you That upon Friday next being the Tenth day of this instant month of June between the hours of Eight and 12 in the aforenoon of the same day you safely conduct the said Bridget Bishop alias Oliver from their Majesties jail in Salem aforesaid to the place of Execution and there cause her to be hanged by the neck until she be dead, and of you doings herein make return to the Clerk of the said court and precept. and hereof you are not to fail at your peril. And this shall be your sufficient Warrant, Given under my hand and seal at Boston the Eighth day of June in the Fourth year of the reign of our Sovereign Lord and Lady William and Mary now King and Queen over England etc. Annoq Dom 1692. William Stoughton[53]

Weel thar now, mee, Bridget Bishop, war judged guilty o' witchery ond condemned to hang by mee neck 'til dead. Mee 'ave had mee day in court. Mee war told if mee repented, God may grant mee forgiveness ond war advised to confess mee sins for mee souls sake. When the verdict war read, mee turned to Judge Hathorne ond blasted, "If mee am a witch, ye'll soon know it." Tauntin' hecklers waited at the bottom o' the Salem courthouse stairs. They shoved mee as mee passed. One stranger stuck out his foot ond tripped mee. Mee tumbled head first, but the gaolers caught mee 'afore mee head hit the ground. Mee guess the gaolers wanted to save mee neck for mee noozin'. Mee warn't given the

three days for appeal 'afore mee execution what later defendants
war. Mee enemies ond the Puritan judicial system wanted mee
dead. Thomas Putnam sounded off for all o' 'em, "We want to
clear all Massachusetts of its witches."

After the verdict, whispered voices passed the word around
Salem gaole, Bridget war goin' to 'ave a hearty choke ond caper
sauce for breakfast. Cold chills went through the othar felons
ond the gaole walls seem to reel ond rock around us. On 9 June
1692, the night 'afore mee execution, an ominous silence fell
over the gaole. Mee thinks mee bunkies all had a wretched,
sleepless night. In the mornin', a large farm cart drew up 'afore
the small, filthy gaole on Prison Lane in Salem Town. George
Corwin, the sheriff, entered the gaole, knocked the iron pins out
o' the darbies 'bout mee legs ond took mee away. Freed o' mee
fetters, mee legs war lame from the leg chains ond mee hobbled
painfully through the dimly lighted gaole. Due to the crowded
conditions ond noe convenience for keepin' ourselves clean,
mee stench war whiffy. After eight days o' confinement in the
Salem pigsty, totterin' through the outer door into the open air
war verie invigoratin' to mee. Outside the gaole, a crowd had
gathard to see mee emerge from mee irons. A gaspin' sound, like
a sudden breeze, arose as mee appeared in the door. Mee hand
chains rattled as the sheriff prodded mee up the plank, placed to
form a ramp onto the cart floor. Just a few o' the chained gaole
prisoners had a view o' the outside through barred slots-like
windows. They war able to see Sheriff George Corwin push
mee into the horse-drawn cart ond force mee to stand soe the
hundreds o' spectators could see mee better. As mee cart drove

off, it had difficulty gettin' through the narrow Prison Lane owin' to the great multitudes o' people. Salem Town ond Salem Village war the second largest settlement in Massachusetts Bay. On Saint Peter Street, the Salem militia steppin' to the fife ond drum, joined mee at side o' the cart, John Hathorne, on horseback, war a prominent figure in the procession what followed mee to Gallows Hill. As the cart turned from St. Peter's Street, mee eyes met even more people linin' the main street. From our path down Essex Street mee could see waer mee ol' house ond business once stood. Mee cart jolted up Boston Street 'til Gallows Hill come into mee view.

A tide o' Puritan viewers had flowed in from great distances to view mee noozin'. Today, all the Salem Town shops waer tradesmen 'plied thar goods war closed. The shipyards ond wharves war silent o' hustlin' feet. The only sound war the creakin' o' moorin' lines as they lunged at thar beckets bein' moved to ond fro by burst o' waves. The streets war packed five deep w'th mee Puritan neighbors dressed in thar austere dress; the women in thar somber-colored dresses opposed only by the white-winged caps, aprons, collars, ond cuffs; the men war clad in dark, dull coats ond plain high crowned hats. Thar faces war blank. Farmers ond townspeople jeered ond pelted mee w'th vegetables as the cart passed the throng over the rough road what twisted severall miles towards the west. Mee clung to the sides o' the cart to keep from bein' toppled by these missiles. They hurled hateful words sich as, "witch confess yer sin," "repent, repent, wicked witch," ond "the devill can't save ye now." Outside the town, the cart turned from the main street onto Boston Road, past the North River, crossin' over the town bridge, turnin' off the main road onto a track o' common land what led up to a small rocky hill. The town dwellin's had thinned out ond thar war farmhouses in the distance fields ond pastures. Occasionally, in the crowd, mee would catch a glimpse o' a familiar face who would return to mee a fearful stare. Mee know they war thinkin' thar association w'th mee might brung a future accusation thar way. The crowds what lined the streets closed in behind ond followed the cart road. Mee turned mee gaze to the rocky outcroppin's what stood out starkly against the sky, for its high bare ledges had prevented the growth o' many trees. From all over the countryside, an excited mobility had collected on the barren ond rocky elevation on the western side o' the villages. It war named Gallows Hill—the place o' twistin'. The horses pullin' the cart strained at mee load in order to brung the cart to the gallows. Gallows Hill would later come to be called "Witches Hill." 'Cause o' the shame ond embarrassment o' the citizens o' Salem Town ond Salem Village, who didn't want to be held accountable for the 19 executions on this hill, the location o' Gallows Hill war buried in minds ond forgotten. At the crest, the cart jolted to a stop at last ond backed up to a hastily constructed wooden platform. The people spread 'emselves out all around the rocks ond boulders. As mee climbed the ladder to the platform, mee took a long last view o' the scene what spread 'afore mee. Thar war the vast expanse o' sea, Salem Harbor, Salem Town, Salem Village ond its fields ond farmhouses, ond woodlands to the west. It war a commandin' view o' places familiar what mee dearly loved. Mee hard cold-hearted

Magistrate Hathorne whispered to Reverend Noyes what "death is eternally fascinating. There she stands, licking her lips in terror, and yet a moment from now she will become a useless bundle of rags." Ravenger Sheriff Corwin war pokin' 'bout the rocky outcroppin's, to tag a spot amid the rocks whar hee could throw mee remains. Mee hands war tied behind mee back ond black sack war placed over mee eyes. As mee neck neared the nooze, the drummers started beatin' thar snares. Assistant Reverend Nicholas Noyes snickered as hee slipped the nooze o' the hangin' rope around mee neck. Noyes war mee across-the-road neighbor 'afore mee moved from Salem Town to Ipswich Post Road. Mee felt his eyes war always on mee comin's ond goin's. Hee war the biggest nitpicker against mee way o' livin'. Mee felt the roughness o' the rope's strands against mee neck. The sheriff tightened the noose around mee neck. The crowd's eyes war riveted to mee person by unseen forces what would not lett 'em look away. The drummers continued beatin' thar drums; sweat oozin' down thar faces. Reverend Hale gave mee a final chance to confess mee crime. It waren't forthcomin'. Noe dismal ditty for mee. Mee shot a volatile curse at him. Mee claimed mee innocence ond warned, "Ye 'ave God's divine punishment to fear." The drums beat faster. Mee hart raced to match the rhythm. The crowd had recovered its voice ond war screamin' vile curses, along w'th throwin' cabbages ond rotten apples. These projectiles found thar markes on mee dress, face, ond arms. Even Sheriff Corwin slunk back in surprise. Nicholas Noyes, famous for his departin' taunts to witches, seemed to enjoy the gruesome spectacle by the crowd. Then a sudden hush swept over the crowd. Beneath the hot summer sun the hangman received the deadly signal. The drummin' stopped. The crowd fell still. Mee war turned off from the platform. The crowd gasped. Thar war a sickenin' drop, a convulsive jerk, the rope tightened on mee throat ond cut off mee breathin'. Mee body thrashed violently for a few moments o' strangulation, ond then mee hung limply. Mee 60-yar-old body morrised 'afore the crowd. A slight gust o' wind billowed mee skirt exposin' mee lacy mish. The watchin' mob nodded. Mee enemies war content what Salem war rid o' Bridget Bishop, alias Oliver, thar first witch. The upright men o' Salem war rid o' one less disciple o' Satan to plague thar parishioners. Mee would noe longer corrupt the yeng o' the area. Mee 'ave a feelin' those who dispersed down the slopes o' Gallows Hill s'd to 'emselves . . . shee sold her soul to Satan, shee had to die. Mee am sure they tryed to rationalize; it reads in the Bible "Thou shalt not suffer a witch to live." Yet did doubt nag 'em? What if I warn't a witch?

Mee body war cut down ond thrown into a shallow, unmarked grave what had been dug amang the rocky crevices close by. Noe eternity box for mee. Mee body war hastily covered over w'th dirt by the moabites 'avin' charge o' mee execution. Mee received noe prayers over mee grave. Mee had been executed accordin' to the stern vengeance o' Puritan lawe in Massachusetts Bay Colony. Now the townsmen o' Salem could sleep in peace, sure what mee spectre wouldn't press 'em, throw 'em around a room, or press mee cold lips to thar mouths. Cast out witches war not allowed burial in church burial grounds ond thar deaths whar not recorded. But mine war.

The sheriff seems to have proceeded, immediately after the execution, to the clerk's office, and indorsed his return on the warrant. According to the within Written precept I have taken the body of the within named Bridget Bishop out of their Majesties' Jail in Salem and Safely Conveyed her to the place provided for her Execution and caused the said Bridget to be hanged by the neck until she was dead all which was according to the time within Required and So I make Return by me. When he wrote it, he added, after the word dead— and buried her on the spot.

On its occurring to him that the burying of the body was not mentioned in the warrant, he drew his pen through the word dead and added—and buried her on the spot.[54]

This war important to mee, however, as indicatin' to mee descendants, the burial place o' mee body.

Mee husband ond children war charged the hangman's wage for all transportation costs to the hill, mee rope, as weel as the executioner's fee ond burial charges. Can't say mee husband war too long in mournin', as hee war married w'thin eight months o' mee death to Elizabeth Cash, 9 March 1693.

Mee tryall ond the proceedin's o' the court must 'ave caused some discord amang the justices. Justice Nathaniel Saltonstall become alarmed by the continued arrests ond possible deaths. Mr. Saltonstall resigned from the court after mee tryall. Jonathan Corwin war his replacement. Hee war one o' the magistrates what cross-examined mee at mee pre-tryall. The Oyer ond Terminer court war now packed w'th four justices who war committed to use spectral evidence ond findin's o' the pre-tryalls to convict. Upon return to his home in Haverhill, Saltonstall spoke out strongly against the hysterical witch hunt. Saltonstall questioned the use o' spectral evidence. Hee felt the circle o' girls fits ond spectral evidence warn't a good source for hard evidence. In time, the afflicted girls started to cry out against him. They claimed falsely his spectre war in attendance at severall witch meetin's. Puttin' aside these falsehoods, the fearless Saltonstall continued to oppose the court proceedin's ond tryed to convince othars to take a stand similar to his. 'Cause Saltonstall war feelin' guilty for mee blood on his hands, hee took up the drink, becomin' a maudlin from then on. Followin' mee execution, thar war severall o' mee townspeople who courageously signed petitions on behalf o' those sitten in the gaoles, who they felt war innocent. It warn't long 'afore a number o' Boston justices refused to serve on any witchcraft cases, statin' what they would rather resign thar commissions than be responsible for condemnin' good citizens on the type o' evidence presented in the previous tryall. Some members o' the court war hard talkin' low ond insinuated what if spectral evidence had been barred from Bridget Bishop's tryall, shee would 'ave been convicted for little more than wearin' a red frill, permittin' shove ha'penny ond shovelboard in her ordinaries, ond gettin' herself talked 'bout, all offences, perhaps, but hardly capital felonies. How lucky wee victims war to 'ave two voices rise against this witchcraft madness. They war Bostonians, Robert Calef, a Baptist, ond Thomas Brattle, a Harvard graduate ond current treasurer o' Harvard. Both o' these verie smart respected men, at thar own expense, attended many o' the examinations ond tryalls, talked to folks who war acquainted w'th the legal court cases, ond kept a whopper amount o' notes on what they larned. On 8 October 1692, Mr. Thomas Brattle laid it all out in a published letter to a non-existent minister. Hee took it to those ol' justices ond othar high-barn men in the colony condemnin' the legal proceedin's ond procedures o' the pre-tryalls ond court jury tryalls ond concluded his letter by sayin', "I am afraid that ages will not wear off that reproach and these stains which these things will leave behind them upon the land." Mee thinks this letter war one o' the most important factors in bringin' the witchcraft hysteria to an end.

The court took a short recess after mee execution, accusations slowed down for a time, ond more than a month passed 'afore thar war any more executions. Increase Mather's Boston sermon to his parishioner wharin hee counseled 'em to look inside to thar own weaknesses ond not to those o' thar neighbors around 'em, fell short o' suggestin' people halt thar accusations.

Due to the fact what the entire populace war swept up into a passion, all those who war accused in the first series war quickly convicted ond executed. Magistrate Hathorne had spent the summer o' 1692 holdin' his pre-tryalls as hee done since March. The final convictions come on 17 September 1692. Three days after Giles Corey's pressin', 22 September 1692, eight more war hanged, includin' Giles's wife Martha. 'Bout 150 accused witches war left in the local gaoles.

The end o' the summer, October, brung Sir William Phips return from Maine to the colony. Thar war quite an outburst o' public kick goin' on when hee arrived. Governor Phips prohibited the arrest o' any more accused persons. Hee forbade furthar executions, pendin' orders from the king. Phips tryed to persuade William Stoughton to change the court's methods—to stop relyin' on the spectral testimony o' the bewitcht. Stoughton apparently refused. Governor Phips consulted Increase Mather, his most trusted adviser, ond larned what the burnin' issues war the court's admission o' spectral evidence ond the trustworthiness o' the circle o' girls' spectral visions. Mather shared his essay, *Cases in Conscience,* w'th Royal Governor Phips. This may 'ave been a blessin', 'cause when the tryalls resumed in January, Mather's published work influenced Phips's decision to exclude spectral evidence, touchin' tests, ond to require proof o' guilt by clear ond convincin' evidence.

Historian Marion Starkey has great drift on this occasion:

> It was not that these God-fearing Puritans had ceased to believe in the reality of witchcraft, but a great many had come to believe that this was no way to combat it. Phips put a stop to the trials until the magistrates and ministers could find a more rational basis to continue them. The girls were no longer consulted in these deliberations. They only knew their services were less in demand than they had been. However, early in October, while the trials were still in abeyance, they were invited to Glouster to uncover its witches . . . they will listen no more to distracted children. Were they liars? John Hale stated "the devil is a liar and the children could only report the devil's delusion." We go by new rules of evidence. Afflicted could be heard at the pre-trial examination, but not the trial. No longer spectral evidence. It will not be enough to testify that the shape, the spirit of the accused has been doing evil deed. The body presence must be proved. What defense have we if we can be convicted on what your daughter saw in dreams?[55]

In the meantime, it war clear what thar war open disagreement 'tween Chief Justice Stoughton ond some o' the judges on the one hand, ond the ministers ond severall laymen on the othar. For one, the justices had ceased seekin' tryall advice from the clergy. Secondly, Increase Mather gave up his former stand when his wife war accused o' bein' a witch. Mather finally buried what ol' hatchet ond conceded innocent lives had been sacrificed. Increase Mather's essay, *Case In Conscience Concerning Evil Spirits Personating Men,* war delivered to a counsel o' ministers wharin hee expressed a strong disapproval o' usin' spectral evidence in the witch tryalls, callin' it unreliable. This essay may 'ave prompted this council o' ministers to propose what the court disallow spectral evidence ond debar the circle o' girls performin' thar antics while the court war in session. Alsoe, public opinion amang the townspeople 'emselves war shiftin' from accused bein' witches to accused bein' possessed.

Phips dismissed the court 'afore the end o' the month. W'th the Court o' Oyer ond Terminer dissolved, executions come to an end, thus endin' one o' the most disastrous results o' the witch hunt. Royal Governor Phips admits, "When I put an end to the Court there were at least 50 persons in prision in great misery by reason of the extream cold and their poverty, most of them having only spectral evidence against them and their mittimusses being defective, I caused some of them to be let out upon bayle and put the Judges upon consideration of a way to relieve others and to prevent them from perishing in prision, upon which some of them were convinced and acknowledged that their former proceedings were too violent and not grounded upon a right foundation . . . The stop put to the first method of proceedings hath dissipated the black cloud that threatened this Province with destruccion."— Governor William Phips, 21 February 1693[56]

In November, the General Court o' Massachusetts created a superior court to judge the cases what remained. Governor Phips's new instructions war to "give very little weight to spectral evidence." Mee hard tell, Governor Phips had what ye might call a fuss heat . . . his own good wife war accused o' witchcraft on spectral evidence.

In January, the new Superior Court o' Judicature, Court o' Assize ond General Gaole Delivery commenced in Salem w'th Stoughton at its head. Chief Judge Stoughton ordered all matrons who had been exempted 'cause o' thar pregnancy to be tryed. Royal Governor war quick to deny this order. W'th spectral evidence not admitted, thar war an acquittal, then anothar acquittal, then a third, fourth, fifth, ond soe on. Stoughton war enraged ond angrily pressed on relentlessly against those accused. The Superior Court jurors convicted three o' 52 persons tryed in January. Stoughton condemned these three ond signed the death warrants o' five othars, four o' 'em war confessin' witches. Phips stayed all the executions. Forty-nine o' the 52 war pardoned 'cause thar arrests war made on spectral evidence. Mee guesses ye might put the lid on this ol' pot by sayin' many folks war fearin' spillin' innocent blood more than sufferin' a witch to live. The court sat againe in April 1693, but thar war noe more convictions. When the 49th acquittal war delivered, Stoughton gave up. In May 1693, Phips signed a general pardon for the accused or convicted o' witchcraft who war lyin' in great squalor awaitin' tryall. Phips's demand to discharge all o' the prisoners awaitin' tryall war welcomed news. By order o' the Royal Governor, these people war to be released when thar gaole ond court costs war paid. But many o' the prisoners war forced to stay in gaoles 'til thar families could pay thar release fees. Mee weekly fee at the Boston gaole war two shillin's, sixpence a week, plus processin' fees ond fees for mee darbies ond chains. This weekly chunk war more than relatives could hope to scrape up in a week by back-breakin' labor. It war cold in the winter ond many o' mee bunkmates had to pay extra for blankets. Prisoners war charged dearly for maintenance, clothin', fuel, transport to the gaole, court ond prison fees, discharge from the gaole, ond even reprieve from execution. Many o' the prisoners war soe financially ruined what they couldn't pay for thar own freedom. Innocent people had been robbed o' property, family, health, money, ond social standin'.

Mee accountin' o' the victims o' this witchy madness are reported:

Executed

10 June 1692	Bridget Warsselbe Oliver Bishop
19 July 1692	Sarah Solart Poole Good, Elizabeth Jackson Howe, Sarah Averell Wildes, Rebecca Towne Nurse, Susannah North Martin
19 August 1692	Reverend George Burroughs, Martha Allen Carrier, John Proctor, George Jacobs Sr., John Willard
19 September 1692	Giles Corey (pressed)
22 September 1692	Martha Corey, Mary Towne Easty, Alice Parker, Mary Ayer Parker, Ann Greenslit Pudeator, Wilmot Read, Margaret Stevenson Scott, Samuel Wardwell

It war reported to mee what the witchcraft tryalls took an economic toll on all the communities around Essex County. Soe many o' the townspeople, civic officials, ond farmers abandoned thar normal work, beginnin' in March 1692, to attend the yar-long pre-tryalls ond court jury tryalls. Mee guess it took a few yars o' everieone workin' verie hard to reverse the losses. Poor crop yars ond epidemics continued to rain down on the colonies. Puritan ministers preached it war 'cause "God was punishing them for the deaths of so many innocent people."

Many 'ave speculated 'bout what caused the strange fits o' the accusin' girls ond testimonies o' the tryall witnesses. Mee know the fits war to cover over the white magick they war practicin'. The othar tryall witnesses in mee case war motivated by revenge ond jealousy.

Ann Putnam Jr., one o' the principal accusers, who accused people who had been in conflict w'th her family, confessed, in 1706, what shee had been deluded by the devill, ond shee publicly acknowledged her share o' responsibility for the sheddin' o' innocent blood. Ann Putnam Jr. apologized 'afore her congregation by sayin':

> I desire to be humbled before God for that sad and humbling providence that befell my father's family in the year 1692; that I, then being in my childhood, should, by such a providence of God, be made an instrument for the accusing of several persons of a grievous crime, whereby their lives were taken away from them, whom now I have just grounds and good reason to believe they were innocent persons; and that it was a great delusion of Satan that deceived me in that sad time, whereby I justly fear I have been instrumental, with others, though ignorantly and unwittingly, to bring upon myself and this land the guilt of innocent blood; though what was said or done by me against any person I can truly and uprightly saw, before God

and man, I did it not out of any anger, malice, or ill-will to any person, for I had no such thing against one of them; but what I did was ignorantly, being deluded by Satan. And particularly, as I was a chief instrument of accusing of Goodwife Nurse and her two sisters, I desire to lie in the dust, and to be humbled for it, in that I was a cause, with others, of so sad a calamity to them and their families; for which cause I desire to lie in the dust, and earnestly beg forgiveness of God, and from all those unto whom I have given just cause of sorrow and offence, whose relations were taken away or accused.
—Ann Putnam[57]

Mee feel saddened what this family accused soe many close associates, friends, ond neighbors who war innocent o' witchcraft. The powerful Putnam family actively promoted the witch accusations upon those w'th whom they war feudin'. Ann Putnam Jr. war the leader o' the circle o' girls ond the prime finger-pointer ond accuser. Shee testified in court ond signed many affidavits.

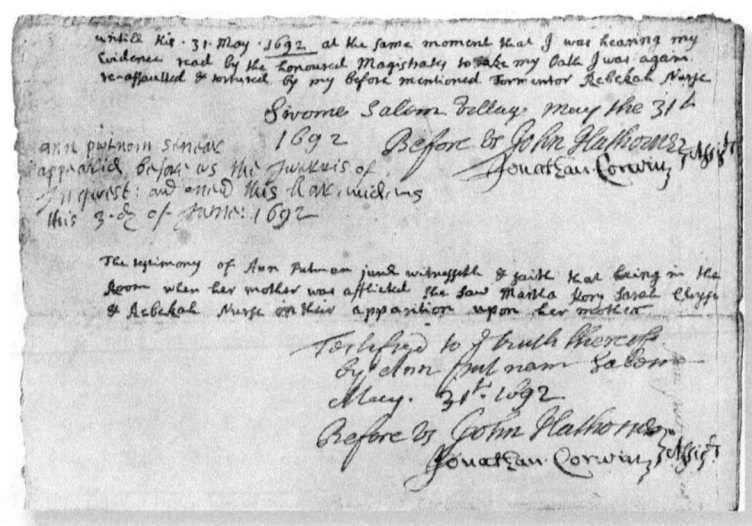

Deposition of Mrs. Ann Putnam Sr. and her daughter, 1692

Thar war times in court what her mothar, Ann Sr., would alsoe become afflicted. Those ol' girls war pretty good actors. The othars who witnessed against mee at mee tryall alsoe recognized thar grievous mistake, recanted, expressed contrition, ond 'ave sought apology ond forgiveness for the injustice done to mee.

Most o' those who had participated in the terrible deeds o' the precedin' summer confessed the great wrong what they had done to soe many innocents; but confessions couldn't restore the dead. It warn't long after the tryall ended what the courts ond churches declared days o' penance ond prayer, passed lawes, harped on forgiveness, ond reversed excommunication from the parishes. The bigoted Cotton Mather, in a vain attempt to justify heeself 'afore the world, wrote a discourse in which hee voiced his great thankfulness what soe many who had cast spells over othars had met thar fittin' fate. Mathers'd wee all died by a righteous sentence. It war payback time for all o' us who war accused, when Cotton Mather war denied bein' president o' Harvard College. Alsoe seven yars later, 1699, the deaths o' Ann Sr. ond her husband w'thin months o' one anothar o' an unknown infectious disease war rumored the result o' a curse o' God for all thar lyes durin' the witch tryalls. In 1694, the General Court o' Massachusetts declared that witchcraft war noe longer an offense in the colony. In January 1696, 12 o' the witch-tryall jurors signed a statement o' contrition, admittin' what: "We confess that we ourselves were not capable to understand, nor able to withstand the mysterious delusions of the Powers of Darkness and Prince of the Air; but were for want of knowledge in ourselves and better information from others, prevailed with to take up such evidence against the

Accused, as on further consideration, and better Information we justly fear was insufficient."[58]

The followin' yar, on 14 January 1697, the first formal fast-day war held. On what day, Judge Samuel Sewall repented his role in the tryalls, publicly declarin' in church his feelin's o' blame ond shame ond asked God to pardon him for his sins. Othar personages involved in the tryalls later expressed remorse.

In 1697, Robert Calef, a Boston merchant ond a critic o' the witch tryalls, wrote in *More Wonders of the Invisible World:* "And now to sum up all in a few words, we have seen a bigoted zeal stirring up a blind and most bloody rage, not against enemies or irreligious profligate person, but again as virtuous and religious as any . . . and this by the testimony of vile varlets as not only were known before but have been further apparent since by their manifest lives, whoredoms, incest . . . etc. The accusations of these, from their spectral sight being the chief evidence against those that suffered. In which, accusations were upheld by both magistrates and ministers."[59]

Mr. Calef's book alsoe attacked religious leaders like Cotton Mather, who encouraged charges o' witchcraft rather than tryein' to determine the truth. It strikes mee funny what Increase ond Cotton Mather thought they could rid the colonies o' Calef's book by burnin' 'em publicly in Harvard Square. Aw shucks! It only increased thar popularity—mum for that.

Calef aggravated the dispute even furthar by printin' *Another Brand Plucked From the Fire,* an account o' conversations ond wrighten correspondence 'tween Mather ond him. Calef attacked Mather for takin' supposedly bewitcht girls into his own home ond encouragin' thar testimony against accused witches durin' the tryalls. Mather war deeply offended by Calef's charge, ond hee spent the remainder o' his life tryein' to justify his actions.

In 1711, Massachusetts granted compensation, 578 pounds, to be divided amang the heirs o' the victims. Mee heirs received noe compensation ond never petitioned for reimbursement. In 1957, the General Court o' Massachusetts formally admitted wee may 'ave been illegally tryed. The legal system o' ye day, in mee opinion, would judge parts o' mee tryall unconstitutional. Mee taint war finally removed when in 1960, a brief war attached to house bill No. 91 by Representative Buczko o' Salem on behalf o' John Beresford Hatch what follows:

"Mr. Speaker, under leave to extend my remarks in the record, I wish to include the statement of John Beresford Hatch of 15 Harbor Street, Salem, Massachusetts, as the petitioner for house bill No. 91 filed in the Massachusetts Legislature for the adoption of resolutions memorializing the Government of the United States for redress of certain grievances by reason of the illegal arrest, gaoling and execution of persons suspected of witchcraft in the year 1692 and 1693. Historic transgression which was a gross violation of every legal right these people had inherited by the Magna Carta of 1215 and the Bill of Rights of 1641 . . . Its Court of Oyer and Terminer stands out glaringly as one of the most laweless tribunals in the history of British jurisprudence."[60]

Mee fancy the judicial events o' mee tryall had a profound impact on notions o' justice in the New World. Mee gets fire in mee belly when mee thinks 'bout justices assumin' what people war guilty 'til proven innocent. Mee pin mee hopes upon a day when a legal system will be developed war victims are innocent 'til proven guilty.

Writer Nathaniel Hawthorne, while attendin' Bowdoin College in the 1820s, altered his name officially from Hathorne to Hawthorne, but hee never gave reason why. Some o' his close associates s'd it war 'cause hee war soe embarrassed o' what his great-great-grandfather, Judge Hathorne did; but othars asserted it war 'cause o' the intimidatin' curses on the Hathorne family name by many o' the sentenced witches as they stood on the gallows platform.

Mee hard what Sheriff George Corwin's relatives had to bury him in a secret unmarked grave soe the loved ones o' the executed witches wouldn't dig him up ond tear his body to shreds.

Mee thinks man's inhumanity to man arn't altered since ancient times. Humankind's mentality o' wantin' retribution, bein' vengeful, ond blamin' othars for misfortunes seems to exist throughout human history. Those ol' Romans had similar avengin' desires. They called upon thar gods to inflict violence upon those they perceived had mistreated 'em. Thar wrighten curses would be recorded upon tablets what war deposited inside shrines ond temples. Tablets containin' murderous cursin' sich as "destroy, crush, kill, strangle" 'ave been found. Flaws in human nature sich as the desire o' human bein's to project evil on othars, define 'em as outsiders, ond punish 'em horribly are timeless. Ideology determines the form the evil takes. Suspicions, accusations, indictments, ond depositions all stem from revenge, jealousy, ond greed; human frailties what everieone has to some extent noe matter how pious they are. Mee guess people in yer day may 'ave participated in similar hateful, ruthless mass murders. Curator Alison D'Amario gives a good rundown: "Tolerance is at the root of a free society. Therefore Salem learned the lesson that led to the creation of the United States." Mee am thankful what Salem war the last huge witch craze in the English-speakin' world.

Even though mee lost mee life wrongly, mee hopes ye will remember mee as an emancipated woman who dared to stand up ond demand equal rights ond respect in a society war women had noe rights ond war considered inferior ond subordinate to thar husbands, fathers, or religious leaders; a society whar women war to be seen ond not hard. Mee did not yield to judicial pressure even though a confession would 'ave freed mee from prison ond execution. Mee could 'ave sidestepped the worst o' the noozin' if mee had pleaded "benefit of clergy" ond recited the first line o' Psalm 51: "Have mercy upon me, O God, according to thy loving kindness." Mee showed noe remorse ond protested mee innocence up to the verie moment o' mee hangin'.

Salem Village changed its name in 1752 to Danvers. Mee wonder if it war 'cause its residents felt a new name would help 'em to forget.

The city o' Salem has been uncomfortable 'bout rememberin' the accused witches, except in terms o' tourist promotion. The disappearance o' soe many official documents made it difficult for historians to restore the dignity to witch-hunt victims. Through the combined efforts o' Wayne E. Higley ond Howard Thomas Hay, president o' the Sons ond Daughters o' the Victims o' Colonial Witch Trials, a Salem Witch Trials memorial statue war erected in Salem in 1992 in honor o' thar ancestors ond many like mee who war put to death durin' the Salem witch tryalls in 1692. Mee exoneration come in 2001 w'th Chapter 122 o' the Massachusetts Acts o' 2001, which included mee name, clearin' mee o' the felony o' witchcraft.

Mee would like to turn the clock back to reflect on sum o' mee feelin's 'bout the Salem witch tryalls. What happened in Salem Village/Danvers can be attributed to many sources. At its fountainhead war an inflamed, hysterical witch hunt ond the uncanny power what some individuals can wield over the lives o' othar human bein's. Salem Village/Danvers war a whole community o' people what felt itself beset by the devill's influence. 'Cause o' fear ond gossip, the residents o' Salem Village lost the capacity to discern 'tween innocence ond evil. Mee Puritan neighbors' two-fold religious beliefs turned the scale. Namely, what God controlled everythin' ond when calamities occurred they war bein' punished by God. Ond second, Satan war the author o' these calamities ond God allowed Satan to inflict in order to brung those who had strayed from community regulations ond norms back into the fold. God had forsaken Salem Village ond Salem Village had forsaken thar God.

Dr. Griggs war right in his identification . . . thar war witchcraft at work in Salem. Witchcraft war responsible, but it war the girls' use o' witchcraft as they appealed to a non-Christian source to 'ave thar fortunes foretold. The guilt-stricken girls fear o' bein' caught in thar mischief opened the door to bein' possessed by the devill. Thomas Hutchinson suggested what the "girls were suffering from bodily disorders, which affected their imaginations." Today, thar strange fits might be labeled mental illness ond physical illness. Methinks a better label is deception.

Intelligent, reasonable judges become prime movers who chose to believe in witches ond witchcraft what caused strange agonies ond grievous torments ond to deliver death sentences w'th little or noe visible hard evidence, only invisible evidence. It sure are mystifyin' what these women who made a confession o' witchcraft all lived ond those o' us who denied practicin' witchcraft war hanged. Thar now mee reader, mee 'ave noted these facts three separate times. Marke 'em in ye mind, as it is verie grave.

Massachusetts Bay Colony's fear o' religious suppression by English monarchs who had power to manipulate charters, bloody conflicts w'th the French ond Dutch, ond local hatreds 'tween the farmers o' Salem Village ond Salem Town forged a cauldron what when set to fire by stresses o' nature, boiled over into a day o' reckonin'.

Lastly, mee flamboyant lifestyle, shameful conduct, ond exotic manner o' dress sowed the seeds o' revenge ond vindictiveness. As a result o' mee malice, many o' the tradesmen ond merchants who knew mee war terrified o' mee ond had thar hallucinations as a result o' what terror. Mee thinks thar hallucinations war a result o' believin' in the devill ond allowin' him to take control o' thar minds. The opinion o' othars 'bout mee brung accusations, mee arrest, mee interrogations, mee tryall, mee conviction, ond mee demise. Mee war not a practicin' witch. Mee war innocent. Mee know nothin' 'bout witchcraft, ond mee don't even know what a witch is.

Notes

1. Holy Bible (King James version).
2. Henry Wadsworth Longfellow, *Giles Corey of the Salem Farms.*
3. Tim Lamber, "A Brief History of Norwich," *A World History Encyclopedia,* and http://www.ancestry.com (http://www.localhistories.org/Norwich.html).
4. Nathaniel Philbrick, *Mayflower* (New York: Penguin, 2006), 8–10.
5. Helen Ellerbe, "The Witch Hunts: The End of Magic and Miracles, 1450-1750 C.E.," *The Dark Side of Christian History* (Morningstar and Lark, 1995).
6. Cotton Mather, "The Education of Children," http://www.spurgeon.org/~phil/mather/edkids.htm.
7. Charles Hudson, *History of Town of Marlborough* (Boston Press, 1862), 65–86.
8. Cotton Mather, *On Witchcraft* (1692; reprinted by Bell Publishing Company) 106–107.
9. Chadwick Hansen, *Witchcraft at Salem* (New York: New American Library, 1969) 75, 95–96, 139–140.
10. Winfield S. Nevins, *Witchcraft In Salem Village in 1692* (New York: Burt Franklin, 1971), 268.
11. "The Revocation of the Charter," *Chronicles of America,* 1684.
12. Mary Lou Lustig, *The Imperial Executive in America: Sir Edmund Andros (1637-1714)* (Fairleigh Dickinson University Press, 2002), 160, 164.
13. George Bancroft, *History of the United States from the Discovery of the American Continent* (Boston: Little, Brown and Co., 1874-1878), 8, 50, 51, 85.
14. Leo Bonfanti, *The Witchcraft Hysteria of 1692* (New England Historical Series, Vol 1), 9, 14–16, 53.
15. David Levin, *What Happened in Salem?* Second Edition (New York: Harcourt, Brace & World, Inc., 1960), 15–17, 20–34, 110–111.
16. Charles W. Upham, *Salem Witchcraft* (New York: Frederick Ungar Publishing Co., 1859; 1867; Ungar Pub Co New York, 1959, 83–85, 191–197, 211, 253, 266.
17. Ibid., Mather, 106–107.
18. Ibid., Upham, 241–242.

19. Winfield S. Nevins, *The Witches of Salem* (1892; Stamford: Longmeadow Press, 1994), 70, 73–74, 268.

20. Peggy Saari and Elizabeth Shaw, eds., *Witchcraft in America* (2000), 194.

21. Ibid., Levin, 20.

22. Paul Boyer and Stephen Nissenbaum, eds., *The Salem Witchcraft Papers* (Volume 1: verbatim transcripts of the legal documents of the Salem witchcraft outbreak of 1692), http://etext.virginia.edu/etcbin/toccer-new2?id=BoySal1. sgm&images=images/modeng&dat.

23. Ibid., Levin, 22–23.

24. Ibid., 20–21.

25. Marion L. Starkey, *The Devil In Massachusetts* (New York: Anchor Books, 1949,1969, 1989), 26–178. Marion Starkey, *The Visionary Girls,* Fifth Edition (Boston: Little, Brown and Co., 1973), 15–49, 128, 148.

26. Dr. Peter C. Hoffer, *The Salem Witchcraft Trials: A Legal History* (University Press of Kansas, 1997).

27. Dr. Bryan F. LeBeau, *The Story of The Salem Witch Trials* (Pearson, 2009).

28. Heinrich Kramer and James Sprenger, *Malleus Maleficarum* (Speyer, Germany, 1487).

29. Cotton Mather, *The Wonders of the Invisible World* (1693) http://en.wikipedia.org/wiki/Wonders_of_the_Invisible_World.

30. Robert E. Cahill, *New England's Witches ond Wizards* (Peabody: Smith Pub House Inc.), 26.

31. Paul Boyer ond Stephen Nissenbaum, *Salem Possessed* (Harvard University Press, 1974), 192, 971.

32. Ibid., 1:108; Bonfanti, Vol. 1, 35; Levin, 21, 23; Essex County Court Archives, Vol. l, No. 136.

33. Ibid.

34. Ibid.

35. Ibid., Mather, 223.

36. Ibid. 223–224.

37. Ibid., Levin, 20, 21.

38. Ibid., 25–27.

39. Ibid.

40. Ibid., 23–24.

41. Ibid., 24, 35.

42. Ibid.

43. Ibid., 27–28.

44. Ibid.

45. Ibid., 32.
46. Ibid., 30.
47. Ibid., 28–29.
48. Ibid., 31.
49. Ibid.
50. Ibid., 30–31.
51. Ibid.
52. Ibid. Kramer and Sprenger.
53. Ibid., Nevins, 156–158.
54. Ibid., 158.
55. Ibid., Starkey, 15–49, 128, 145, 146.
56. Francis Hill, *The Salem Witch Trials Reader* (Da Capo Press, 2000), 108.
57. Ibid., Saari, 70. Frances Hill, *A Delusion of Satan,* 99.
58. Robert Calef, Nath. Hilllar, *More Wonders of the Invisible World,* Part 4 and 5 (Princess-Arms in Leaden-Hall-Street, England, 1700).
59. John Beresford, "Remarks of Honorable Tomas J. Lane of Massachusetts in the House of Representatives, Wednesday, January 20, 1960," *Salem Witchcraft, Fact or Fictions?* (Hatch, 1963), 10–13.

Bibliography

"1651 – Navigation Acts." Stamp Act. http://www.stamp-act-history.com/timeline/27/.

Alderman, Clifford Lindsey. *The Devil's Shadow.* New York: Archway Paperback, a division of Simon & Schuster, Inc., 1975, fifth printing.

Adams, J.T. *The Founding of New England,* first published 1921.

Alderman, Clifford Lindsey. *The Devil's Shadow.* Archway Paperback, 1967.

Anderson, Robert Charles. *The American Genealogist,* no. 64, (1989): 207.

Baker, Kevin. "Cruel and Usual." *American Heritage Magazine* (July 2006): 22–23.

Barillari, Alyssas. "Tituba, Salem Witch Trials in History and Literature (an undergraduate course). University of Virginia, Spring Semester, 2001.

Barnes, Viola Florence. *The Dominion of New England: A Study in British Colonial Policy.* New York: Frederick Ungar.

Bishop, Edward Jr. "Follett & Devalska/Develski/Kisseron Family Tree" (entry 2055). RootsWeb (An Ancestry.com community). Last modified July 22, 2012.

Blake, John B. "The Inoculation Controversy in Boston." *The New England Quarterly 25:4,* (December 1952): 489–502.

Bodge, G.M. Soldiers in the King Philip's War, 3rd ed., 1891, 1906, 1967.

Boston Record Commissioners' Report, 9 [1883]: 98.

Boyer and Nissenbaum, eds. *Salem-Village Witchcraft.* Salem Church records, March 27, 1692.

Boyer, Paul and Stephen Nissenbaum, eds. *Salem Witch Papers.* NewYork: Da Capo,1977.

Bourne, R. *The Red King's Rebellion,* 1990.

Breslawe, Elaine G. *Tituba, Reluctant Witch of Salem.* New York: New York University Press, 1996.

Brown, David. *A Guide to the Salem Witchcraft Hysteria of 1692.* 1984.

Bulletin of the History of Medicine 80 (2006): 148–247.

Burns, Ivan and Gilbert Geiss. *Trial of Witches: A Seventeenth Century Witchcraft Prosecution.* (Kentucky: Roultedge, Taylor, and Francis Group, 1997).

Burr, George Lincoln, ed. *Narratives of the Witchcraft Cases 1646-1706.* New York: C. Scribner & Sons, 1914.

Burr, George Lincoln. *The Salem Witchcraft Papers.*

"Census of Prisoners & Dates of Prison Transfer." Essex County County Court Archives, vol. 2, No. 134, James Duncan Phillips Library, Peabody Essex Museum, Salem, Mass.

Cahill, Robert E. *New England's Witches and Wizards.* Peabody: Smith Pub House, Inc., 1983.

Cahill, Robert Ellis. *The Horrors of Salem's Witch Dungeon.* Peabody, Mass.: Chandler-Smith Publishing House, Inc., 1986.

Campbell, Donna M. "Puritanism in New England." *Literary Movements.* Dept. of English, Washington State University. Last modified March 21, 2010. http://public.wsu.edu/~campbelld/amlit/purdef.htm.

Chaitkin, Anton and John C. Smith Jr. "Bancroft and the Treason School of History." *American Almanae* (November 1997): 50–51, 85.

Collins, Gail. *America's Women: 400 Years of Dolls, Drudges, Helpmates, and Heroines.*

Cotton Mather on Witchcraft. New York: Bell Publishing Co. First published 1692.

"Cry Innocent: The People vs. Bridget Bishop." History Alive! http://cryinnocentsalem.com/additional-information/character-bios/bridget-bishop.

Daly, Donald R., *Recipes from Seventeenth Century Kitchen,* 1992, Salem, Mass.

Daniels, Bruce C. *Puritans at Play, Leisure and Recreation in Colonial New England.* Palgrave Mcmillan, 1996.

David Goss, interview by Laura Jo DeMordaunt.

Demos, John. "Entertaining Satan." *American Heritage* (August/September 1978): 14-23.

Drake, Samuel G. *Witchcraft Delusion.*

"Dominion of New England." Family Search. https://www.familysearch.org/learn/wiki/en/Dominion_of_New_England.

"Dominion of New England." United States History. www.u-s-history.com/pages/h546.html.

Earle, Alice Morse. "Customs and Fashions in Old New England." Echo Library, 2009: 37,41,44,216, 224,290-294, 315-318,320 321.

Ellis, G.W. and J.E. Morris. *King Philip's War,* 1906.

Elson, Henry W. *History of the United States of America.* New York: Macmillan Co., 1904.

Encyclopædia Britannica Online, s. v. "Half-Way Covenant," accessed January 20, 2013.
http://www.britannica.com/EBchecked/topic/252432/Half-Way-Covenant.

Ferguson, Henry. *Sir Edmund Andros.* Kessinger Publishing, LLC, 2009.

Fraustino, Lisa Rowe. *I Walked in Dread (Dear America).* New York: Scholastic Inc.

Green, David L. TAG 57:129-38.

Grose , Francis. *1811 Dictionary of the Vulgar Tongue.*

Guiley, Rosemary. *Encyclopedia of Witches and Witchcraft.*

Hamilton, Donny L. "The Port Royal Project: History of Port Royal."
http://nautarch.tamu.edu/portroyal/PRhist.htm, 2000.

Hansen, Chadwick. *Witchcraft at Salem* (A Mentor Book). New American Library.

Hanson, J.W. *History of the Town of Danvers to the Year 1848.*

Hatch, John Beresford. "Extension of Remarks of Honorable Thomas J. Lane of Massachusetts in the House of Representatives, Wednesday, January 20, 1960." *Salem Witchcraft, Fact or Fictions?* 1963: 10-13.

Hather, C. "Bridget Bishop," *Witchcraft Delusion.*

Hill, Francis. *The Salem Witch Trials Reader.* DaCapo Press, 2000.

"History of Town of Medfield." http://www.medfield.com.

Hurd, D. Hamilton. *History of Essex County, Ipswich.* Philadelphia, 1888.

Hutchinson, Thomas. "Salem Witch Trials." *Twentieth Century Encyclopedia,* 1st ed., 1948.

Jackson, Shirley. *Witchcraft of Salem Village.*

Jehle, Paule. "Were Biblical Laws Responsible for the Satan Witch Trials?" (Forerunner TV), YouTube, 2010.

Juergens, Tom. *Wicked Puritans of Essex County.* Charleston, South Carolina: History Press, 2011.

Kent, Zachary. *The Story of The Salem Witch Trials (Cornerstones of Freedom).* Chicago: Childrens Press.

"In Search of History: Salem Witch Trials." (A & E Television Networks, 1998), VHS.

Lanham. *Protestant Kingship: 1688-1776.* Lexington Books: 69.

Leach, D.E. Flintlock and Tomahawk, first published 1958.

"Legends of America, Witches of Massachusetts."
   http://www.legendsofamerica.com/ma-witches-c2.htm.

LeVack, Brian P. *Witchcraft—History.*

Lewis, Jone Johnson. "Bridget Bishop - Salem Witch Trials." About.com.
   http://womenshistory.about.com/od/salempeople/p/bridget_bishop.htm.

Linder, Douglas O. "Famous Trials,"
   http://law2.umkc.edu/faculty/projects/ftrials/salem/ASA_PUT.HTM.
   http://lawe.umkc.edu/faculty/projects/trials/salem.

Lobell, Jarrett A. "Curses!!!," *Archaeology* (September/October 2012): 16.

Mason, John and Paul Royster, ed. *A Brief History of the Pequot War,* 1736.

Maxwell, P. G. *Witchcraft in Europe and the New World.*

May, Robert. *The Accomplished Cook,* 1660.

Melton, J. Gordon. *Magic, Witchcraft ond Paganism in America.* Port Royal,
   Jamaica: University of the West Indies Press, 1974.

Mintz, S., & McNeil, S. (2012). *Digital History.* http://www.digitalhistory.uh.edu.

"Modest Enquiry, Reverend John Hale in Burr." 343, *Narratives:* 413.

Mornul, Michells M. *Dictionary of American History, Colonial Charters.*

Murdock, Kenneth Ballard. *Increase Mather: The Foremost American Puritan,* 1971.

Nevins, Winfield S. *The Witches of Salem.* First published 1892. Stamford, CT:
   Longmeadow Press, 1994.

New England Ancestors. Vol. 9, no. 1. (Spring 2008): 26.

"New England's Witches and Wizards." Salem Collection. Salem Public Library
   [133.4N]: 23. *New World Encyclopedia.*

Norton, Mary Beth. *In The Devil's Snare.* New York: Knopf, 2002.

"Note on the Charter of Massachusetts Bay, 1629." AMDOCS: Documents for the
   Study of American History. Scanned and converted to HTML by D. Barnhoorn for
   The American Revolution – an .HTML project. http://www.vlib.us/amdocs/texts/
   massbay_note.html.

O'Connell, Margaret F. *The Magic Cauldron.* New York: S. G. Phillips, 1975.

"On the problems of successive ministers: Boyer and Nissenbaum," *Salem Possessed*: 45–79.

Original Lists of Persons of Quality. New York, 1874.

Perley, Sidney. *The History of Salem Massachusetts.* Vol. III, 1671-1716. Salem: 1928. Reprinted byPanarizon Publishing Corp., 1979.

Pickering, David. *Cassell Dictionary of Witchcraft.* Cassell Publishing, 1996.

The Post Register, November 1, 1988. A-8.

Price, Benjamin Lewis. *Nursing Fathers: American Colonists Conception of English,* 1999. "Puritan Women." Google Images.

Rappeport, Laurie. "Lives of the Puritans After the Salem Witch Trials." eHow. Last modified October 06, 2011.

Ray, Benjamin. "Witchcraft In Salem Village." http//etext.lib.virginia.edu/salem/witchcraft.

Records and Files of the Quarterly Courts of Essex County, Mass., 4:90; 7:329 f. Salem College Public Library.

Records of the Quarterly Courts of Essex County, Mass. [Salem 1911-75] 3:385.

Richardson, Katherine W. *The Salem Witchcraft Trials.* Salem: Essex Institute, 1983.

Ridpath, John Clark. *A Popular History of the United States of America From the Aboriginal Times to the Present.* A.M. Jones Bro & Co., 1877.

Rinaldi, Ann. *A Break With Charity.* Gulliver Books/Harcourt, Inc., 1992.

Roach, Marilynne K. *The Salem Witch Trials: A Day-By-Day Chronicle of a Commmunity Under Siege.* Maryland: Taylor Trade Publishing, 2002.

Robinson, Enders A. *Salem Witchcraft.* Heritage Books, Inc.,1992.

Romona E. Worsencroft to Laura Jo DeMourdant.

Roper, Lyndel. *Witch Craze.* New Haven: Yale University Press, 2005.

Rosenthal, Bernard, ed. *Records of the Salem Witch Hunt.* Cambridge Press, 2009.

"Salem at Peace." *American Heritage* (October 1992): 28–29.

"Salem, Maritime Salem in the Age of Sail." National Park Service (in cooperation with the Peabody Essex, Museum) U.S. Department of the Interior, 2009: 21-27.

Salem Witch Trials Documentary Archive and Transcript Project. http://www2.iath.virginia.edu/salem/home.html.

Shaw, E. *Witchcraft in Colonial America,* 2001.

"Smart Living." *Post Register*, March 6, 2011.

Starkey, Marion L. *The Devil In Massachusetts.* New York: Anchor Books, 1969.

Thorndike, Joseph Jacobs Jr. "My Ancestor, The Wizard." *American Heritage* (August/September 1984): 81–85.

"Three Cheers for Juries." *American Heritage* (February/March 1985): 8,10.

"Tituba's Story." *New England Quarterly.* Vol. 71. no. 2 (1998).

Todd, Mabel L. *Witchcraft in New England,* 1997.

Upham, Charles. *Salem Witchcraft.* New York: Frederick Ung Publishing Co., 1859.

Valletta, Frederick. *Witchcraft, Magic and Super.*

Weber, Paige. "A History of Fashion ond Costume." *Early America,* vol. 4: 47.

Weisman, Richard. *Witchcraft, Magic, and Religion in 17th Century Massachusetts.* Amherst: University of Massachusetts Press, 1984.

Westwood, Mai-Linh Gonzales. "A Sketch of Bridget Bishop." College of Humanties & Natural Sciences, Loyola University, New Orleans. http://chn.loyno.edu/sites/chn.loyno.edu/files/A%20Sketch%20of%20Bridget%20 Bishop.pdf.

Wikipedia,

"Ann Putnam Jr.," http://en.wikipedia.org/wiki/Ann_Putnam_Jr.

"Bury St. Edmunds Witch Trials," http://en.wikipedia.org/wiki/Bury_St._Edmunds_witch_trials

"Dominion of New England," http://en.wikipedia.org/wiki/Dominion_of_New_ England

"Half-Way Covenant," http://en.wikipedia.org/wiki/Half-Way_Covenant

"Massachusetts Bay Colony," http://en.wikipedia.org/wiki/Massachusetts_Bay_Colony

"Massuchusetts Bay Colony," http://en.wikipedia.org/wiki/Massachusetts_Bay_ Colony#Revocation_of_charter

"Massachusetts Charter," http://en.wikipedia.org/wiki/Massachusetts_Charter

"Pequot War," http://en.wikipedia.org/wiki/Pequot_War

"Puritans," http://en.wikipedia.org/wiki/Puritans

"Restoration (England)," http://en.wikipedia.org/wiki/English_Restoration

"Salem, Massachusetts," http://en.wikipedia.org/wiki/Salem,_Massachusetts

"Spectral Evidence," http://en.wikipedia.org/wiki/Spectral_evidence

"Salem Clothing and Food"

Witten, Suzy. *The Afflicted Girls.* Dreamwind Publishing, 2009.

Worsencroft, Mary Esty. *An Echo From Salem.* Horseshoe Bend, Arkansas.

Yool, George Malcolm. 1692 Witch Hunt—*The Layman's Guide to the Salem Witchcraft Trials.* Maryland: Heritage Book, Inc., 1992.

Acknowledgments

Bridget Bishop, otherwise Oliver, Warselby, Playfer, accused of bewitching, has never had her story told. Ironically, Bridget's death warrant is carefully preserved under glass in Salem Superior Court for all the public to see. In spite of this prominent public exhibition, Bridget's vindication was delayed hundreds of years by the Salem community. In 1711, Massachusetts granted compensation to the heirs of the victims. Bridget's family was never compensated or reimbursed for her suffering. In 1957, the General Court of Massachusetts formally admitted that the victims had been illegally tryed. Bridget was amang four others who were not exonerated. In 2001, the Massachusetts government finally cleared Bridget of felony charges, 309 years after her infamous execution in June 1692.

As her ancestor, I feel that Bridget, along with the other 19 victims who were wrongfully accused and executed, were our first American heroes. Each of them bravely refused to yield to judicial pressure, even though a confession would have freed them from prison and execution. They died rather than admit falsely to witchcraft, "when all about thee owned the hideous lie!" (as said by John Greenleaf Whittier). In contrast, Tituba confessed her witchcraft and freed herself and continued to feed the fires of the witch-hunt hysteria by accusing and implicating others during this darkest page of New England history and Anglo-American jurisprudence.

I have spent almost 35 years researching Bridget Bishop's life, environment, arrest, trial, conviction, and execution. I have read other author interpretations, both traditional and recent objective reviews too numerous to mention. I acknowledge the scholarship and diligence of these authors, both early on and more recently in recording the events that took place. Their written words have filled my subconscious and placed fuel on my fire.

But from the perspective of a descendant, I have felt that I could perhaps put together a more complete story of an early feminist woman torn between individualism and conformity.

A special thanks to Lisa-Ross Akoury, my publisher, Shannon Miller, my editor, Bryce Lowry and Randy, my illustrators, and others at SDP Publishing Solutions for helping me turn my ideas into a historical novel. They made this journey an enjoyable one. Thank you to those whose faithfulness in keeping records made my research credible.

About the Author

Laura Jo DeMordaunt has been a lifelong student of the history of New England. With ancestors arriving on the Mayflower, others in 1626 and thereafter, a good portion of her lifetime has been spent researching and writing histories of their struggles and triumphs in the New World, specifically Salem, Massachusetts. Her ancestor, Bridget Bishop, has been a 35-year research project. The vaults of many of New England's museums, public offices, libraries, and genealogical societies have become her friends.

After encouraging her six sons and one daughter to achieve advanced degrees, Mrs. DeMordaunt returned to college at the age of 57 and graduated from Lewis-Clark State College in Idaho with a Bachelor of Science degree, emphasis in Education. She loves to serve in her church, flower garden, travel, and spend time on the family cattle ranch she shares with her husband, Roger. She is very proud of her 27 grandchildren. Roger and Laura Jo have just celebrated their 51st wedding anniversary.

Thou Shalt Not Allow a Witch to Live

Laura Jo DeMordaunt

www.laurajodemordaunt.com

Publisher: SDP Publishing

Also available in ebook format

TO PURCHASE:

Amazon.com,
BarnesAndNoble.com,
SDPPublishingSolutions.com

SDP Publishing

www.SDPPublishingSolutions.com

Contact us at: info@SDPPublishing.com

www.ingramcontent.com/pod-product-compliance
Lightning Source LLC
Chambersburg PA
CBHW020531270626
47155CB00025B/3048